McAlister's Spark

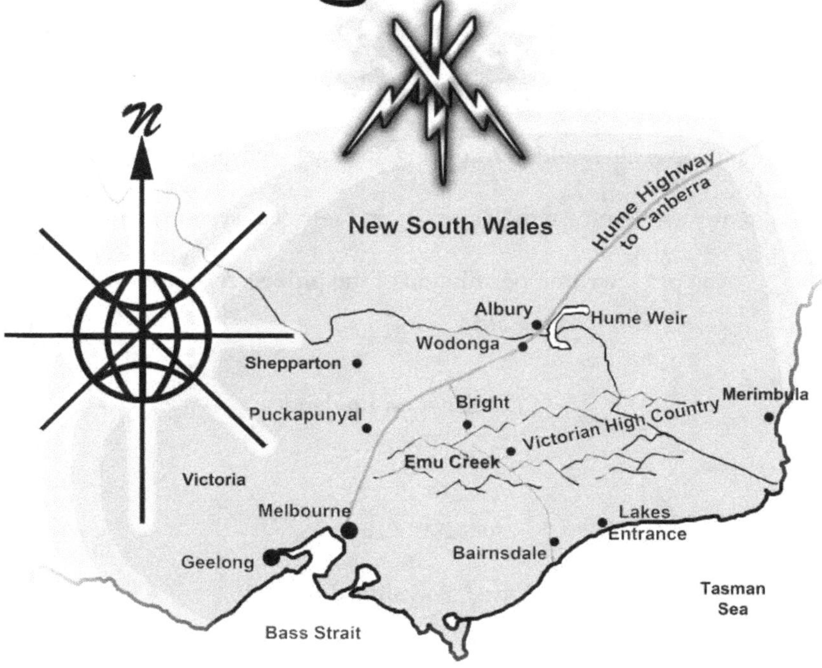

Richard Marman

Cover design, artwork and graphics by Richard Marman

Published in England

by

ABELA PUBLISHING

Sandhurst, Berkshire, England

Email: Author@RichardMarman.com

Website: www.RichardMarman.com

ISBN 13: 978-1-92568-0-928

Republished in 2018 with Ocean Reeve Publishing

First Edition, 2013

Acknowledgements

Once again I'd like to thank the usual suspects: my wife Judy and my daughter Sally for following the plot and ironing out any initial discrepancies. Wendy Kleine and Sheila Yong for proof reading and Judy Bandidt for the final edit. Also, a big thank you to the lovely Brooke Bowtell and handsome Mitch Reynolds for allowing me to use their portraits on the jacket design. And thanks to John Halsted for getting this series of novels off the ground.

**This book is dedicated
to my wife Judy
and my daughters
Sally and Elizabeth**

Glossary

AC	Alternating electrical current
ANZAC	Australian & New Zealand Army Corps
Brumby	Australian feral horse equivalent to an American mustang
Bundy	Bundaberg rum – distilled in Central Queensland
Charlie	Viet Cong guerrillas
CO	Commanding Officer
DC	Direct electrical current
DI	Detective Inspector
Diggers	Australian troops
DPP	Department of Public Prosecution
GI	American soldier – derived from *General Infantry*
GPS	Global Positioning System
IGA	Independent Grocers of Australia
Jackaroo	Expert horseman, cattle and sheep musterer
Klicks	Kilometres
MC	Military Cross (Army award for bravery)
NLA	National Library of Australian
Puka	Puckapunyal Army Base, Victoria
Punji Sticks	Sharpened poled hidden in underground pits as a booby-trap
RAN	Royal Australian Navy
RAR	Royal Australian Regiment
Reveille	Early morning bugle call to wake up troops
RSL	Returned Serviceman's League
Russel Street	Victorian Police Headquarters
QC (Silk)	Queen's Council – hot-shot expensive barrister

SBS	Special Broadcasting Service (Australian free-to-air TV station specialising in local and ethnic programmes)
SES	State Emergency Service
SOG	Victoria Police Special Operations Group
Tommy	British soldier
VB	Victoria Bitter – a popular Australian lager style beer

Prologue — Cosmic Onslaught

Planet Earth

Everyone thought trigger-happy super-powers, an Islamic Jihad or maybe global warming would destroy civilisation on earth, but that's not how it happened in the end.

The North Atlantic was far and away the busiest strip of oceanic airway anywhere in the world. Not quite the busiest in the world, flights over the European and the United States landmasses had that honour. Every day countless con-trails streaked across the skies like lines of white, ice-crystallised spaghetti. At night navigation and anti-collision beacons flashed as a thousand blips echoed from ATC radars and on the traffic avoidance screens that were mandatory equipment for all jet airliners. But worldwide many more planes carved their way across the stratosphere bearing holiday-makers, businessmen, movie stars, politicians and world leaders wherever they wanted to go.

Giant luxury cruise ships and super-tankers gouged through the planet's oceans, laden with revellers, oil, grain and containers carrying an infinite variety of cargo including heavy machinery, vintage wine, industrial paraphernalia, illegal migrants and drugs. Whatever the mighty vessels' shipments might be, good or bad, they all had a reason for being where they were.

Ashore, road and rail transport cluttered national highways, railways and traffic-light ridden high-rise cities. These buildings blazed in an electronic orgy that made spectacular viewing from manned satellites that glided around the globe in their silent orbits. The metropolises' splendour was only over-shadowed by monstrous thunderstorms that ringed the equator drifting north and south with the sun's annual passage between the Tropics of Cancer and Capricorn. The planet lit up the solar system like a giant disco-ball. From the satellite point of view the world may have looked huge, but logistically it was a very small place indeed.

All that was about to change.

Before pilots and mariners started a flight or voyage they were supplied with reams of computer printouts telling them about anything notable they might encounter along the way. Phenomena such as volcanoes, severe thunderstorms, strong winds and high seas and unserviceable navigation aids were all included in those bulletins. Meteorologists and astronomers had predicted unusually high sun spot activity which was nothing new and really didn't affect modern inertial and GP navigation systems as it did much older electro-magnetic compass-based equipment. Consequently nobody took a lot of notice and it was business as usual for seaman and aircrew with a little milk and sugar in their coffee, thank you very much.

There was another astronomical event that had gained interest and a good deal of media coverage. A comet from a distant galaxy approached. It was named after a long forgotten German scientist who'd predicted its arrival fifty years previously when it was less than a speck on even the mightiest and probing inter-stellar telescopes. The comet was expected to be accompanied by a spectacular meteor shower. Once again there was nothing to worry about. The comet would pass a few million kilometres clear of Earth and the meteors were all expected to burn up on impact with the atmosphere in a spectacle rivalling the northern and southern auroras. So, sightseers and scientists alike were ready with binoculars and cameras at hand, not to mention folding chairs and thermos flasks full of hot tea laced with brandy, if you please.

That was until the comet, for some unfathomable cosmic reason of its own, decided to change course. It powered straight through the solar system causing gravitational and magnetic mayhem as it flashed past leaving the universe in general chaos and the earth in particular peril.

The comet's tail was a light-year long and consisted of countless electrostatic spikes of over a billion volts each. Immense lightning bolts forked into anything they passed and the earth was to be bombarded for decades, maybe even centuries to come.

Not a single earthly device requiring electricity was immune. Every transformer, anode, diode, transistor, volt, watt, farad and amp was immediately rendered inoperable. The world's magnetic field was thrown into random fluidity as each electro-magnetic pulse pierced the earth's crust and plunged into the magma core right down to its molten centre. In a period of twenty-four hours all electrical generation ceased. Efforts to restart emergency supplies proved useless as more spikes blazed in from outer space.

With one swift blow the entire planet had collapsed and returned to the Stone Age.

Aircraft instrument panels went blank, and with no information to guide their computers or power their flight controls, they simply plunged from the sky. Super tankers wallowed in ocean swells and mega-cities were instantly blacked out. Patients died on operating tables and in hospital wards with no electrical power to keep life-support systems going. AC or DC, it made no difference. Even household torch batteries were rendered useless. Cars and trucks jammed the world's freeways, although that might have taken a little longer to notice. Spark-plugs, distributors, engine computers and headlights simply shut down. Only some old diesels rattled on valiantly until their fuel ran out.

Every piece of modern technology no longer worked!

How long was it before panic set in? No one really knew, but it may have ranged from minutes to hours. In any event a total social breakdown was well under way within forty-eight hours. Millions died in the first moments as every plane smashed into the earth's surface, many colliding in mid-air. The roads were carnage. Police and emergency services were completely helpless. Their communication networks ceased to exist and the chain of command disappeared. The military was in the same, parlous situation. Generals were unable to contact their units and issue orders. What would those orders be anyway?

Shelter, water and food — in that order — are man's basic survival needs, and it didn't take long for survivors of the initial death-toll to realise that. In short order they realised only the most desperate and ruthless were going to make it, and that was exactly who emerged as the world returned to tribalism. With their natural brutality and street cunning, criminal gangs were on the front foot when it came to establishing their survival priorities and techniques. Inevitably the faithful flocked to their churches for sanctuary, only to find that their prelates had no answers other than prayer. They appealed to the urban gangs for help and discovered that charity was indeed a bygone notion. The meek certainly weren't going to inherit this new earth.

South-Eastern Australia was no exception.

Part One — Blackout

Chapter 1 — Aftermath, the Beginning

Excerpt from Probationary Constable Mike Farrow's Memoir:

Bob Brenan was our desk sergeant when Karen Davenport and I came straight out of Glen Waverley Academy. We were temporarily assigned to Emu Creek, a two-ute town a couple of klicks up a dirt track off the Great Alpine Road in the Victorian high country. There'd been a spate of cattle-duffing and Bob suspected the Harrison clan was behind it. We'd been on stake-out duty for a couple of days, but nothing had turned up so far. Bob was a great beefy bloke who stood 185cms at least, with a booming voice and ruddy complexion. He'd been a DI once, but was busted to uniform sergeant after threatening to thump the living daylights out of a DPP silk who'd muffed a drug bust his team had sewn up tight. The trouble was Bob claimed the QC had been nobbled by the mob and he's done it right outside the High Court with a dozen media cameras rolling. Nothing was proved and, although the commissioner probably agreed with him and managed to save his job, he still exiled Bob to what was essentially a senior constable's post — out of sight, out of mind maybe.

Bob was sanguine about his situation and even enjoyed the independence isolation brought. He reckoned racing around the countryside kept him fit and saved him from going to fat. He fancied a beer, but he liked Bundy rum best. At first he was a bit of a chauvinist where Karen was concerned, but she gave as good as she got and they soon became good mates.

Bob's mobile rang on the morning just before everything stopped. He listened for a few minutes, grunting occasionally.

'Come on, drop everything!' he roared, snapping the mobile cover shut. 'Morrie Sparrow's knifed Sandra Watkins, his de facto and taken off with their two kids. She's serious, but stable, at the doc's place. He's called Myrtleford for an ambulance. Goodness knows when it'll get here. Two lads from traffic followed him up to a shack along the Alpine Highway not far from here. They need some help.'

We put the station phone on 'answer' and took off like a shot — paperwork flying everywhere. I think Bob was doing about eighty before we got the car doors shut. I was in front while Karen piled into the back seat.

'Buckle up,' Bob admonished. 'Just because we're coppers doesn't mean we can flout the law.'

That was typical of the bloke.

The traffic boys filled us in. Morrie was a habitual low life with continual form for violence, drug abuse and sexual offences. He'd baled up in an abandoned shack with the kids and was threatening to kill them if provoked. Russell Street was arranging a Special Operations Group team to be airlifted in and they thought the media had got wind of it somehow.

'They'll be all over us like slime,' Bob hissed, and ordered the traffic guys to guard the property gate and prevent any unauthorised people coming too close.

'Karen, get on the loud hailer and try to make contact,' he added. 'He might be a sucker for a girl's voice.'

Karen rolled her eyes, but did what she was told.

'Ahoy inside!' she called. 'This is the police, we're here to help. No one need get hurt if we all remain calm …'

She was interrupted by a tirade of verbal profanity that would have curdled milk, but the gist of it was that Morrie wasn't coming out for anyone.

'He sounds pretty unstable,' I commented. 'What now, Sarge?'

But Bob had disappeared. Neither Karen nor I had seen him go as our attention was fixed on the shack. Where was our boss when we needed him? We were just two rookie cops.

'Where the blazes ..?'

My voice trailed off as two shots echoed from inside the shack.

'Morrie's done for the kids,' Karen yelled. 'Come on, Mike. No time for negotiating now.'

We hit the verandah at full tilt and flattened ourselves against the wall either side of the front door with our revolvers drawn.

Victorian police were being issued with new Smith & Wesson M&P .40 semi automatic pistols, but along with some other country coppers, we were still armed with .38 revolvers.

'On the count of three,' Karen panted. 'Boot the door in Mike, and I'll go through. You follow, OK?'

I didn't have time to say I'd go first — she was already counting.

'One, two …'

'Hold your fire!' Big Bob bellowed as he kicked open the door from inside and emerged holding a boy of about seven in one arm and a girl maybe a year or so younger in the other. They were sobbing and terrified, but otherwise seemed unhurt. With unexpected gentleness Bob handed the kids to Karen who naturally seemed to know exactly how to comfort them and say the right things.

'They should be okay in time, provided some counsellor doesn't get hold of 'em. Least-said-soonest-mended, I reckon,' Bob growled. 'Morrie won't be bothering anyone again. Saves the DPP a job anyway, but there'll still be a mountain of paperwork and the Commissioner will be pissed off. By the way, get a haircut, Mike.'

I have no idea how that big man got inside the shack so quickly and stealthily, but he did and was now quietly walking back to our car. He didn't want to be around when the press arrived and left the traffic cops in charge of the crime-scene. We followed with the kids. I thought I heard the distant beat of chopper rotors — the SOG team was on its way, but it never arrived — nor did the media or anyone else. Morrie Sparrow wasn't the only person to die that day …

I have to commend Sergeant Brenan. We'd be in a poor way without him. The town has shut down. Our car stopped before we got back to the station and we had to walk. Nothing works. No phones, no lights, no fridges, nothing. It's chaos. Dr Nandamuri thinks he can save Morrie's girlfriend, but it's touch and go. The ambulance from Myrtleford will never get here now, that's for sure. At least her children are being cared for by a local family. The sarge has taken charge and rallied everyone into the RSL hall for a briefing. No one knows what's happened and they're all scared stiff. Worse than the bush fires a few years back. Shelter and water are no problem. We have clean streams and the town relies on rain-water tanks anyway. Food might be another matter

...

The SOG choppers had gone down of course. One smashed into the convoy of press vehicles struggling up the narrow road to Emu Creek and erupted in a gigantic fireball. Those who weren't killed instantly died from burns and fractures as there was no one to help them. The following day Sergeant Brenan ordered Constables Mike Farrow and Karen Davenport to grab a couple of bicycles and pedal down to the crash site, but there was nothing they could do. Most of the bodies were charred mulch in the wreckage while those who had staggered away had died shortly afterwards. Amid a blizzard of bush-flies, crows, ravens, peregrine and falcons even a couple of wedge-tailed eagles flocked among the dead. A dingo slinked away, but he'd be back. The police officers didn't even try to drive the scavengers away. What was the point? The sooner they cleaned up the mess, the better. Emu Creek's residents had become primitively pragmatic after a mere twenty-four hours. They really had no other choice

'What's happening, Mike?' Karen asked.

Her shoulders dropped as she stared helplessly at the horror before her.

'Looks like the world's just stopped,' he replied, wondering if it would ever start again. That night the sky had been ablaze with meteorites slamming into the earth's atmosphere and lightning bolts that struck even though there were no storms in the area. They could still see flashes in the morning sky. Most homes had backup generators and Emu Creek residents fired them up as soon as the power lines went dead. But it was hopeless. The generators either exploded or simply failed to start. Maybe an ancient Massey-

Ferguson or John Deere diesel tractor could be coaxed into action, but what then? Electrical power was what they needed.

'C'mon Karen, let's get back up the hill and report this to the sarge. Dunno what he'll make of it.'

Luckily they were both young and fit having recently finished a gruelling training regime at the police academy, so getting around on bikes was fine by them. Bob had organised the townspeople to preserve and store food and water supplies. He'd also arranged for all perishable food to be stored in the IGA store (it was hardly a supermarket) and the local pub cool rooms, although nothing would stay cold for long. Any ice was packed in as well while Dr Jagadbandu Nandamuri advised everyone on health issues.

'You know what the worst part about this is?' Bob said after his two coppers had returned. 'The bloody beer will be warm in no time.'

After the horror they'd witnessed, Karen and Mike weren't amused.

When they got hungry, the two traffic cops had abandoned their useless motorbikes and hiked into town from Morrie's shack. They were senior constables Jim Pike and Wally Everett, but it was Karen and Mike's patch and the two traffic cops were just as nervous and confused as anyone else. Bob told them to take the bicycles and pedal to Bright, which was the closest town, and see what was going on there. They never returned.

In the meantime life at Emu Creek settled into a boring routine. There was no TV, no iPods, no telephones and no motor transport. The lyrics of Gordon Parson's 1958 song rang prophetically true because a pub with only warm beer was just as bad as a pub with no beer at all. A few of the more enterprising local lads took a few slabs of VB down to the creek the town was named after and decided the beer was drinkable after cooling all day in the icy water.

Within a week, a feeling of complete isolation descended over Emu Creek. The night sky was spectacular, but no one rejoiced at the display. They all knew that somehow it was responsible for the tragic events of the pass few days. Most people remained calm, either from shock, bewilderment or plain resignation. There was the occasional panic attack, but Dr Nandamuri had enough sedatives for the time being. After a week, Bob saw that although the town's supplies would last some time if properly managed, they were dwindling perceptibly. Tom Palmer, the local mechanic periodically tried to start various pieces of machinery, but with no success. Meanwhile Bob was disturbed that no news had filtered up to Emu Creek even though it was the end of the line. So once again he called the town together at the RSL hall.

The entire town shuffled in and sat where they could. Emu Creek's population numbered about 200, but the police beat covered all the country from the top of the Ovens Valley across the Bowen Range to the Snowy Mountains on the New South Wales border. It was a huge area for three coppers to patrol. They had relied heavily on chopper support from Melbourne or Sale when they needed to look for felons on the run, lost bush walkers or people stranded by floods and fires. Now, without the use of their 4-wheel drive, trail bikes or quads, that task had become impossible.

Bob opened the meeting after the townsfolk had settled down. There really wasn't much he could tell them that they didn't already know.

'Look, I'm in the dark just as much as you,' he admitted. 'I know you're all frightened about the power failures and you're concerned about friends and families elsewhere. I think we're lucky in one way. We have enough food to keep going for a while. I'm sure this will be over by then and we should get some help. The army and SES should be onto it right now, they're really good at this sort of thing. Nothing those blokes like more than roughing it. All I can say is conserve what you've got while I ration groceries to those who need help. Anyone who has a veggie patch, keep it going and I'd recommend everyone else start.'

The crowd look doubtful about that, surely the power would be back before then.

'I don't know what happened to Constables Pike and Everett. Maybe they were needed elsewhere. They weren't stationed here after all. But, Karen Davenport and Mike Farrow are *our* coppers, even if they are on temporary transfer. So I'm sending them to Wodonga to find out what's going on. And they'll come straight back if they know what's good for them.'

There was a smattering of nervous laughter.

'Sarge, what do you reckon if we go south to Melbourne?' Mike suggested. 'We can take the Ovens Highway to Bairnsdale. It'll take a bit longer, but we can get to Russell Street Headquarters and if they don't know what this is all about, no one will.'

'Okay, Mike. Fair call if you're prepared to go the extra way. There are some bloody steep climbs over the Hotham Heights. You game Karen?'

'It'll be fun going down-hill on the other side,' she replied.

Pike and Everett had taken the best mountain bikes in town, but there were several others to choose from. Mike and Karen checked their condition and decided what they'd need to carry.

Emu Creek was a popular starting point for bush-walkers and trail-riders so there was a specialty shop catering for campers in the main street. They would travel light in track suits and sneakers with a backpack each for food, a two-man tent and parkas in case of rain. They both pocketed a Swiss army knife for good measure. Bob suggested they carry several boxes of safety matches, it could get cold at night and rubbing two sticks together wasn't the quickest way to get a fire going. The bikes were both fitted with brackets for water bottles and the two police officers decided to forgo crash helmets in favour of military-style giggle hats.

'Special case, Sarge,' Mike said cheekily.

'Like your stubble and hair. You look like a bloody hippy,' Bob replied.

They also took their police badges, side-arms and extra ammunition. Half the town was there to see them off. Bob shook Mike's hand and even gave Karen a big-brother hug, which was unusual because he wasn't a *touchy-feely* kind of guy.

'Good luck.'

'See you in a couple of weeks, Sarge.'

'You bet,' he whispered under his breath as they pedalled away. They were good kids, they were his coppers and although he wasn't a religious man, he prayed that they'd be okay.

Farrow and Davenport left this morning. Emu Creek is relatively stable. Luckily there are plenty of horsemen in the area, so the local farms are running at least, although they still relied on electricity when it comes right down to it.

I'm no jockey, but fortunately I can ride, so I'll borrow a horse and head north to see if there is any sign of Pike and Everett. The town should be safe enough. Everybody seems calm. I'll have my service pistol, but I'll take a rifle and a shot gun as well. You can't be too careful. I'll need provisions for a couple of days as I don't want to be away longer than that ...

The Road to Bright

Bob Brenan travelled via the Great Alpine Road. *The Great* bit obviously described the view, because the road was very ordinary, two-lane bitumen in need of repair in many places. Highway maintenance had obvious fallen to the bottom of the Victorian Government's to-do list. Indeed the road to Emu Creek was still gravel. Bob came across several abandoned cars, a four-wheel drive and a truck. The drivers had decided to take their chances on foot and try to make it back to civilisation — wherever that might be now.

Property owners had left all the farm houses he passed except one that was occupied by a confused, elderly couple who said their son had ridden to Bright to see why the SES hadn't fixed the wires yet. Until then, they were sitting tight. After determining they had enough food, Bob decided it was best to leave them where they were.

He camped by the roadside and made a fire. His mount had to rely on what it could forage, but rain had been heavy lately and there was an ample grass supply. The sky was once again ablaze with meteorites as he reflected on what might lie ahead, but had no real idea. He wondered how long the fireworks would last and of course there was no answer to that either.

The following morning he arrived at Bright. The town had once been a picturesque Victorian showpiece, popular with sightseers especially in autumn when the deciduous tree foliage was truly spectacular. Now it was a wreck. The boutique shops, art galleries, restaurants, B & Bs and delicatessens were ransacked and most homes bore the scars of smashed windows and random destruction. The war memorial was desecrated with human filth which an elderly couple was trying to clean up. The community was in shock and it had been unlucky.

An outlaw motorcycle gang, who called themselves *Satan's Scrotum*, or *SS* for short, had camped outside town for a week before the lights went out. Although they'd taken over most of the pubs, they generally behaved themselves. Unfortunately they collectively lost control when their Harleys failed to start, taking their frustration out on anyone and anything close by.

They stormed the local police station and overpowered the cops, locking them in their own cells before looting shops and beating up anyone who got in their way. The town garages were ransacked and their owners left bleeding and bruised when they couldn't fix the bikes. After pillaging what they wanted, the entire pack pushed their Harleys along the Ovens Highway to Wangaratta where they hoped they might find more competent mechanics. It was going to take them a long time and many wouldn't make it.

Ironically the brewery had survived intact. It was closed for major refurbishment and its signage had been temporarily removed. The doors were barred and bolted. The brewery looked just like a corrugated iron shed. With so many other soft targets at their disposal, the bikers had shown no interest in the building. The gang was from Melbourne and hadn't been through Bright before. Obviously they hadn't done their homework or they'd surely have known about the brewery.

Bob was met by a small group of town officials and liberated police officers who admitted the place was totally out of control. He knew most of them as colleagues or from various civic meetings in the past. Local people had joined the looting and helped themselves to what the bikers left behind. Many homes were trashed and some reduced to smouldering ruins.

'Over half the townsfolk got out and headed for friends on farms or tried to get to Wangaratta for help. No one's come back and everyone left has gone mad, Bob,' Ted Harrison, a town councillor said. 'They've turned feral. It's as if they think this is the end of the world.'

'They might be right, who knows?' Bob replied.

'Yeah, well the town's a wreck and you're not going to like what I've got to show you next.'

Bob tethered his horse and followed Ted to one of the town churches although he couldn't remember which one it was afterwards. The bodies of Constables Pike and Everett lay beside the altar. They were covered with white, blood stained sheets. Each man had been shot twice, a double-tap, chest and head. Their weapons were missing and Bob was convinced they'd been shot with their own guns.

'We brought them here because it's one the coolest places in town,' Ted said apologetically. 'The minister says we'll have to bury them tomorrow.'

'Yeah, okay,' Bob said eyeing the small pile of personal belongs lying on the altar. 'Dunno how I'll get in touch with their families. I think they were based at Wodonga. What happened, Ted? This is execution style.'

'There's been a mass breakout from Beechworth Correctional Centre. Two hard noses made it here, took these boys by surprised and killed them for their guns and bicycles.'

'But Beechworth is for low-risk crims, inmates coming up for parole.'

'Not these two apparently. They were being held awaiting transfer to Melbourne to stand trial for rape, torture and murder. Seems they led the escape and stirred up the rest of the prisoners. Now we've got desperate men running all over the countryside and some of them are armed.'

'And I've got no way of letting anyone know ... What a bloody shambles.'

With no other ideas, Bob decided to return to Emu Creek and warn as many people as possible about the danger. He was going to have to form a horse-powered posse just like the Wild West, which was exactly what rural Victoria had become.

Chapter Two — Road Rage

Omeo Highway, Gippsland, Southern Victoria

Aafter the events of the past week, pedalling through the Victorian high country was surreal for Karen Davenport and Mike Farrow. The weather was fine and cool and they made good progress. The road was unsealed until they reached Omeo, a small town about twice the size of Emu Creek. The town was in a daze and many people had left to find relatives and friends elsewhere. Those who'd remained barricaded themselves indoors and were disinclined to talk to anyone. A couple of old bushies, who *were* inclined to talk, weren't able to tell Karen and Mike anything they didn't already know.

Initially they travelled through temperate forests of giant gum trees, but as they descended into the Gippsland coastal plain much of the land had been cleared for agriculture. They checked any farms they passed and found it was business as usual in the more remote places, but some effects were evident. Dairy farmers had come to rely on automatic milking techniques and now it took all day just to milk their herds. Cattle with swollen udders bellowed continually and shuffled around the milking yards tussling to be first in line.

'We can't keep going like this,' one harassed property owner complained. 'I'll have to put some stock down.'

'You might find yourself eating them before long,' Mike replied. 'I've got a bad feeling that supermarket shelves will be bare when you get to town.'

Mike and Karen camped for the night a couple of hours cycling from Bairnsdale, the first large town they'd pass through. They lit a fire, boiled a billy for tea and heated a can of baked beans.

'You know what the problem is?' Karen said as they watched the usual evening light show.

'Which particular problem would that be? I mean I can only think of about a billion right now.'

'Everyone thinks the trouble will end shortly and the world will return to normal, but we've got no guarantees. No one has the slightest idea how long this crisis will last.'

'Yeah?'

'So the only solution is to assume it'll be indefinite and the sooner we plan permanently the better.'

'What, like go back to the dark ages?'

'No you goose, I mean people lived without electric power only two hundred years ago. It was that Benjamin Franklin bloke with his kite and Thomas Edison who started it all. They used fire, water mills and steam technology for energy before that. We'll have to learn to do the same.'

'You think it'll come to that?'

She shrugged.

'Just as long as I don't have to wear a powdered wig, those silk knee pants and stockings like they did back then. You'd look good in one of those fancy ball dresses though.'

'Like Cinderella?'

'Yeah, why not?'

'Come on, Prince Charming, it's time to turn in.'

'It's gonna be pretty squishy in that dinky little tent.'

'Just watch where you put your grubby hands then, big boy.'

Karen needn't have worried. Mike was asleep in seconds and she decided it was best one of them stand guard while the other slept. After a couple of hours she didn't have the heart to wake him and fell asleep as well. They weren't bothered during the night, but in the morning she told him it was probably the last time they'd have that luxury. He agreed that one of them should always be lookout in future.

It had been downhill most of the way, but the number of abandoned vehicles grew steadily until they cluttered the road so badly that the cyclists had to swerve left and right to avoid crashing. They eventually arrived on the outskirts of Bairnsdale. The town had once been a small, compact community, but now suburban sprawl seeped outwards like everywhere else in Australia. It was almost as if developers thought they could just keep building houses until they all joined up in 700 square metre blocks across the entire continent.

Approaching from the north east, they passed an area where the roads, curb-and-guttering and drainage had been completed.

There were even a few 'sold' signs around although no construction had started yet. Bairnsdale's population was close to 12,000 and as Karen and Mike rode nearer to the town centre, they soon saw clues that large communities were not fairing as well as small, isolated ones. The sky was black with soaring crows, and that could only mean one thing.

Sure enough as they entered the first built-up street, the road was littered with the bodies of men, women and children. No one was spared. Karen gasped and Mike gagged as the corpses were bloated and growing ripe. Flies swarmed and droned like a thousand buzz saws. Dogs were everywhere feasting on the victims.

'What the blue blazes ...?' Mike was dumbfounded.

They pulled up and leant their bikes against a telephone pole. It was going to take a moment to get their heads around what lay ahead. The street was quiet. They saw no one alive.

'Let's check out a few of these houses before we head into town,' Mike suggested. 'Maybe someone is hiding. They might be able to give us the low down on what happened here.'

Karen didn't argue. She was in no hurry to discover what she was dreading. They opened the nearest gate and stepped into the yard. It was well manicured, although the lawn needed a trim, but the garden beds were ablaze with roses, camellias and rhododendrons. The house was neat and had been freshly painted, but all was not well. The front door stood ajar and the place had been ransacked. A middle-aged woman lay sprawled in the hallway and a grey-haired man was slumped over the dining room table. Both were dead, and both looked as if they had been bludgeoned mercilessly. The kitchen cupboards were bare — anything edible had been stripped from the shelves.

'Shit ...' Karen whispered. She never swore, not even an occasional *damn*.

They checked the next two houses, which had also been looted, but there was no one home. They tried one more place, but as they approached the front door a rifle shot cracked from the front window. The bullet slammed into the concrete pavers just ahead of the police officers and ricocheted away across the street.

'Don't come any closer, you heathen bastards,' a woman's voice called from behind the curtains. 'Next shot goes into your guts. I ain't kidding and I've got plenty of ammo.'

'Hold on, we're the police ...' Karen said as calmly as she could, considering she was standing in front of a trigger-happy, crazy woman.

'Yeah, pull the other one. You don't look like no coppers to me.'

'We're from Emu Creek in the high country ...'

'I know where that is, I ain't no moron. Lived around 'ere all me life, ain't I?'

'Okay, but we've come down here to try and find out what's going on.'

'The whole bloody town's gone raving mad, that's what's happened.'

'Look, it's best we talk inside. Here, we'll show you our badges.'

'You could have stolen them.'

'Yeah, right.'

Karen reached for her badge.

'No tricks or I'll blast yer. Don't think I won't. You've seen what's been going on out there.'

Karen and Mike waved their police badges at the window and that seemed to satisfy the woman, if not entirely.

'Leave them guns outside,' she ordered.

'No way,' Mike said. 'I'm not abandoning my weapon. Especially not here.'

That convinced the woman, it sounded like something a copper would say.

'Okay,' the woman conceded, 'but keep 'em holstered.'

'Fair enough.'

The front door creaked ajar and a .22 rifle barrel poked through the crack, followed by a woman well over retirement age. She was dressed in a grubby tracksuit and looked and smelt as if she hadn't bathed in days. That probably made her much like everyone else. The old woman relaxed after a few moments and offered her guests tea. She had a small LPG burner and started boiling a kettle. She placed the rifle against a wall.

'Belonged to me old man,' she said by way of explanation. ''E's dead now, but he used it for rabbitin' and such. Ain't got no licence though.'

'I think that's academic under the circumstances,' Karen replied. 'And we're fact-finding not booking people right now.'

'Sorry about takin' a pot-shot at yer, but yobbos have been prowling around. You can see what they done in the street. I was just lucky they missed me, but they'll be back. Seems there're no coppers around to help now.'

'Well, we're coppers, aren't we? I'm Constable Davenport and this is my partner Constable Farrow, Mrs ...'

'Blunt, Ruby Blunt,' the old woman replied. 'Blunt by name and blunt by nature. I don't hold with fanciness. Call me Ruby.'

'Okay, Ruby. I'm Karen and this is Mike.'

It was always easier for police when they were on friendly terms with the public. Karen and Mike sat in Ruby's lounge room sipping tea (sorry no milk) and they refused sugar, saying Ruby had better eke out her supply for as long as she could. It seemed ridiculously incongruous considering the carnage on her doorstep, but they listened as she told them what had befallen Bairnsdale.

Mike took notes as any conscientious young copper would.

Excerpt from Constable Farrow's Notes, Ruby Blunt's Evidence:

Bairnsdale's citizens were as confused and frightened as everyone else. At first, people simply wandered around the streets trying to fathom the mystery. They asked each other questions to which there were no answers. Just like Sergeant Brenan, the local police inspector converted to pedal-power to gather as many of his officers, SES volunteers and emergency services people together as he could. The big challenge was that a population of 12,000 was a lot harder to control than 200.

<u>Mistake 1</u>. He thought the problem was only temporary and delayed any action for three days, hoping things would return to normal or help would arrive from Melbourne.

<u>Mistake 2</u>. He allowed his officers to return home to their families in the calm before the storm.

<u>Mistake 3</u>. Once he determined there was a protracted, ongoing problem he fragmented his force. He sent officers east and west along the Princes Highway to get help, leaving only a skeleton crew at Bairnsdale.

Had Bairnsdale's police inspector acted differently it was still a moot point whether things would have worked out any better. His force of officers would probably have been too small to deal with the mass panic that ripped Bairnsdale's heart out before the week was up. Initially looting was widespread although random, but gangs formed with alarming speed. Soon the town was divided into about a dozen factions who immediately went to war over the spoils in Bairnsdale CBD.

The police tried to maintain order, but with so few officers left they were quickly overcome, battered unconscious and left to die in the streets. A number of female officers were gang raped before being beaten to death. By the first week the town was defenceless. The mass hysteria escalated into desperate clashes between rival gangs that left a trail of dead and maimed bodies in its wake. Homes were raided and looted. The occupants were crushed mercilessly. The gangs had ceased caring who lived or died.

Not surprisingly the gang leaders were the town's low-life, but amazingly people who had been normal, law-abiding citizens only a week before, flocked to join them. It seemed survival relied on numbers. By the time Karen and Mike arrived in town the police inspector was dead and Bairnsdale's population had been reduced to less than half. Four main gangs remained and they'd carved the town up into their respective territories around the main shopping malls. There had been fierce battles around the local market-gardens. The victors enslaved the producers, but those plots were limited food sources and only of use while they could be defended. That was pretty much how the status-quo would remain until supplies ran out and the gangland wars would rage until it was literally a case of the last man standing.

Ruby Blunt's Living Room, Bairnsdale

'So, whatcha plannin' to do now?' Ruby asked as she poured a second cup of tea. 'I mean you ain't gonna stand up to them yobbos. Not just the two of youse.'

'We'll have to think about that,' Karen said, 'but right now I'm going to get our bikes and hide them in your back yard if you don't mind. We don't want anyone nicking them, do we?'

She went outside, checked the street and dragged the bikes behind the house.

'More importantly, what are you going to do, Ruby?' Mike asked while Karen was gone.

'I'm packing up and heading out of town. Taking anything I can carry and this .22. Me old man had a place in the hills. It's a long hike. I might make it or I might not. Don't even know how long I'll last up there anyway. But one thing's for sure, I won't be makin' it 'ere at all. I've 'ad a good innings and I miss the old man, even if he could be a right pain at times. If it's the end of me days, I'd rather spend them in peace and quiet than in this mad house.'

'I wish there was something we could do to help.'

'Don't fret, love, just seeing your friendly faces was enough. It's been nice chatting to you, but I'll be off as soon as it gets dark. You're welcome to stay 'ere as long as you like, but I can't see what good it'll do ya.'

'Ruby's right,' Karen said as she entered the room. 'We can't hang around here for long. What do you reckon, Mike?'

'I honestly don't think we'd make it to Melbourne with just the two of us. We'll need a squad at least, but we should at least check out the town thoroughly. We'll have to report this back to the sarge.'

'OMG!'

Yes, Karen actually said, '*Oh ... Em ... Gee.*' It seemed blasphemy was also against her rules. Although she was no more religious than Bob Brenan, she was simply a nice girl who didn't need a gutter-mouth to get by. She'd managed through Glen Waverley Police Academy, but right now she was pushed to the limit.

'If it's like this in a small place like Bairnsdale,' she said, 'what sort of mess is Melbourne in? Mum and Dad are there!'

What could Mike say? His folks lived in Stawell near the Grampian Range in Western Victoria. He had a brother at sea with the Navy and a sister who was a recent medical graduate working as a voluntary locum way up at Kowanyama in the Gulf Country.

'They should be okay if they keep under the radar,' he replied without sounding too convincing about it, so he changed the subject. 'Are you up for a look around town tonight?'

She nodded, but he saw despair in her eyes.

'It'll be dangerous,' he warned.

'Remember on graduation day, the commissioner said there'd be bad times as well as good. I don't think he quite expected this, but we'd better get used to the idea that it's going to be dangerous all the time from now on. Maybe things aren't as bad as you've painted them, Ruby.'

'Maybe,' Rudy said without conviction.

By nightfall Ruby had packed as much as she could carry. She took off on an ancient bicycle loaded down with supermarket bags stuffed with provisions. The bike was fitted with a basket on the handlebars and panniers so she had enough to last a month if she was careful. She strapped the .22 across her back and ensured she'd got all the spare ammunition in the house. She waved cheerfully and disappeared. The two police officers never saw her again.

'She seemed happy enough,' Mike said after Ruby was gone. 'I suppose she's glad to be out of this mess.'

'She's a lovely old lady. I hope she makes it.'

Their staple diet was muesli bars and they ate a couple each for dinner before refilling their water-bottles from Ruby's tank. It was one plus in a world full of negatives. There had been severe nationwide drought and water restrictions during the first decade of the century. As a result most homes had installed rainwater tanks that quickly filled once the drought broke. Now that regular rainfall had returned to constantly replenish the tanks, water wasn't going to be as critical as food in the coming months. They also needed a greater variety of weapons. Their service pistols were all well and good, but they were noisy and there was only a limited ammo supply. They also carried ASP 21 expandable police batons, but both agreed you couldn't have too much fire-power for what they were planning to do.

After combing half the back yards in the street Mike scrounged around and found two axes. He removed the heads and gave one to Karen who'd commandeered a pair of decent kitchen knives that she sharpened with a steel.

'Good old Ruby,' she said. 'Not everyone has these old-fashioned sharpeners anymore.'

They took turns trying to get some sleep although it was fitful at best. There was a lot of yelling, crashing sounds and gunshots,

but by midnight they both had a couple of hours rest and it was
time to go.

Chapter 3 – Bedlam in Gippsland

Bairnsdale, Gippsland, Victoria

Mike and Karen left the bikes hidden at Ruby's place and headed into town on foot. They hugged fence lines, hedgerows and shadows as they crept towards the CBD. They'd been in luck arriving from the north-east along the Omeo Highway. The largest portion of Bairnsdale lay to the west of the Mitchell River and that was where all the action was fomenting. They met no one before reaching the river where a road bridge accommodated the Princes Highway. Although there were no streets lights, the town was illuminated by dozens of camp fires and the occasional building that had been set ablaze out of pure vandalism.

An immediate problem faced the police officers. One of the new warlords had decided controlling the bridge was a good idea and had posted armed guards across its span. Their silhouettes stood out against the flickering light from town. Karen and Mike crouched behind some native bushes.

'What're we gonna do about that lot?' Karen hissed.

'Swim?'

But, it didn't come to that. Although the road bridge was guarded, no one had thought to man the old railway bridge situated about fifty metres to the south. Crossing the Princes Highway proved easier than they expected as the bridge guards were all drunk and not at their vigilant best. They edged their way along the track and scuttled across without being spotted. Once across they turned right and headed north along the riverbank.

The west bank of the Mitchell River was fringed with parkland and a boardwalk that was a popular attraction for tourists and townsfolk alike. Now it was littered with rubbish, broken glass, crushed beer cans and a few bodies that were either dead or sleeping off the booze. Smashed and upturned supermarket trolleys were strewn everywhere. The stench of urine and human defecation was pretty awful, but the police officers were so pumped with adrenaline, they hardly noticed. It was impossible to remain silent as trash scrunched underfoot with every step.

'Mind your step,' Mike whispered, but Karen just glared at him.

They entered town at the junction of Riverine and Nicolson Streets, shuffling in the building shadows until they reached Bailey Street. There they stopped dead and dived behind a pile of upended wheelie-bins with trash scattered all around. It looked like a turf war was in full swing. A crowd of fist and knife wielding drunks was moving south. They numbered about two hundred while another equal sized gang tramped north. It looked like they'd meet right at the intersection.

Karen and Mike eased back along Nicolson Street into shadowy blackness. It was just as well. The gangs halted right at the cross roads and some people spilled into Nicolson Street. Knives were not the only weapons-of-choice. They brandished clubs, garden tools as well as cricket and baseball bats. It seemed bullets were precious and few firearms were evident. Everyone was liquored up and stood several metres apart roaring obscenities across the gap. It was impossible to tell who the leaders were in the mayhem. No orders were given, but with a cacophony of screams, the two sides suddenly surged forward.

This was no random bar-room scuffle or even a trade-union protest like those Karen and Mike had broken up often enough in the past. The two sides slammed together with unbridled ferocity and desperation. Heads were smashed and knife victims crumpled to the pavement only to be trampled by friend and foe alike. Teeth went flying, skulls caved in, ribs cracked and lungs were punctured. The sheer brutality of the assault was mind blowing. The gang members were not only men, but included many women and children barely in their teens. No quarter was asked or given. The only positive aspect of the fight was that the true horror was veiled by semi-darkness.

'Well, we're not going to stop that,' Mike said, barely audible over the row even when he yelled directly into Karen's ear. 'Come on, girl, it's time to get out of Dodge. We've seen all we need to. We'll be lucky to get ten steps if we try to head for Melbourne through that lot.'

They high-tailed it back to the river and thought they were going fine, until they ran into the bridge sentries who were returning to town to reinforce whichever gang they belonged to. When they were only metres apart, the guards hesitated, wondering which faction Karen and Mike came from. The guards certainly didn't identify them as coppers and if they were fugitives from a rival pack they needed dealing with. Never mind, when in doubt shoot first and ask questions later. There were half-a-dozen of them and three were armed with rifles. Before they could unsling their weapons, Mike drew his revolver and fired, hitting the leading rifleman in the chest. Karen swung her axe-handle and landed it across the jaw of another armed guard. His teeth shattered into crimson shrapnel as he dropped, spewing blood and gurgling hideously.

'Don't even think about it,' Mike snarled. 'Drop the weapons.'

The thugs must have guessed he was a copper then. No one except policemen say, *'weapon'*, but it didn't matter. Mike was pointing a gun and he'd proved he could use it. The armed guard dropped his rifle. Karen thought of tossing the gun into the river, but decided to hang onto it.

'Ammo!' she yelled, brandishing the axe-handle.

The guard pulled a box of .22 shells from his pocket and dropped it beside the rifles.

'Now bugger off,' Mike hissed, 'and be thankful we don't blast you here and now.'

The four guards needed no encouragement and raced towards town leaving their injured companion writhing on the bridge. Karen looked doubtful, but Mike holstered his service revolver before grabbing the rifles and ammo. He handed one of the weapons to Karen.

'C'mon, Karen, before they come back with some mates. We took 'em by surprise, but we won't be so lucky next time.'

They took off for Ruby's house. There was no time to waste. Their packs and bikes were safely where they'd left them. They were pedalling for all they were worth within minutes. It was just as well because right then a gang of about fifty louts came charging over the Mitchell River Bridge bellowing for blood. It seemed the bridge guards belonged to the winning side of the street brawl in town.

Once again the sky was ablaze with meteorites and thunderstorms were billowing all along the Great Dividing Range. The storms were vast surges of electric-static energy that simply vaporised as soon as the first lightning bolt streaked from the cumulonimbus thunderheads. This resulted in short, torrential downpours that dissipated as quickly as they formed. It seemed natural phenomena were not immune to cosmic interference either. This made riding a bike on a dark road with no street lights more hazardous than it might seem.

With no reliable light, staying on the sealed surface was difficult. The last thing Karen and Mike wanted was to damage their bikes or themselves by falling into a ditch. But with the gang so close behind they wanted to put as much distance between themselves and Bairnsdale as possible. Hopefully the pursuers would lose interest and head back to town. That indeed seemed the case as the clamour from behind grew dimmer and finally stopped altogether.

They rode for half-an-hour, but after bumping into countless obstacles, were forced to stop until daybreak. They hunkered down behind a Holden sedan and waited. It was only a couple of hours away in any event. The automobile was part of a six-vehicle pile-up and wreckage was crumpled together so tightly it was impossible to tell one car from another.

'Funny, we don't even really know what time it is,' Karen whispered. 'My watch is useless.'

'We need to find some good old clockwork jobs then. We'd better keep quiet though in case some of those scoundrels are prowling around out there.'

Scoundrels? I can think of a lot of other things to call 'em.

But, he never swore intentionally in front of Karen.

'Hang on — I've got an idea to deter 'em if we need to.'

The Holden's boot was ajar and after some scrambling Mike found a handful of oily rags. He investigated a couple of petrol caps until he came to a van that lay on its side. 91-octane had gravity-fed back along the refuel pipe and pooled at the cap. Mike doused the rags with petrol before ramming them into the gas-nozzle tightly enough that no more fuel leaked out.

In the pre-dawn light when they could make out the barest shadows it was time to go. They were just about to mount up when a black figure leapt across the car bonnet screaming his lungs out. Mike dropped his bike and grabbed his axe-handle. He swung with all his strength, shattering the attacker's skull and smashing his brain to a scarlet spray of fleshy pulp. Karen looked beyond the Holden and saw a swarm of crazed almost zombie-like figures streaming towards them. She and Mike aimed the commandeered .22 rifles and squeezed off four or five shots each. A man flung up his arms and pitched onto his back while a woman slumped over a car bonnet. The rest of the gang dived for cover.

Silently thanking Bob Brenan for insisting they bring extra matches, Mike struck one and set the petrol-soaked rags ablaze. The flames flared with agonising slowness until suddenly the whole car was enveloped in a fireball.

'That should distract them,' Mike said as they mounted up.

Mike and Karen pedalled out of town. The frenzied gang members howled as they dodged between or clambered over the abandoned cars. The police officers heard a dull thump followed by a blast of scorching air as the van's petrol tank exploded. More eruptions followed, instantly accompanied by the crack and clatter of falling metal while other scraps whizzed past the cyclists. Karen and Mike didn't look back. They needed their full concentration to dodge other wrecks on the highway.

Fortunately the number of vehicles quickly reduced the further they went and soon they were able to reach full speed, leaving the screaming mob behind. Still they didn't stop for over an hour and that was only for a swig of their water-bottles before taking off as quickly as possible. They made another brief pause to gulp down a packet of dried fruit each and then kept going until nightfall.

By that time they had started uphill and found a truck-stop giving them a good view back to the Gippsland plain almost as far as Bairnsdale. There was no sign of pursuit anywhere as far as they could see. A billowing tower of smoke marked where the car crash now smouldered to a blackened mess of ruined metal and molten plastic.

'Never thought to bring binoculars,' Mike said, 'but I don't think anyone's after us.'

'Let's put that tent up in the bush,' Karen suggested. 'We can hide the bikes as well.'

'Yeah, best not light a fire, looks like another cold can of beans for dinner tonight.'

They erected the tent and opened the beans, taking turns eating spoonfuls with their Swiss army knives attachments. They hadn't mentioned the horrors of Bairnsdale, but finally Karen felt she needed to talk about it.

'Can you believe how those people have become so savage that quickly?' she said.

'Dunno whether I'm going to judge 'em. We were really lucky to have been in Emu Creek when this whole melt-down started.'

'You were pretty quick back on the bridge. You saved our lives when you shot that guy. The car bomb was neat too.'

'Something I learnt from the sarge when he sorted out Morrie Sparrow. Make a decision and then get on with it. Can you remember all that stuff they taught us at Glen Waverley? You know, about giving the bad guys every chance to surrender ... I think that's all over now.'

'I've never been so scared in my life.'

'You too? I thought it was just me.'

'You were pretty decisive a few times back there.'

'The inner brute, you mean...'

'No, silly ... well *yes* in a way.'

'C'mon, you'd better turn in, I'll take first watch. We want to be up at first light.'

'Mike?'

'Yes.'

'Will you sleep with me tonight?'

He hadn't seen that coming. He certainly liked Karen and she was a drop-dead gorgeous girl, no doubt about that, but she was a colleague. At the academy she'd kept her private life exactly that -- private. She had a reputation as an ice-queen, but Mike hadn't really thought about it. He'd tried to avoid romantic attachments with fellow cadets, it could get messy. His brother who commanded (or had commanded) an RAN patrol boat had often told Mike he spent more time dealing with 'red-light' harassment accusations from female crew-members than actually running the ship. Mike had taken his big brother's advice. There were plenty of girls around who didn't wear a uniform.

Karen saw his hesitation.

'Don't you like me?'

'Yes of course I do, but what about guard duty?'

That sounded pretty lame and Karen giggled.

'We should be okay hidden away here for a while. Look, who knows what will happen tomorrow? I'd hate to ... well you know ... miss this opportunity.'

Mike did mention he hadn't thought to bring any condoms along with the binoculars either and that it wasn't a particularly good time to risk a pregnancy. She laughed again and took a blister pack from her breast-pocket.

'First thing I did after we arrived at Emu Creek was to have Dr Nandamuri make sure I wouldn't run out of "the pill".'

Who'd have thought it?

'I *have* had a couple of boyfriends before, you know,' she insisted.

That was quite enough discussion on the matter in Mike's opinion. It was time for action.

'Now I'll show you what a bad girl I can be,' she whispered.

'Just leave the hand-cuffs where they are, okay ..?'

So one primeval survival urge took over from all other primeval survival urges. That night's watch wasn't as attentive as it might have been and Karen and Mike were certainly a little more relaxed than they should have been. It was at least an hour after dawn when Mike stuck his head out of the tent flap and headed a discrete distant away to relieve himself.

He wasn't gone long, but when he returned three strangers stood at their camp site. Karen was standing in front of the tent dressed only in her underwear. She was staring down the snub-nosed barrel of a Victorian police issue Smith & Wesson .40 semi-automatic pistol. Two of the men carried pistols while their companion was armed with a cricket bat. Unfortunately Mike was unarmed. Both revolvers were still in the tent.

One of the intruders swung round and pointed his pistol at Mike.

'Well, well,' the man snarled, 'you the boyfriend then?'

'Maybe,' Mike tried to stay calm. He weighed up his chances of successfully diving for the tent and winning a shoot-out. Pretty well zero and Karen would be the first to go. 'What do you want?'

'Yer food of course, yer blithering idiot and we'll take this pretty little sheila too. It's been a long time in the slammer.'

'Gaol? I know you two, don't I?'

Stalling for time was one thing, but it was easy to slip up as well. Mike recognised two of the men from police files. They'd tortured, raped and murdered a young woman in Geelong, but weren't the sharpest tacks in the box. They'd stolen a custom-built vintage Falcon GT0 and headed north. The car was a cop-magnet especially careering along the Hume Highway at nearly 200 kilometres an hour. They were picked up on a radar trap just outside Wangaratta, but failed to stop and a chase ensued. A police chopper from Albury joined in along with units from Southern New South Wales towns along the highway. The pursuit ended badly for the crims when they rolled the car and both ended up in Albury Base Hospital.

When they were fit enough they were immediately taken to Beechworth Gaol awaiting transfer to Melbourne for trial.

Unfortunately they were the two villains who led the breakout when all power failed. Mike and Karen didn't know it then, but these were the men who'd murdered Constables Pike and Everett for their guns and bikes. They'd run into the biker gang who were in a murderous mood, so the fugitives decided to backtrack. They'd sneaked past Emu Creek undetected, picked up a fellow escapee with a stolen bicycle along the way and were now heading south. The third villain was a petty felon and not particularly comfortable in the company of hardened criminals, but tagged along in desperation.

'Yeah, you're the Mooney brothers, who's your mate?'

'How'd you know that, you a bloody copper or what?'

It was probably a bad time to divulge that particular piece of information.

'Newspapers. Unlike some people, I can read. Tom and Derek Mooney, right. This other bloke obviously isn't important enough for the media to bother with.'

'Yeah I was,' the third guy blurted out. 'M'name's Cedric Bean and I got me picture in the paper too.'

'The *Shitsville Gazette* doesn't count, Cedric,' Mike goaded.

'Well tough shit to you, professor, 'cos we're gonna take yer stuff and yer girl.'

Out of the corner of his eye he saw Karen edging back to the tent, so he pretended to slip drawing the gunmen's attention a little further away from her. Derek Mooney waved his pistol under Mike's nose and Karen made her move. She was quick, but not quite quick enough. Tom and Cedric dived after her.

Derek was distracted for a second which gave Mike the chance to land a right hook onto his jaw. Derek dropped his gun and went down, but was only mildly dazed. Mike's fist hurt like blazes and the impact jarred up his arm, but there was no time to worry about the pain. Mike flung himself at Derek and started raining punches wherever they'd land.

While they tussled the tent erupted in a flurry of flailing arms and legs as Tom and Cedric wrestled Karen into submission. She fought back in a fury, clawing, biting, and kicking until a gunshot cracked from the tent. There was a scream as another shot blasted a bullet through the tent's nylon fabric. Cedric hopped through the tent-flap with blood pouring from his thigh. Karen had managed to grab one of the revolvers and got off two shots before Tom overpowered her.

'That bitch shot me ... the bitch ... the bitch!' Cedric howled

'Shaddup, yer whinin' bastard,' Tom roared dragging Karen from the tent with his pistol jammed against her skull. 'Okay, Professor, get off 'im or yer girlfriend's arse is grass.'

Derek rolled from under Mike. He was surprisingly tough considering the punishment he'd taken. Derek staggered to his feet and booted Mike in the ribs before he could get up. The escapee picked up the pistol and aimed at Mike.

'I reckon they're bloody cops,' Tom bellowed.

'You don't say. Well, now you're gonna get it now, pig ...' Derek growled as he cocked the weapon.

Chapter 4 — A Horseman Rides By

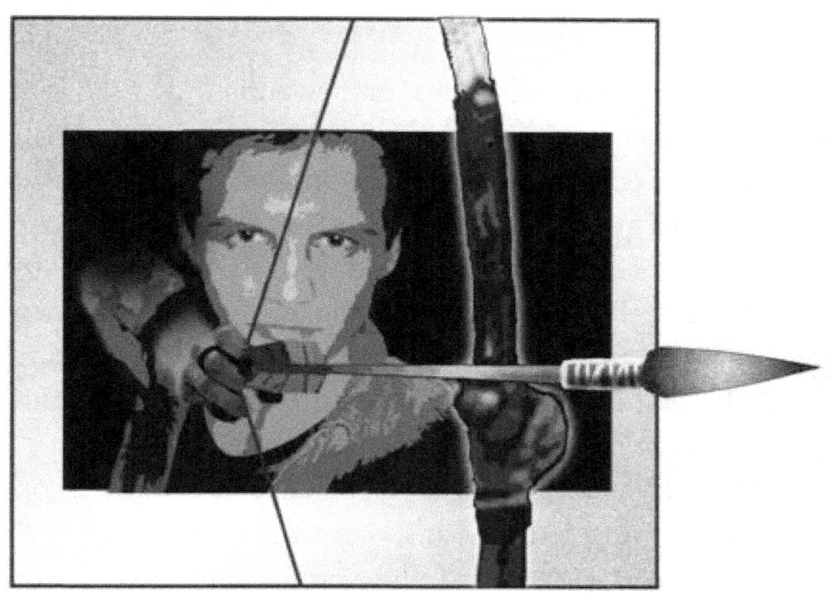

Blam!

A .40 calibre bullet blasted from Derek's pistol muzzle at a velocity of 370 metres/second. Two screams rang across the bush. One was from Karen as she stared in horror, the other came from Derek as he crumpled to the ground with an arrow impaling his thigh. The shaft had penetrated right up to the fletching. In shock Derek had fired wide and the bullet zinged away into the bush. With two crims out of action, Karen elbowed Tom in the guts, turned and drove her knee into his groin. He groaned, released his hold on her and staggered back a few paces, but he was still standing and levelled his gun, aiming between Karen's eyes.

'Bad move, sunshine,' a voice said calmly from only a few metres behind the tent. 'Don't even think about it or you're a dead man. Drop the gun.'

A man who looked in his mid-twenties sat astride a black horse. He'd re-arrowed his bow and held a firm bead on Tom. The stranger kept a rock-steady aim and Tom knew he stood no chance. He relaxed the grip on his pistol and let it drop to the ground. Derek's gun lay beside him and Mike went to retrieve it.

'Just leave the guns where they are for the moment,' the stranger said, transferring his aim to Mike. 'We seem to have restored the status quo. I'm pretty sure I know what this is all about, but fill me in anyway. Quick version will do.'

Karen told him. The stranger listened, but didn't comment. He dismounted and tethered his horse before picking up the two automatic pistols. He herded the three escapees close together sensing Karen and Mike weren't his immediate threat.

'New uniform?' the stranger asked with just the hint of a smile as he passed Karen. She disappeared into the tent, dressed and was back in seconds.

'Police issue?' he asked holding the guns towards Mike for inspection.

Mike nodded and the stranger turned to Tom. Derek and Cedric were no use. They simply moaned and nursed their wounds.

'Where did you get these guns?' he asked.

Silence.

The stranger put a bullet through Cedric's skull.

'You were saying ..?'

He sensed Karen and Mike were ready to move.

'No heroics please,' the stranger said without raising his voice. 'I can kill you just as easily.'

That pulled them up short. It was the sheer decisive finality and self-assurance of the man. No one was in any doubt he meant exactly what he said. No warning, no second chance.

'We can't let you shoot people. We're police officers ...' Karen stammered.

'Not anymore,' the stranger observed. 'You're just survivors — same as the rest of us.'

He turned back to Tom.

'Now, where were we? Oh yes, the guns. Where did you get 'em?'

'Took 'em off two coppers back in Bright.'

'And they just let you?'

'Naw, we 'ad to persuade 'em, didn't we?'

'You murdered them?'

'Yeah, so what? What's it to you? Like yer said there ain't no cops no more.'

The stranger shot Tom through the temple, turned the gun on Derek and put a bullet into his heart. He rifled through their pockets and collected any spare ammunition he found. It was all the three villains carried that was worth anything. He emptied the magazines, handed one weapon to Mike and pocketed the other along with half the bullets.

'Half each,' the stranger said, 'that seems fair to me.'

Karen just stared at him.

'They were baggage,' he said.

'Who *are* you?' she managed at last.

'Not the Lone Ranger that's for sure. My name's Zach McAlister. I live with my grandpa and his girlfriend Ange over Merimbula way. They're pretty well self-sufficient. Grandpa's in his eighties now, but he's a fit old boy, so is Ange. Merimbula, Eden and Bega — whole south-east corner for that matter — are all pretty much basket cases, but Grandpa's armed and got his place booby-trapped. A few mates and their families have moved onto his farm so they're doing okay, I guess.'

'It's lucky you happened by when you did,' Mike said.

'Oh, I didn't just happen by. I've been following you since yesterday — checking you out. Nice touch blowing those cars, by the way.'

'We didn't hear you last night.'

'I heard you all right,' Zach grinned as Karen's cheeks reddened. 'Don't worry, I kept a discrete distance. I found your pal Ruby in a shack not far from here and stayed the night. She told me all about you — said to say "hello" — She has quite a soft spot for the pair of you.'

'How's she doing?'

'Okay by the looks of things. She knows how to trap rabbits and has already started a veggie patch. She's got as good a chance as anyone, I'd say.'

'That was quick. She only left Bairnsdale a couple of nights ago.'

'I'd say it's a case of *the-quick-and-the-dead* these days. No one has time to hang about and Ruby knows that.'

'What are you doing way over here then?' Karen asked, eyeing him with interest. He was a handsome young bloke and a week's stubble just added to his rugged attraction. He was tall, muscular and uncompromisingly masculine – a man without a feminine side. Mike noticed her expression with suspicion, although he was realistic enough to know last night's passion didn't necessarily mean any commitment. He didn't quite know how he felt as he'd had his eye on a couple of Emu Creek girls, although they weren't in Karen's league.

'Same as you, it appears — reconnaissance. Looking for some friendly faces and you're the first I've come across. I've had Jet here since she was a foal. She can live off the land and she's a great cross-country horse, so I volunteered to have a look around. The world's gone belly-up and it's only going to get worse. Anyone who's made it so far will need allies. It was lucky I saw those bastards creeping up on you. Your tent was well hidden, but not quite well enough.'

'Would you like to come back to Emu Creek with us then?' Karen offered brazenly as Mike rolled his eyes almost through the back of his head. 'We can do with big strong men like you and I'm sure Sergeant Brenan will be interested to hear what you've got to say. He's sort of taken over now.'

'You'll need a good leader. A committee's no use anymore and you can kiss democracy goodbye. I'm not sure it wasn't overrated anyway.'

'What about them?' Mike ventured.

'Crow bait. I'm not wasting time on rubbish.'

Zach dragged the arrow through Derek's leg and inspected the shaft.

'I'll have to re-fletch it, but it should be okay,' he muttered to no one in particular.

He returned the arrow to the quiver clipped to his saddle and mounted up. The animal was a hardy Snowy Mountains Stock Horse from Jindabyne and a natural high country bushland survivor. Zach didn't wait for Mike and Karen to pack up, but rode away at an easy walk.

'Emu Creek straight ahead, I take it,' he called over his shoulder. 'I'd bring a couple of those other bikes along. They look like quality kit and you might be glad of them later.'

It didn't take long for Karen and Mike to stow their gear and prepare to follow. They worked in silence, but there was, if not tension, a tacit atmosphere between them.

'What ..?' Karen snapped at last.

'Nothing,' Mike replied with a grin. 'Just noticed how you looked at him, that's all.'

'Well, I wasn't looking at anything special. Now get on your bike.'

It took a little while to get used to riding one bike while gripping the other stolen one by its handlebars. Initially they wobbled all over the road, but eventually got into a rhythm. They caught up with Zach in less than an hour. He wasn't in any hurry, keeping alert and not rushing into trouble.

Emu Creek, Victorian High Country, SE Australia

'Busy few days, I take it,' Sergeant Bob Brenan said, handing out creek-chilled beers all round. 'You've earned these by all accounts.'

Zach refused, saying he didn't drink alcohol.

'Didn't take you for a wowser,' Mike said, a little too sharply in Karen's opinion, although Zach didn't appear to take offence.

'Not a moral-high-ground issue, I just don't like the taste,' he replied.

Bob's place was an alpine-style chalet at the edge of town where Karen, Mike and Zach were tucking into barbequed sausages, jacket potatoes and tossed salad. It was the first decent feed they'd had since leaving Emu Creek. The sarge had listened to their report without interruption, taking thorough notes as the story unfolded. Once a copper, always a copper and he wanted to keep records, especially as all other communication media was no longer available. He was especially interested in what Zach had to say. He concluded that Emu Creek must become self-sufficient without delay. They needed to have enough food to last through winter and make sure they grew winter crops during the colder months.

'We'll have to co-ordinate the farms as well. They have the agricultural knowledge. They'll have to work a management programme for slaughtering livestock and rely heavily on game. It's not as if there's a scarcity of roos around here. The local jackaroos will be the best blokes for hunting I guess. Every aspect of food supply will have to be considered in the context of not lasting day-to-day, but year-to-year.'

'I never thought I'd say this,' Mike said absently, 'but I'm going to miss a Big Mac.'

'Yeah, we sure took a lot for granted.'

'What irks me most is those lay-abouts up in Nimbin will probably do alright,' Zach said. 'I mean they don't bother with soap much and they're so juiced up most of the time, they probably don't even know what's happened yet.'

'They'll wake up to it when their dole cheques stop coming,' Bob replied. 'They're not half as independent as they think. Beats me why they slag off against the government all the time when it's their prime source of income.'

He began analysing every aspect of town life and how Emu Creek could survive. It was going to take time, but Bob was proving he was not only a man of action, but a half-decent administrator as well. He planned to do the rounds of town and talk to everyone individually. He wanted to pick their brains separately before gathering them together for a town meeting. He knew that large groups spent too much time talking around in circles and achieving nothing. Synergy was all well and good, but it had to be managed.

'You know that if you make this work, sooner or later someone is going to come and try to take it off you,' Zach said.

'It's human nature,' Bob agreed.

He liked Zach because the young man saw the facts of life with absolute clarity. He was under no rose-coloured illusions about what people were capable of when they were desperate. Just like Bob, Zach's world was in black-and-white.

'Always been the same,' Zach surmised. 'Cavemen pushed the Neanderthals out. Persians, Egyptians, Phoenicians, Greeks, Romans were all pushing one another out at some time. Saxons and Angles pushed the Celts out. Normans and Vikings all did their share of pushing. Then Europeans up and pushed Indians around in America and the Aborigines right here. The Islamic extremists were having a red-hot go at pushing everyone out of everywhere and would probably have done all right except the lights went out and spoilt it for them. I'm not blaming them, it's just the way people are. *Civilised* people have grown soft and complacent, now they'll need to toughen up fast or die. Only the strongest and most ruthless will come out at the end. No more Mr-Nice-Guy from now on. We have to get that through our heads.'

'Well, look at you, the little historian and philosopher,' Karen giggled, nudging Zach in the ribs. It didn't take much beer to make her tipsy.

'Not my words really,' Zach said. 'My Grandpa's girlfriend, Ange Holyman, was once a big-shot doctor and professor. She knows all sorts of stuff. She used to be a religious nut until she worked out it was all mythology. She may be an old girl now, but she's got a head full of knowledge that we can't afford to lose. She started writing stuff down as soon as *The Spark* went out. According to her we've got to save as much knowledge about everything we can. Everyone should keep journals.'

'*The Spark?*'

'Yeah, it's a term she coined.'

'Your grandfather has a girlfriend?' Karen said with a hint of admiration.

'Sure, why not? She's kinda his age and they get along great. He'd known her when he was younger and they got together again after my Nan died.'

'Where are your family?'

Zach shrugged.

'Sydney I guess. I don't want to talk about it. I can't afford to dwell.'

'Dwelling's a girl thing anyway,' Bob said

'What?' Karen challenged.

'Girls think too much about things. They worry about consequences, right and wrong and stuff like that. Sure, we've got to plan, but we have to act decisively if we're threatened. I agree with Zach that it'll be the most hardnosed who survive this.'

Karen let it slide.

'Do you think this could really be The Apocalypse? You know, "The End of Days" that the prophets wrote about in the Bible,' she asked.

Bob shrugged.

'It's as good a theory as any,' he said.

'Which makes us the chosen ones,' Mike said. 'I wonder if that's a good thing or not.'

Maybe it was the beer, but she was exhausted. The last few days had caught up with her. She and Mike shared a two-bedroom unit beside the police station where Bob had lived until be bought a place of his own. Zach was staying the night in Bob's spare bedroom, so Karen and Mike headed home. She crashed and slept for twelve hours. When she awoke she realised she was a changed woman.

Excerpt from Mike Farrow's Memoir:

All Karen's firmly held beliefs have been comprehensively shattered. She joined the police force with a genuine desire to help the community — to make a difference. She'd maintained that goal throughout her time at Glen Waverley despite the hazing and sexual harassment. She was so focused she was able to ignore all the rubbish from other cadets and get on with her training. I got to know her a bit and I was happy when we were assigned to Emu Creek together.

Our night of passion? I think that might be just what it was. Maybe girls get just as big a testosterone rush as guys after cheating death the way we did. I dunno. Also there's no doubt she fancies Zach McAlister. She can't keep her eyes off him and doesn't think

I've noticed, but who wouldn't? Am I jealous? Hell yes, but there's no hope of competing with Zach in the macho stakes. Pity. I mean, Karen's a babe and she sure handled herself well on patrol, I couldn't ask for a better partner.

But, Zach's just so in control, and that bow-and-arrow thing. Probably reckons he's Robin Hood although I don't reckon there's any giving to the poor involved. Zach says he learnt archery on his grandpa's farm. They'd put up a shooting range for guns and bows and it's just as well. He's a crack shot with any weapon as far as I can see. I reckon I can hold my own in a fight now, but wouldn't like to take Zach McAlister on.

Bob's taken to him as well and they're off somewhere checking Emu Creek's defences and organising the farmers. There are six properties surrounding town and they're to be our forward look-out posts. Luckily the owners have large families and there is a good stock of jack-and-jillaroos to patrol the bush and add muscle to our defences although some of the more isolated families haven't always seen eye-to-eye with the law in the past.

Quite a few of the young Turks have spent a night or two in our lockup after some drunken disturbances. Hopefully we can use that aggression to our advantage. One thing is for certain, I'm going to have to learn to ride a horse.

Chapter 5 — Respite

Emu Creek, Victorian High Country, SE Australia

Bob left Karen and Mike to maintain order in Emu Creek. There was some discussion about their status under the circumstances, but Bob told them to wear their uniforms. He said it was a psychological thing, a bit like airline pilots. Passengers would be uneasy if they turned up in shorts and singlets, it was the same with coppers, unless they were TV detectives of course. Bob had asked Zach to accompany him. It would at least relieve some of the alpha-male tension in town.

'Just patrol the beat on your bikes,' Bob instructed Mike and Karen. 'A police presence should keep everyone calm. Help out where you can. Hearts-and-minds and all that stuff.'

The best thing Bob had done was take control from the start, keeping a lid on panic. Emu Creek locals saw that they weren't in immediate danger of starvation, so they didn't resort to the irrational mob-rule Karen and Mike had witnessed in Bairnsdale. Many townsfolk, especially the older ones, were already preparing alternative ways of getting by. Wood fires were of course common in alpine homes, so warmth wasn't an issue. Every house had a blazing fire and enough fuel to last for months. An old guy was reinventing the Coolgardie Safe and hessian waterbags. Zach had told them it was that sort of knowledge Ange Holyman insisted was vital to preserve. People were starting to experiment with other non-electronic mechanical devices.

'Our hope for the future,' Mike commented.

'Sarky,' Karen retorted.

'No, I mean it. We've got to start somewhere and these people are doing just that. They're not sitting around feeling sorry for themselves or contemplating suicide. They're having a go. They're staying as a community where Bairnsdale fragmented. They're thinking ahead, not in the past. That's what we've got to do too.'

They dismounted and wheeled their bikes for a bit. All quiet on Main Street, so they patrolled the side roads.

'Mike,' Karen said after a short silence, 'you said "we", did you mean everyone or us?'

'Both if you like.'

'Back on the road the other night ... I loved every minute ... but ... my past relationships haven't gone well. My first boyfriend dumped me because I joined the force and the second one because I wouldn't quit. And I thought men liked women in uniform,' she smiled sadly.

'The fantasy doesn't necessarily transfer to reality. It's hard to keeps dates with the hours we work. But, you don't have to explain anything to me. We were both pumped and that affects people. I don't have any regrets though.'

'Neither do I,' she smiled.

'Look, there's nothing I'd like better than for us to have a steady relationship, but you've got to be sure it's what you want. Any time you're ready to share a bedroom, just let me know.'

'Thanks, Mike, you're sweet.'

'Hey, I dunno about those other guys, but *I* like women in uniform.'

That was his stroke of genius. He'd let her know exactly how he felt, without any pressure and he made sure he didn't mention the enigmatic Zach McAlister. No point in putting comparisons into her head. They continued patrolling, helping out where they could and said no more about relationships.

Excerpt from Karen Davenport's Diary:

Mike is a darling and most girls would say I'm a fool
not to grab him without a second thought. He's a hottie
no doubt about that and he doesn't have to prove himself
after our bike patrol. He was so courageous. I don't mean
mindless, animal bravery. I know he was scared just like
me, but he overcame his fear. That's what makes a true
hero in my eyes...and my heart.
Mike's an amazing lover too...mmmmm... ☺...yummy.
Then along came Zach. He's such an awesome hunk
and, boy does that complicate things. The silly part is I'd
move in with Mike in a flash if it wasn't for Zach and
he only seems to think I'm funny. Just a gawky

schoolgirl. I know Mike cares, but Zach is so indifferent and cruel. But. ..?

I know the Mooney brothers were bogan dags, but Zach was so heartless. 'Baggage' he called them. Would he shoot anyone else if he thought they were baggage? Would he do the same to me? He said he'd have strung them up and saved the bullets, but he wasn't sure whether we'd try to stop him. Would he have shot us too if we got in his way?

OMG, the world's falling apart, our families are probably gone and here I am worrying about potential boyfriends! ☹

Some people wanted to leave Emu Creek and try to find their families, but after we returned from Bairnsdale, Bob talked them out of it. Now I think everyone is too numb to think about it anymore. Bob just said, 'Hope for the best and prepare for the worst.'

It's a bit of a cliché, but what else can we do?

The Harrison Place, 10 Kilometres North East of Emu Creek

Bob and Zach visited all the outlying farms and warned the owners to watch out for the Beechworth fugitives in particular and anyone else in general. All strangers were to be considered enemies until they established otherwise.

'Don't take any chances,' Bob admonished each family in turn. 'If in doubt, shoot first and ask questions later. I'll be making regular checks, but if you're at all concerned, come into town as fast as you can. My coppers will patrol, but we can't be everywhere at once so I need you to be my eyes and ears. Anything fishy going on, let me know straight away. It doesn't matter how trivial, right now there are no false alarms.'

Most of the farms understood the need for concern and had already taken precautions. They bred large families out where TV reception had been poor, so along with a few hired hands, most places had the numbers to deter anyone snooping around and up to no good.

The last place they visited was the furthest away along the road to Bright. Phil Harrison was Bright Councillor Ted Harrison's brother and the two men couldn't have been more different. Phil was a sullen, foul-mouthed bully whereas Ted was a regular bloke who genuinely wanted to help his community. Phil wasn't a particularly tidy farmer or a very good one either. The house was over a kilometre along a rutted track from the road and in a pretty rundown condition. They were met by a careworn woman and her two sullen, teenage daughters. Sharon Harrison knew Bob Brenan well. She'd been into town often enough to bail out her drunken old man and wayward sons. Sharon had four sons aged fifteen to nineteen called Gary, Andy, Joe and Clarence respectively. The girls eyed Zach lustfully.

'Phil and the lads are roundin' up stock, but they'll be back for tea. You wanna come in for a cuppa?'

'Thanks, don't mind if we do,' Bob replied. Being sociable with those on the cusp of the law was a good way of keeping an eye on them and maybe gleaning a hint about what mischief they might be planning next.

'Hi, I'm Norma,' one of the girls said as she shoved ahead of her sister towards Zach.

'And I'm Charlene,' the other girls said, elbowing Norma in the ribs.

'Nice to meet you, ladies,' Zach replied, causing the girls to giggle.

'Don't know if we're ladies,' Charlene said, 'but we're women enough for you I guess.'

As neither of them looked older than sixteen, Zach had his doubts. He was well advised to steer clear of the girls who were in fact well-developed fourteen-year-old twins.

'Quit the skank act and get inside you little sluts,' Sharon snapped and the girls scuttled through the door.

'Nice happy little family,' Zach observed as they followed.

'They're just bored,' Bob replied. 'I mean there isn't much social life out here, so they haven't had a chance to learn many airs and graces.'

They sat around the kitchen table. The farmhouse was served by a wood-burning stove so boiling a kettle was no problem. While Sharon Harrison poured tea, the girls shuffled each other aside to be closest to Zach. Sharon sported a black eye, but that was nothing new. Phil Harrison was a surly brute and had a reputation for knocking his missus around along with anyone else he took a disliking to.

'Phil's been at it again,' Bob observed. 'You know I can't do anything if you don't make a complaint. Why do you let him get away with it?'

'He's all I got,' she replied feebly. 'I caught him pawing the girls, so I gave him a mouthful and got a fistful in reply.'

'You should have come to me. What sort of example is he setting the boys? No offence, but they're easily led into strife.'

'None taken. They're not so bad when their father isn't around.'

'We can take care of ourselves,' Charlene insisted. 'Dad weren't hurtin' us none.'

'He shouldn't be touching you at all,' Bob said.

'You keep out of it, copper,' Norma said. 'We look after our own.'

'So I see by your mother's shiner,' Zach said.

'Look, it's better now the lights have gone out,' Sharon said. 'The boys have to work twice as hard without the trail bikes and quads. They're so shagged out at the end of the day, I just feed 'em and they're asleep in no time.'

'Alright,' Bob said, 'but I'm still the law around here, so for heaven's sake come and see me if you're worried about anything happening again.'

There was a clatter of hooves outside, heralding the arrival of Phil Harrison and his four boys. Sharon looked about nervously. Entertaining the local filth wasn't on Phil's to-do list for her.

'Don't worry,' Bob said heading for the door, 'I'll let him know you didn't call us. How could you anyway?'

Phil Harrison and his boys met Bob on the verandah steps. They were ready for a fight. They were always ready for a fight. They didn't need a reason.

'Whatcha want, copper?' Phil snarled.

'And good day to you too,' Zach said.

'Who's the kid with the mouth?'

'Phil, meet Zach McAlister,' Bob said. 'Someone you don't want to get on the wrong side of – same as me.'

'Yeah, heard you popped Morrie Sparrow. Pretty tough eh, Brenan?'

'Whatever. I've got better things to do than trade pleasantries with you, Phil. I've come to warn you.'

'What can you tell us that we don't already know?'

'You heard about the Beechworth breakout as well, then?'

'Bunch of penny-ante bottom feeders. We can handle 'em.'

'Maybe, but remember they're desperate and hungry bottom feeders. You've got Sharon and the girls to think about.'

'Yeah, but when are we gonna get the power back?' one of Phil's boys blurted.

'Don't hold your breath, Gary,' Bob replied. 'PCs Davenport and Farrow just got back from Bairnsdale and the place is a mess. Bright's a ghost town after a biker gang hit it, so who knows what's going on further afield.'

'Is Ted alright?' Sharon asked then bit her lip when Phil glared at her.

'He's okay. Trying to sort out the mess though.'

Unable to think of anything further to say, Gary and his brothers just looked hostile and shuffled sullenly on the porch.

'Look, Phil,' Bob said, 'I know we don't always agree, but I need you farmers to be the town's lookouts. Don't under-estimate anything, especially marauding gangs. You see anything suspicious, get word to me quick-smart, okay?'

'What's in it for us?'

'Your lives most likely.'

Bob and Zach mounted up and rode back to the farm gate.

'I hope we don't have to rely on that bunch for our future gene-pool,' Zach remarked when they were out of earshot. 'You think they'll do what you asked, Bob?'

'Probably not in Phil's case, but if Sharon is worried enough, she might.'

They rode back to Emu Creek.

Excerpt from Karen Davenport's Diary:

Mike is growing a beard. It suits him just as well as
Zach McAlister. OMG, men are lucky ducks, they
require so little. We girls seem to need so much back up.
My legs are overdue for a shave, and I don't want to
think about my under-arms. As for a bikini wax – well
forget it! ☹
Ugh! I don't want to go feral.
List of things I'll have to ration or find a substitute for:
Toilet rolls
Deodorant
Toothbrush and paste
Soap
Tampons
Dishwashing detergent (no more dishwashers)
Toilet cleaner
I'm sure I'll be adding to this list in no time.
We have to flush the loo with bucket water because there's
no pressure. Bob and some town brainiacs are working
out ways to store milk, meat and vegetables. Thank
heaven for the old fashioned housewives around here who
can still make butter. Cheese is proving more difficult,
but some folk are giving it a go. Most women can bake
bread in camp ovens, but I don't know what'll happen
when the flour runs out.

Now Dr Nandamuri is concerned about hygiene and disease.

Emu Creek, Victorian High Country, SE Australia

It was nightfall when Bob and Zach returned to town and there were already some changes. The high country was always rife with bush flies, but Bob noticed a huge increase during the week.

'The place is starting to smell pretty organic,' Zach remarked. 'Must have been like this in the Middle Ages.'

Dr Nandamuri left his main street surgery and came to meet them.

'I must speak to you urgently, Sergeant Brenan,' he said.

'You look worried, doc.'

'I'm more than worried, sergeant. We have to think of the town's hygiene and we'll have to act quickly before people get sick.'

'What sort of sick are we talking about?'

'Cholera, dysentery and typhoid must be our primary concerns,' the doctor explained. 'They're probably rife in the cities already. We do have one advantage that we're still using septic systems and not sewerage. Human waste is contained, but we must stay vigilant, especially with garbage...'

Dr Nandamuri rambled on with a list of health precautions he thought required immediate attention. Bob understood the doctor's concern, but he was exhausted and all he wanted was a creek-chilled beer. He was relieved to hear that Sandra Watkins, the late Morrie Sparrow's ex-girlfriend, was going to recover and her kids were being well looked after by a local family.

'Okay, doc you formulate a health plan. Bring it the station tomorrow at 9am and we'll get things organised.'

'Nice delegation,' Zach grinned as Dr Nandamuri hurried off to this surgery.

'Maybe, but there'll be a shit-load more delegating I tell you. The doc's right and he's the best man for the job. We'll have to ferret out any other specialist experts and get 'em to co-ordinate what needs to be done. We're going to have to rely on eighteenth century engineering before long.'

'They're probably doing okay at Old Sydney Town then.'

Bob held another council-of-war over dinner at his place that evening. Karen cooked vegetarian pasta. It wasn't the boys' favourite, but given that most of the meat was off she thought it best to play it safe. If they wanted to go eating half-rancid meat, they could, but not when she was cooking. Zach told them he was heading off in the morning. He planned to scout as far as Lake Hume, then back along the Upper Murray River Valley through the Snowy Mountains to his Grandpa's place.

'What's the plan after that?' Mike asked.

'I don't think we have a choice. Just staying self sufficient and defending the place is the best anyone can do. It's going to be tough. We'll have to turn everyone away, thugs and refugees alike. We simply won't be able to feed them.'

'Everyone will become your enemy,' Karen said.

'I think they already have. You are going to have to do the same here. You don't have the luxury of being soft-hearted or you'll be overrun.'

Bob understood and nodded while Mike remembered Braidwood and held no illusions about just how ruthless they must be. Karen shuddered at the thought.

'I'm off to bed,' Zach announced. 'I want to be gone by first light. Goodnight all, it was nice to meet you. Thanks for the hospitality, Bob. I'll try to get by this way when things settle down.'

'If they ever do.'

Zach shook hands with Bob and Mike and kissed Karen. Whether he intended simply a friendly peck on the cheek was unclear, but their lips met. Karen closed her eyes while the kiss lingered until Bob cleared his throat. She turned looking a bit sheepish although Zach just smiled and headed for the spare room. Her eyes followed him until he closed the door. When she turned back to Bob and Mike they were eyeing her with amusement and suspicion respectively. The two policemen exchanged glances.

'What?' Karen said.

Bob shrugged

'I've got a big day with Doc Nandamuri tomorrow, so I'm gonna hit the hay. You two can sort this out by yourselves,' he said and went to bed.

'You want to go with Zach, don't you?' Mike said as they walked home.

Karen paused.

'Oh, Mike, I don't know, it's all so complicated.'

'Too right...'

She turned, flung her arms around his neck and kissed him.

'Look, I don't know about tomorrow, Mike,' she whispered, 'but I know who I want to be with tonight.'

Chapter 6 — The Gathering Storm

Excerpt from Karen Davenport's diary:

Everything takes so long now. Mike came up with this plan to keep clean. We toss a few buckets of water into the bath then boil a couple more. At least we can wash even if we have to use the same bath water. Mike suggested we share the bath which might be fun.☺
We have tank water, but of course no pressure without the pump. Emu Creek runs right past the police house, so we get our drinking water from there. It's so clear and fresh to drink. That's not the only thing that's fresh ...

Emu Creek

Karen awoke early. Mike was still asleep with a silly grin on his face, so she stoked the fire, grabbed a pitcher from the kitchen and headed to the creek. They now boiled water in a saucepan over the lounge room fire. As she approached the creek, she spotted Zach McAlister bathing a little way downstream. The sight of him stark-naked took her breath away. *A body to die for* she later recorded in her diary, *all muscle and attitude.*

'Morning,' he called cheerfully, without the slightest hint of embarrassment.

'M ... m ... morning,' she replied.

'You wanna join me?'

'Don't be silly, it's freezing, you'll catch your death.'

'No, it's fine. I'm used to it. Okay, if you're not coming in, I'll come out.'

He splashed out of the shallows and strode towards her while she stared wide-eyed. He winked as he bent and grabbed a towel beside his clothes.

'Sorry about the view,' he grinned, 'but cold water shrinks everything ... temporarily.'

'It's okay, I took that into account.'

Well, if he was going to flirt, she could too. He quickly dried and dressed and there was an awkward pause.

'Will you be coming back?' Karen finally asked.

'Do you want me to?'

'Yes ...'

It was out before she'd thought about the consequences.

'What about Mike?'

'It's ...'

'Yeah, I know — complicated. Look, I'd ask you to come with me, but I work better alone and you're needed here ... and I don't mean just for Mike.'

'I've only known you for two minutes, why do I feel like this?'

'My animal magnetism?' he smiled. 'Tell you what, if I manage to survive and get back to Grandpa's place and things are fine there, I'll ride back here and then we can see how things are between us.'

'The three of us, you mean.'

'Okay, I'm ready to try new things.'

'That's not what I meant, Zach ... and you know it ...'

He kissed her briefly.

'I'd take you in a flash, Karen, but I don't think you've thought things through yet. I don't think any of us have. Now Bob's scrambling eggs for breakfast, so I'd better dash. I promise I'll be back, and we can talk some more then.'

He left for Bob's chalet. Karen watched him go then turned back to the police house. She saw Mike at the kitchen window.

'You forgot the water,' he said when she entered the kitchen taking the pitcher from her hand. He quickly went outside.

Excerpt from Zach McAlister's notebook:

I'm probably moving on in good time. No doubt about it, Karen is a little stunner, but it's a bad time to form attachments. Grandpa and Ange are relying on me to have a good look around, so that's what I'd better do. I'm not here to white-ant Mike Farrow either.

The last thing I want is to make enemies when I need all the friends I can find. I told Bob Brenan where I was going and that I'd try to get word back if I run into anything that will threaten Emu Creek. He said he was going to have to rely on farm horsemen as couriers. He warned me about the gangs north of his town.

If I travel by road it'll be quicker and I'll be more likely to run into people with news.

I'll be more likely to run into trouble as well ...

The Road to Bright

Apart from the occasional abandoned car, Zach saw nothing unusual as he rode north. After he passed the gate to Phil Harrison's place he was in uncharted territory. He moved at a slow pace and scouted every building along the way, so he was still short of Bright by late afternoon. The properties beyond the Harrison place were all abandoned. Zach knew that some families had moved to Emu Creek, but others had fled elsewhere. In a few cases a note was left on the kitchen table giving a clue to the fate of the families who had lived there. Some messages were brief and some heartbreakingly detailed since Zach had a pretty good idea how the writers would wind up. The notes were handwritten except in one case when an old Remington manual typewriter was used.

Only in the country, Zach thought, *no one in town has one of those things anymore. Looks like they'll be making a resurgence.*

Leaving with Mary and the kids to try and join up with our folks at Shepparton. Taking the horses and set the other livestock loose. Had to put the milker down.

John Bradley
Gone bush. Gangs of vandals lurking
around. They killed the dogs.
The Callum Family

*Food gone, we'll have to get to town. Wife
expecting any day. Got to find a doctor. Need
to feed the kids too.
George and Jenny Weston.*

They were all much alike, how could they be otherwise. They reflected the despair and confusion of ordinary families who were hopelessly ill-equipped to deal with the crisis.

Towards dusk Zach left the road and rode Jet overland to a shack he spied on a hilltop some distance away. The place looked deserted, but he approached cautiously anyway. There was evidence of several fires around the shack, although only cinder piles remained as if they had been hastily extinguished. He dismounted and kicked one of the ash mounds and discovered just how recent it was as it burst into flames when oxygen hit the embers. Zach drew his police automatic.

'Put the gun away, man,' a voice called without sounding particularly threatening.

Zach spun around, but there was no sign of anyone. Zach raised the gun although he had nothing to aim at. Suddenly he heard a *whoosh-whoosh* from one side and something solid smashed into his arm, knocking the gun from his grip. It hurt like blazes and he jumped with shock. His arm wasn't broken, but he'd have a massive bruise that'd take ages to heal.

'Told ya,' the voice said.

'Who are you? What do you want?' Zach yelled into thin air.

The area was silent for a moment before Zach sensed movement all around him. Black figures emerged from nowhere and walked stealthily towards him. He was surrounded by a group of about fifty Aboriginal people -- men, women and children, mothers nursing infants. Their leader was a bearded man around middle age. He carried a .22 rifle although most of his companions were armed with clubs, bows and spears.

Spears! They've got bloody spears!

One of the younger men moved ahead of the others and retrieved a boomerang that lay a few metres from Zach.

'You hit me with that? Jeeze it hurt,' Zach said.

'It was meant to. You shoulda dropped the gun,' the young man mumbled.

Zach's pistol lay at his feet, but no one made a move to retrieve it.

'Didn't want to waste a bullet,' the leader said.

'I'm pleased to hear it,' Zach replied, 'but I don't mean any harm. I know that's hard to believe after what's been going on around here lately.'

The Aboriginal leader said nothing, but stooped and picked up Zach's pistol. He ejected the chamber round and magazine and handed the separate components back to Zach, who picked up the spare cartridge and pocketed it.

'Dunno when I might need it these days,' he said sheepishly.

'Not around us, anyway. We ain't gonna hurt you. Your mob is doing a good enough job of that to each other already.'

'Yeah, hang around a couple more months and you'll probably get the country back.'

The Aborigines thought that was droll which helped defuse any animosity. Zach reloaded the clip into his pistol and holstered the weapon before introducing himself.

'G'day, my name's Apari,' the leader said, but gave no second name. 'Might as well boil a billy. You plan to stay here tonight?'

'Yep, got to find some grazing for my horse first.'

'Plenty of grass in the paddock out the back.'

'Cheers.'

Zach tethered Jet to a fence post giving her enough rope to chew up half a hectare if she wanted to. The Aboriginal people rekindled the fires and prepared a supper of baked beans and fried eggs. Zach added some of his supply to the menu.

'Where's the goanna and witchetty grubs then?' Zach asked.

'C'mon, who do you think you are — Crocodile Dundee? Our mob's the Wiradjuri People, but we mostly live in the Albury and Wodonga suburbs with day jobs just like you. I'm a postman.'

'Why the walk-about out here then?'

Apari frowned. *Walk-about* wasn't a term he'd have used.

'*Actually* we're on our way home from Lakes Entrance. The kids from our local kindie wanted to go to the beach, so we hired a bus and took 'em camping for a week. We had a great time until the bus conked out and the whole place went crazy.'

'You don't know what's going on?'

'Just that the sky's gone nuts, nothing works and there are a bunch of creepy weirdos prowling around the bush.'

'It's all connected.'

'Thought as much. We're just trying to get back to our people, but it's taking longer than we figured. Lucky we had all our camping gear with us.'

'You may not want to go back to Albury. A couple of Emu Creek coppers just came back from Bairnsdale and it's a basket-case.'

'That where you from then, Zach?'

'Passing through, I'm on my way back to Merimbula.'

'You're going the wrong way.'

'I'm going *that way* to check things out and get the big picture. You might be better heading for Emu Creek. At least the local coppers have got a lid on things there.'

'We've got no people there. It's just a washed out gold town that's a stepping off place for bush-walkers now.'

'Pretty much. You might want to take up roo shooting then. It's gonna be messy cutting it up though.'

'No problem, Warra here is a butcher's apprentice. He'll show us the basics,' Apari said indicating the young man who was handy with the boomerang.

'You reckon you can bring down a roo with that thing, Warra?' Zach asked.

'Yeah, I'm pretty good, but why bother when there are plenty of cattle in the paddocks?' Warra asked.

'I've never tried to kill a steer with a club or a spear,' Zach replied, 'but I don't reckon it'd be easy. Your ammo supply won't last forever, so you're going to have to adapt. Lucky I took up archery.'

Apari's people had decided to camp for a couple of days and consolidate their position. As it turned out, despite Apari's remarks, many of his people, especially the women and girls had listened to their elders on bush walks and were able to gather a great variety of bush-tucker, including witchetty grubs.

'They're not as easy to find as people think,' Apari said screwing up his nose. 'Some people eat 'em raw, but not me. They're fine if you toast 'em for a couple of minutes. I guess we're better placed than you whites. We have the old ways to fall back on, even if we're a bit rusty. Our elders'll whip us into shape in no time when we get home.'

'Good luck with that,' Zach said, 'but be careful. The bigger the town, the madder it seems to get.'

'We'll bear that in mind. Tomorrow I reckon we'll slaughter one of them poddies in the next paddock and stock up on beef before we push off.'

'Good idea.'

Excerpt from Zach McAlister's notebook:

Funny how I can lie in a comfortable bed until mid morning, especially on a cold day. Out on the road I'm kipping down just after dark and up at sparrow-fart. It's all so primeval. I wonder if cavemen got to sleep in. Probably not, sabre-toothed tigers to wrestle, hairy mammoths to skin, stuff like that. I reckon we're only a step-and-a-half away from that now.

Ange said I had to write down my thoughts as well as events. She says it's important even if the lights come back on. We mustn't allow this chaos to force us into a historical black-hole.

Approaching Bright, Victoria

Zach set off at first light and reached Bright in just over an hour. He rode down Delany Avenue until it turned into Gavan Street and the commercial centre of town. Initially it looked as if the place was deserted, but as he reached the town centre he saw the first bodies.

Geez, it's just how Karen and Mike described Bairnsdale!

But there was something decidedly odd about the way the bodies lay. They were not scattered randomly, but in small groups of two or three and mostly lying in sheltered spots. Also there were only about a dozen people, which was something of a relief. The next thing he noticed were the number of beer, wine and spirit bottles littered around the prone forms.

Zach tethered Jet where she was hidden by the bush. He crept forward and started when one of the 'corpses' rolled over, belched, farted and went limp once more. Zach noticed small steam clouds from their nostrils and mouths. These people weren't dead. They were sleeping off a heavy night. Dressed in ragged jeans and leathers, there was no mistaking their identity — they were bikers. Their jackets all bore the `Satan's Scrotum` logo. What the hell were they doing in Bright? The gang was supposed to have left over a week ago.

He ducked through the nearest gate and edged his way to the front door. It was unlocked so he cracked it ajar and peered inside. An unmistakable stench of stale sweat, alcohol, urine, flatulence and body odour assaulted his nose. The room was furnished with a lounge suite. All the chairs were occupied by drunken bikers sleeping it off. A half-naked girl lay sprawled across the sofa and there was no doubt as to the purpose she'd served.

Zach could only reiterate his thoughts.

What the blazes are this lot doing here? Bob said they'd buggered off north.

Chapter 7 — Invasion Force

Zach edged back along the pathway to the front gate. His main concern was that the bikers would wake up soon and he didn't want to be around when they did. However he needed to know what they planned to do next. They'd stripped Bright once, so there couldn't be much left and then they'd move on -- but which way? Would they head towards Emu Creek? If they did Bob Brenan would want to know pronto.

Bearded and dressed as he was in a black leather jacket and jeans, he might go unnoticed. The bikers' personal hygiene left much to be desired and Zach wasn't much better after a couple of days without a bath. What he lacked was a bikers' logo. As far as he could see they all wore them.

Zach jogged back to where he'd left Jet and led her further from town. He found a shady spot, well away from any prying eyes. There was ample grazing and a small creek. Jet was now invisible from the road, but close enough for Zach to reach her if necessary. Satisfied that he'd tethered her with enough room to graze and drink when she pleased, Zach slung his bow and arrow quiver across his back before edging his way back to town.

No one had yet stirred. He jumped a fence and edged into the back yard of the first house along Delany Avenue. He scaled one backyard fence after another, hoping he'd reach the town centre unnoticed. A few drunks were waking when he reached the main street. Zach unslung his bow and nocked an arrow to the string. He checked the shop-fronts until he found one unoccupied and ducked inside. The business had once been an art gallery, but the works were nearly all ruined. Years of labour had been wantonly destroyed.

The world might have turned upside-down, but there is no excuse for mindless vandalism. Maybe this is what humans really are and they don't deserve the planet anyway.

It was possible that he was lost in thought or simply focused on the waste around him, but he dropped his guard. He heard footsteps crunching through the debris behind him. He turned, but a micro-second too late. A man stood before him and swung a pool cue. The man didn't look like a biker and he wasn't a natural fighter. He hesitated before landing the blow, giving Zach enough time to raise his arm and fend off the worst of the force. It still stung like hell. He already had a livid bruise thanks to Warra's boomerang, but Zach hadn't time to think about that. The cue knocked the bow from his hands and it clattered to the floor. Zach dived for the man before he could take another swipe. He crashed into the fellow and they tumbled through the wrecked artworks.

The struggle was brief. After Zach thumped his opponent a couple of times, the man went limp and slumped onto his back. He was still conscious, but seemed resigned to his fate and wanting to get it over and done with. Zach sensed he was no longer a threat.

'Who are you?' Zach asked in a whisper.

'Does it matter?' the man replied. 'Why don't you just belt the living daylights out of me, like your mates have done to our town?'

'Firstly, that scum out there aren't my mates ...'

'You're not from the gang?'

'No, I'm just passing through. The name's Zach McAlister.'

Zach helped the man to his feet and dusted some debris from his crumpled suit.

'I'm Ted Harrison, the only town alderman left. Sorry I hit you, but I've been dodging these louts for days.'

'No harm done,' Zach said, rubbing his arm to make sure. 'I'd have probably done the same in your place. Hang on, *Harriso*n? Are you related to Phil and Sharon Harrison?'

'Phil's my brother, although I can't say I'm really proud of the fact.'

'Yeah, he's a bit hard to get along with. Bob Brenan and I visited his place to warn him about the Beechworth breakout.'

'Did he listen?'

'I don't think so. But what are these buggers doing here? I thought they'd left.'

'Well, they came back, didn't they?

Ovens and Hume Highway Junction

The SS bikers had indeed headed for the Hume Highway, the arterial road between Melbourne and Sydney. What they hadn't counted on was the army base at Puckapunyal. Two full platoons of recruits were being transported by truck convoy from a live-round firing exercise in one of their New South Wales training areas. Like every other powered vehicle on the planet, the trucks had ground to a halt when their electrical systems failed. Puka was an armour training unit, so the troops weren't specialist infantryman. Nevertheless, they'd completed two weeks training and were now proficient shots with F88 Steyre assault rifles.

Their commanding officer was Major William 'Roy' Rogers MC, seconded from 7 Battalion RAR for training duty at Puka. He was a combat veteran who'd seen serious action in Afghanistan and Iraq. He was satisfied that the recruits were good enough rifle shots. Next they'd start training on light armoured vehicles. They were great boys' toys and morale was high as everyone was looking forward to getting their hands on the new equipment.

When the convoy shuddered to a halt and no one was able to restart any of the vehicles, Major Rogers ordered the company to lock the trucks and abandon them. The troops shouldered their packs and Steyre assaults rifles, formed up in columns-of-three and started marching back to Puckapunyal. Rogers decided the situation beyond his pay grade so he'd leave it for colonels and generals to deal with. The troops had sufficient rations and water to make the journey with ease. Additionally each man and woman carried two spare 42-round magazines.

The highway was cluttered with hundreds of stranded vehicles so marching was a tedious business. It reminded Rogers of Baghdad in many ways.

The column collided with the bikers just as they were spilling out of the Ovens Road onto the Hume Highway. The bikers were as mean as sin after being forced to abandon their Harleys that were just too heavy to push for more than a few kilometres. They'd been forced to commandeer any push bikes they could and the ignominy of having Harley-Davidson replaced by Malvern-Star was not lost on them. They were out for blood — anyone's blood — but they pulled up short at the sight of fifty disciplined army personnel.

The smart choice would have been to let the soldiers march on by, but the bikers were wasted on grog, speed and ice. Right then common sense wasn't a biker-option and the last thing Major Rogers wanted was a gang of bellicose hooligans tailing his men down the Hume Highway. The soldiers halted.

'Deploy your people — lock and load,' Rogers ordered Lieutenants Goddard and Kildare, his platoon commanders.

The bikers started fanning out like prowling wolves. Obviously they wanted to surround Rogers' company, finish them off and steal their weapons. The gang carried an illegal assortment of pistols, shotguns and hunting rifles, but were outmatched by the soldiers' firepower.

Rogers ordered the platoons to form two ranks. There was no cover right in the middle of the highway, so he manoeuvred his men and women into a square like the old colonial days. It was the best way to hold the bikers at bay and protect their flanks. Soldiers weren't police. It wasn't their job to fire on Australian citizens, however unworthy those specimens might be. But it *was* their job to defend themselves. The troops were nervous. They were new recruits after all. They'd completed rifle training, but facing down a hostile force so soon after enlistment was daunting.

'You people move back along the road there,' Rogers ordered, indicating the Ovens Highway to the bikers. He wanted to see them retreating back the way they'd come. He'd dealt with similar crowds in Kabul and Baghdad and knew that the sight of a company of soldiers bristling with automatic weapons was enough to disperse a rabble. But, mobs were notoriously unpredictable.

The bikers appeared to have no leader and were simply in the mood for trouble. Rogers was met by a bombardment of empty beer stubbies and rocks, accompanied by a chorus of ribald cat-calls and abuse.

And then someone fired a shotgun into the air. Suddenly a biker aimed his pistol and fired. The bullet zinged into the concrete just ahead of Rogers' recruits. The bullet ricocheted and ripped into a front-rank soldier's boot, luckily without hitting his foot, but the air was instantly thick with lead and the staccato rattle of gunfire.

'Hold your fire!' Rogers, Goddard and Kildare screamed in unison.

The engagement was over in seconds. Whether it was justified would never be determined. Three bikers lay dead and a couple more were wounded and wailing in pain. The others fled at full speed. Rogers wasted no time. Right now he needed to put as much distance between them as possible.

'Form up your people, gentlemen and let's march. Double time for the next kilometre,' he ordered his lieutenants.

'What about the wounded bikers, sir?' Goddard asked.

'We don't have the facilities to deal with them. They'd better hope their pals come back and get 'em. It looks like there's a war going on right here at home. Not very glamorous, is it?'

'You think it's come to that, sir?'

'I've got a bad feeling this isn't an isolated incident.'

The recruits marched on to Puka without further trouble, but found the post abandoned. Major Rogers left a hand-written report of what he called *The Highway Armed Engagement* on the orderly room desk. As he couldn't fathom what was happening, he and his recruits marched on to Melbourne and find out. In the meantime, the bikers skulked back to Bright. They were joined by most of the Beechworth escapees along the way. Once again, they vandalised the town, robbing, raping, bashing or murdering whenever they felt like it.

Bright, Eastern Victoria

Ted and Zach were still hiding in the art gallery when Bright oozed into life. The bikers nursed sore heads as they scrounged around for something to eat. Rations were becoming scarce and snarling fights erupted over what was left.

'Reminds me of a pack of dogs scrapping over a bone,' Ted said.

'You reckon we'll be any better if it gets right down to the wire?' Zach whispered. 'How's your supply, by the way.'

'I've got a bit stashed away, you hungry?'

'Yeah, but I'm okay for food right now. What I want to know is what that lot'll do next.'

'They didn't confide in me.'

'How come you're hanging around, anyway?'

'I have nowhere else to go. I love it here. It's one of the most beautiful places in the country – in the world. I have ... had ... a bakery and I've been a town councillor for years. This is my home.'

'Not any more by the looks of things. What about your family?'

'I don't have one, girls don't really interest me.'

Zach raised his eyes, but Ted merely shrugged.

'I'm not gay, if that's what you think. There was a girl once, but she chose someone else.'

'Yeah, I've got a feeling I might have the same problem.'

'No other girls seemed to measure up and I've just been too busy for relationships since then.'

'I think that's going to be a common condition for most people soon. Right now it's time we skipped town, but first I'd like to get an idea of what these guys are planning.'

'How're you going to do that?'

'Mix in. Do they have a leader?'

'Not as you'd tell, but there're a couple of blokes with beards like Dusty Hill and Billy Gibbons — you know *ZZ Top.*'

Zach nodded. Being an enthusiast of retro hard-rock and heavy-metal he was quite a fan of those particular performers.

'They found the Brewery this time. Dunno how, but they missed it before,' Ted said. 'That's where they are now along with a few henchmen who seem to be top of the pecking order.'

'Good choice of location, how do I get there?'

'Just up the street opposite the Bendigo Bank. You can see it from here.'

'Okay, this is what I want you to do. I've got a horse tethered in the bush a kilometre away on the Great Alpine Road back towards Emu Creek. I want you to gather up as much food as you can. Also collect any stuff that you think might be useful for living rough. Guns and ammo if you find them. Then get out to my horse and stay put until I get there. Can you ride?'

Ted shook his head.

'Do you have a bike?'

Ted nodded.

'I like to go trail riding.'

'Good, bring it too. Take my bow and arrows. If I'm not back by tomorrow morning, unsaddle the horse, cut her loose and head for your brother's place.'

'Won't you need the horse?'

'If I'm not back by then I won't need anything.'

Ted took off through the back door while Zach waited and gathered his thoughts. Most of the bikers were awake by then and scrounged around town, smashing any remaining windows and breaking down the last unopened doors. Zach noticed than none of the gang was taking much notice of the others. Considering they're relied on a group-mentality previously, they showed very little cohesion now. Zach waited for an hour telling himself he was casing the street, but in truth he was in no hurry to mix with the members of SS.

Finally, he was forced to move. A biker stumbled onto the side-walk, urinated against the gallery front before smashing through the door. It was unlocked, but he didn't bother to use the handle. He stood facing Zach with an uncertain expression on his face.

'Who the f ..?'

Knowing that the guy who lands the first blow normally wins the fight, Zach kicked the biker in the groin. As he doubled up, Zach grabbed Ted's pool cue and smashed it against the biker's skull. Zach kicked him in the ribs a couple of times to make sure he stayed down. Zach ripped the jacket from the biker. It was feral, but fitted over his own so the lack-of-identity problem was solved.

Now that Zach thought he'd blend in well enough, there was no further excuse for procrastination. Tucking his pistol into the back of his pants he opened the door and stepped into the street. He'd made a timely entrance because the two ZZ *Top* guys were just emerging from the brewery. One of them carried a revolver and blasted a shot into the air. That gained the attention of those nearby and drew others towards the brewery. It was a call to arms or, from what Zach could gather, the nearest the gang came to a plan-of-action. The gist was hard to follow with all the gang members yelling at once and every second word being an expletive. It seemed they planned to stay in Bright until it was stripped bare, then they'd head south on the Great Alpine Road, taking what they needed as they went. There was no army in that direction and nothing big enough to stand in their way. Despite the hullabaloo Zach gathered the leaders' gang-names were *Goliath* and *Sumo*. They were both built to match their sobriquets.

The gang was in agreement and to seal the deal Goliath and Sumo announced free booze all round. There was a roar and the gang poured through the door into the corrugated iron building. Zach was shoved and jostled along and forced inside with the crowd. *Bright Lager* cans, *Hellfire Amber Ale* and *Staircase Porter* long-necks fizzed open as the gang poured beer down their throats. Someone thrust a bottle into Zach's hand.

'C'mon, wanker,' a biker yelled in his ear. 'Bob Hawke it.'

There was no way Zach could skol the beer without gagging and he knew that wasn't the biker way.

'Gotta piss first,' he said and barged through the door.

Zach squeezed outside still holding the beer bottle. Only a couple of stragglers were still arriving at the brewery. Zach heaved a sigh of relief. He'd heard all needed to. Now it was time to get back to Emu Creek and warn Bob Brenan. Just then the biker Zach had tackled burst from the gallery. Blood matted his hair and seeped down his face.

Geez! The way I put him down, he should've been out for a week.

The biker staggered towards Zach screaming a tirade of profanity at the top of his lungs. He recognised Zach right away and other bikers were now pouring out of the brewery onto Gavan Street to see what all the commotion was about.

Chapter 8 — Enemy Territory

The biker forgot his pain and lurched towards Zach who swung the beer bottle. The biker ducked and tackled Zach's midriff. They tumbled to the ground together. Zach knew he was done for as about twenty bikers were now in the street. He thought they'd be on him in a second, but they didn't interfere. As far as they were concerned this was just another dispute between gang-members being settled in the appropriate, time-honoured way. They took Zach for one of their own as he wore the jacket to prove it. No one identified him as a stranger in the confused scuffle.

Zach was on his feet first, but the biker wasn't far behind. He was half way up when Zach launched a kick that landed in the biker's belly. To everyone's surprise the biker took the blow with just a grunt. He grabbed Zach's foot and tossed him backwards. Zach landed flat on his back with a jar that knocked the breath from his lungs although he managed to hang onto the beer bottle. The biker leapt towards Zach who was just able to roll clear and avoid being crushed.

Both men scrambled to their feet and circled each other with cagey respect. What the biker lacked in agility and fitness, he more than made up for in sheer bulk and he was deceptively quick. The biker moved first, trying a rugby-tackle again, but Zach was ready for him. He deftly stepped aside and cracked the bottle onto the biker's head to the cheers of the onlookers. In movies bottles shatter, but in reality they're a lot tougher than that. This one stayed intact.

The biker didn't get up at once, but groaned as he lay face down in the street. He stirred and staggered to his knees. Zach grabbed him by his hair and cracked the beer bottle into his jaw. This time the bottle shattered and the biker went down for good with shards of glass embedded in his chin and beer foam trickling onto his chest. Zach stood panting and still gripping the broken bottle firmly. The other gang members were all cheering and calling Zach to come back inside for another drink.

'Maybe next time,' Zach said, tossing the jagged bottle neck aside.

He turned on his heel and sprinted back along Gavan Street. After a hundred metres he realised the biker's jacket was stifling, restricting and slowing him down. He stopped, ripped the jacket off and tossed it onto the road. Until then the bikers had been merely curious and amused by Zach's antics — dope does funny things to people. He'd just fought a good fight and everyone loved a winner, but tossing a biker jacket aside was tantamount to using the Holy Grail as a chamber-pot. The jacket and logo were powerful symbols for gang members. They'd all had to go through some gruelling, painful and often unsanitary initiations to earn the right to wear their jackets. Zach had just committed biker-sacrilege.

With a collective roar of indignation the bikers charged after Zach who normally would have easily outrun them. They might have been champion arm wrestlers, but were a sedentary lot, prone to beer-bellies. Hanging around bars guzzling and cheering skanky girls in wet t-shirt contests didn't develop a high lung capacity or athletic stamina. A fortnight on foot had however toughened some of them up and they were hot on Zach's heels. About twenty kept pace with him as he dashed through town to where he'd left Jet. Zach considered himself pretty fit and would still be able to keep ahead of the bikers, but he'd been on the go for hours without breakfast, so he tired more quickly than he expected. Worse still, half-a-dozen bikers who hadn't made it to the brewery joined into the chase as Zach raced by. Strangely it never occurred to them to grab some of the bicycles lying around town. Pedal-power was still an unfamiliar and dishonourable concept.

Zach was about a hundred metres from Jet and running out of puff. Several bikers were so close now he could hear their rasping breath, occasional profanity and dire threats of what they'd do to him when they caught him. One biker reached out and grabbed Zach's collar.

He was about to yank Zach to a halt when he screamed and released the jacket. He covered his left eye-socket that was now reduced to blood-squirting mush. The biker crumpled to the road and three others tumbled over him. Zach heard a zing as another biker dropped to the ground with a crimson patch forming in the centre of his forehead. A third biker was hit by the mysterious missiles and the gang surged to a halt.

What the ... I didn't hear shots, but ...

'C'mon you duffer,' Ted yelled from the bush.

Ted stood astride his mountain-bike beside Jet whose reins were tethered to the cross-bar. He was aiming a sling-shot at the bikers and fired another pellet. He was a crack-shot and the bikers dived for cover when another one yelped as he was hit.

'Mount up, Zach!' Ted yelled, untying the reins.

That was one of those superfluous statements people seem to make when they're under stress. Zach vaulted onto Jet in a single bound without bothering with the stirrups. He could have kissed Ted. All his kit, including his bow, was strapped neatly to the saddle and panniers. Ted wore a back-pack and had a water bottle attached to the bike frame, ready for a quick getaway. Jet thundered down the Great Alpine Road at full gallop with Ted pedalling doing his best to keep up. His bike was fitted with more than twenty gears so he kept up a decent pace.

The bikers remembered their bicycles after seeing Ted pedal away. They scrambled over each other to get any bikes they could lay their hands on. However, by the time they took up the chase, Zach and Ted were long gone. The gang soon gave up the pursuit -- what was the point just to beat the crap out of a couple of locals? It wasn't as if it was a co-ordinated chase. Goliath and Sumo hadn't even left the brewery. The bikers returned to town to finish off the beer.

Great Alpine Road South of Bright

After a couple of kilometres, Zach was satisfied they'd outrun the bikers so he slowed Jet to a trot. Ted soon caught up and was grinning from ear-to-ear. Zach couldn't help chuckling too.

'Ted, you're a legend.'

'Not bad even if I do say so myself. I use the shanghai to get feral cats and I can even hit crows now and they're tricky buggers. Works on feral humans too.'

Ted gulped from his water bottle then handed it to Zach who, realising he was parched, finished the water off. Ted refilled the bottle from the Ovens River that ran parallel to the highway. Zach found his canteen and did the same. He allowed Jet to drink as well.

'We'd better keep going,' Zach said and remounted.

As they rode on at a walk, they often checked behind them, but no one followed. Zach broke open a packet of Jatz Crackers and munched on a few. He hand the carton to Ted who took a handful. When he finished he fished into his bike-panniers and found two apples. He handed one to Zach and chewed on the other.

'All your basic food groups, eh?'

They camped with Apari's people that night and warned them to look out for bikers. Apari agreed it would be wise if they travelled cross-country and avoided roads on the way home.

'White people naturally use roads,' he explained. 'So do we actually, but we'll go overland. We'll be fine. We're pushing off tomorrow.'

The aborigines had indeed slaughtered a poddy calf and roasted most of it over a roaring fire.

'Warra says it should be hung for three weeks, but we're all pretty hungry.'

The meat was a bit gamey, but no one complained.

After dinner some of Apari's people pulled out guitars, ukuleles and tambourines and started singing country songs. Someone played a didgeridoo that fitted well with the music. They were great fans of Lee Kernaghan and Troy Cassar-Daley who'd won heaps of golden guitar awards at Tamworth Country Music Festivals. Zach was more of a heavy-metal fan, but had heard most of the songs. He even joined in with a few rock-a-billy licks his Grandpa had taught him. Grandpa Danny was a country music fan with a large CD collection. His iPod was full of country and early rock 'n' roll tunes. Of course he couldn't listen to them anymore. It looked like acoustic instruments were making a comeback and music had returned to its original, primitive roots.

'You know, some good has come of all this,' Apari said. 'Pretty soon all the booze is going to run out.'

'Can't say it will make any difference to me,' Zach replied.

'Maybe not, but our people don't do well on it, especially in places where there's no work. Gov'ment hands out cheques that get recycled straight back into grog-shops. We'll be better off without it.'

'So will we,' Ted said. 'I don't mind a beer occasionally, but that lot back in town prove my point.'

'I reckon brewing booze will be the first thing someone works out how to do,' Zach said. 'I mean you don't need electricity, just a good, roaring fire.'

'People will miss TV,' Warra added. 'I do.'

'Nope,' Zach said. 'I'll miss a live rock band. Don't get me wrong — a camp fire sing-along is great, but there's nothing like a Gibson Les Paul belting out through a Marshall stack.'

'Head-banger,' Apari said.

'Hillbilly.'

'Boy, you blokes really know how to sling the insults around when you're all steamed up,' Warra laughed. 'You know there are caves all round the world where the acoustics are so good, you don't need amps. There's one on an island off North Scotland where some old, dead composer dude used to go to for inspiration.'

'And you know that for a fact?'

'Sure do, I saw it on one of those SBS TV shows.'

'Trouble is no one can get to North Scotland now.'

'No one can get anywhere much,' Ted lamented. 'I liked being a tourist. I've been to Europe, the States and loads of places. Funny how we took globe-trotting for granted. I think that's what *I'll* miss most.'

'I thought you love Bright?'

'I do, but that doesn't mean I don't like visiting other places. Anyway "loved" might be a more appropriate word now.'

'The bikers will move on,' Apari said. 'What do you plan to do then, Ted?'

'Maybe go back to town and see if I can get anyone left to rebuild the place. In the meantime, I'll go to my brother's property and help out there if I can.'

'Do you two get along?' Zach asked thinking how different Phil and Ted were.

'Not so well, but mostly we keep out of each other's way. I guess desperation will make strange bed-fellows.'

*

The following morning the Aboriginal people started packing up, but they were in no hurry. Ted and Zach were about to say goodbye and head for the Harrison place with rather more urgency. Zach wasn't sure he really wanted to call in. Ted was perfectly able to warn Phil and his family, but events forced him to go along anyway.

Just after breakfast Andy, Joe and Clarence Harrison rode into the Aborigines' camp. Andy carried a .22 rifle in a saddle scabbard, but hadn't drawn it out. The boys we scowling and turned mean when they saw the remains of the poddy carcass. Ted and Zach walked forward to meet them.

'Morning, boys,' Ted greeted cordially enough.

'Whatcha doin' 'ere, Uncle Ted,' Andy demanded.

'Coming to visit you. More to the point, why are you out-and-about in these dangerous times? Shouldn't you be home to protect your mother and sisters?'

'Dad and Gary are home.'

'On the sauce, no doubt?'

'Nothin' wrong with them havin' a drink.'

Ted shrugged. It all depended on your definition of 'having a drink'.

'We come out 'ere to check the stock and bring 'em back to the long yards. It looks to me like these boongs have nicked one of our calves already.'

Andy had a point. They were on the border of the Harrison property, but the niceties of ownership were problematic at that stage.

'You Abos can bugger off right now,' Andy said.

Whether three teenage boys could force the issue was uncertain, but Apari wasn't looking for trouble.

'We're just on our way,' he said cheerfully. 'We won't bother you again.'

With that he shook hands with Zach and Ted and led his people into the bush.

'That showed them boong bastards,' Clarence said, but even Andy knew it was a hollow victory and told him to shut up.

The boys rounded up the remaining cattle and drove them to the home paddock. Zach and Ted helped them, but it was still well past noon when they arrived.

Phil Harrison had been drinking and was in an even more recalcitrant mood than usual. He staggered onto his front porch and flung an empty scotch bottle into the yard as Ted and Zach approached while the boys herded the cattle into the stock yards. Jet shied away when the bottle clattered into her hooves. Zach calmed her and dismounted. He wanted to smack Phil in the mouth, but curbed the impulse.

'What ya want, Ted?' Phil snarled. 'Still sniffing around after *my* missus.'

Ah, so that explains, 'there was a woman once', Zach thought, although he knew that wasn't the only reason the brothers were estranged. No one could put up with Phil's attitude for long, but Ted ignored his brother's taunts.

'The bikers are back, Phil,' Ted explained. 'Apparently they were stopped by the Army. Most likely they'll come this way because they've no other option.'

'Oh yeah? How far off are they?'

'We left 'em in Bright, but they'll have bled the town white in a couple of days – tops.'

'We're a way off the road. They'll probably pass us by.'

'Maybe,' Zach said, 'but they'll know your gate leads somewhere and they might just come looking. Lone properties will make prime targets. That's where the last of the food supplies will be.'

'And I'll be ready with a 12-gauge for the bastards.'

At that moment Sharon walked around the verandah from the rear of the house. Her sleeves were rolled up and she carried a full laundry basket. The bruises on her face had faded, so it looked as if she'd managed to keep out of Phil's way.

'Why, hello Ted, Zach,' she beamed. 'What a pleasant surprise. Has Phil kept you standing outside? Come in and I'll put the kettle on.'

'They're not staying,' Phil growled.

'Of course they are after coming all this way,' she said.

She might have got away with contradicting Phil if he was sober, but a skinful of scotch had turned him draconian. He strode towards her.

'Don't argue with me, bitch!' he roared.

He wrenched the laundry basket from her hands and flung it over the verandah rail. She screamed and reeled backwards when he slapped her across the face. And then pandemonium broke loose. Ted dashed onto the verandah, grabbing Phil before he could hit Sharon again. At that moment Gary, who was every bit as drunk as his father, barged through the front door and tackled Ted. The three men crashed through the hand rail in a melee of flailing fists. Zach was aware of Charlene and Norma screaming in the background as he rushed to untangle the fighters.

Zach grabbed Phil by the scruff of the neck and hauled him off Ted who had his hands full with Gary. Phil took a wild swing at Zach who dodged easily and landed a left jab into Phil's nose. Blood spurted from Phil's nostrils, but Zach planted another punch into the farmer's belly. Phil doubled over and spewed the whisky-imbued contents of his guts onto Zach's boots.

'Oh, nice,' Zach hissed and drew his fist back to finish Phil off.

Sharon's warning came a split-second too late. Zach was suddenly aware of movement behind him. He shoved Phil to the ground, grabbed his gun and spun around in time to see the three remaining Harrison boys charging him down. Zach had no time to aim. One of the boys swung an axe handled that landed at the base of Zach's skull. After an instant of intense pain, everything went black.

Chapter 9 — On the Run

Zach's head throbbed hideously. He felt as if his skull was on fire. There was a lump the size of Ayers Rock and a livid bruise on his nape. He instinctively tried to raise his arm to rub the sore patch then realised his hands were bound behind his back. He struggled and discovered his feet were tied as well. What was going on? His confusion turned to panic when he opened his eyes. His vision was blurred and his head spun. Nausea welled up in his stomach and he vomited onto the floor in front of him. That actually made him feel marginally better.

'That's probably what a bad hangover feels like,' he heard Ted's voice. 'Just stay still for a moment or two and the room should stop spinning.'

Ted's advice proved correct. Zach relaxed, opened his eyes again and his vision cleared. The dirt floor was scattered with hay and horse dung with a pervading organic farm smell.

'We're in the barn,' Ted said. 'Trussed up with duct tape, I'm afraid. I've been trying to free myself for hours.'

Zach noticed that the light was indeed dim as evening approached. He was able to make Ted out in the shadows and he didn't look in much better shape than Zach felt. Ted was bound hand and foot just like Zach. Blood had caked on his jaw and temple.

'Knocked me around a bit,' Ted confirmed, 'but I'll live provided Phil doesn't have his way.'

'What do you mean?'

'It seems like Phil and his boys have laid claim to our stuff and are now debating what to do with the previous owners. Phil wants to get rid of us, but I don't know whether the boys are prepared to go that far.'

'Since when does he consult them?'

'He knows he can't do without them now, so they have a greater say, especially Gary. He's almost big enough to take on his old man.'

'Good for him,' Zach sneered.

'Don't count on it. If push comes to shove Gary *and* his brothers will do us in without a second thought.'

No one came near the barn, so they remained without food or water as darkness descended. The duct tape was impossible to remove no matter how hard Zach twisted his wrists. He was only thankful that he wasn't tied with electrician's cable locking ties. They'd have cut into his wrists and ankles mercilessly.

Just after dark Phil arrived carrying a kerosene lamp.

'What's your bloody game? Cut us loose,' Zach yelled.

'Yeah, c'mon Phil, enough's enough,' Ted added.

Phil merely stared at them through icy, malevolent eyes. He checked to see Ted and Zach were still secure before leaving without a word. They heard the door latch and close and a padlock snap shut.

'Should have asked him for the supper menu,' Zach said.

'He probably thinks feeding us is a waste of resources.'

'We've gotta get out of here tonight,' Zach said. 'I have a feeling the longer we're here the worse our chances are. I didn't like the look of Phil at all.'

'I'm with you Zach. What's your plan?'

'Work in progress ...'

His problem was that every time he wrestled with the tape it crinkled into sharp edges that cut into his wrists. If he continued his arms would start bleeding. Even in his frustration, Zach knew that was an unwise strategy. He tried standing and looking around for something sharp to cut the tape, but the barn was now so dark he couldn't see anything. After a few hops he lost balance and thumped to the floor. He only managed to bash into a wooden pillar on his second attempt.

'This is hopeless,' he muttered followed by a stream of expletives.

'Aren't you a little potty-mouth,' Ted said. 'And here was me thinking you were a good, wholesome lad.'

'Wholesome ain't gonna cut it in the future, Ted.'

'What future would that be?'

They sat in darkness for hours as despair crept over them. Thirst was becoming an issue although Ted was sanguine about his discomfort.

'We'd only be dying for a piss if we had anything to drink and I can't undo my pants tied up like this, so it might be for the best.'

'Shut up, Ted,' Zach said, but grinned nevertheless.

They both head a creak from the rear of the barn.

'What the ..?'

A lot of scratching and thumping followed and then a crack as one of the weatherboards sprung open. A thin wisp of moonlight filtered inside. Ted and Zach's pupils had dilated in the pitch black barn and the shaft of light illuminated the interior sufficiently for them to make out details. The scraping continued before another weatherboard snapped open. They heard a thump as the plank landed somewhere outside. After the third board disappeared, part of a head silhouetted in the opening.

'G'day ..?' a voice hissed from the night. 'Anyone home?'

'Warra!' Zach called back. 'What the blazes are you doing here?'

'Saving your sorry white arses by the looks of things. I can't see a bloody thing in there, where are you? Are you blokes tied up?'

'Yeah, hands and feet with duct tape. Can you get through?' Zach asked.

'Hang on I'll have to get rid of a couple more planks.'

There was more wrenching and tearing followed by the clatter of weatherboards hitting the ground.

'Sssh! You'll wake 'em up.'

'This is gonna take too long,' Warra hissed. 'Can you make it to the hole and I'll cut you loose.'

With enough moonlight to see by, Zach hopped to the opening. He was able to turn around while Warra reached through the wall and cut his wrist bonds with a pen knife. It took a little sawing as the knife wasn't particularly sharp. Once free Zach took the knife and stabbed the tape with the knife point. It was a more efficient method than sawing and his feet were soon free. Zach scrambled back to release Ted.

'I'm going to try the door,' Warra whispered through the opening and disappeared.

He was only gone for seconds when he stuck his face back through the weatherboards.

'Someone's coming!' he hissed.

'Bugger.'

Zach and Ted spun around as they heard a key click in the padlock. They ducked into the shadows behind some hay-bales and crouched ready to at least take the Harrison boys by surprise. Zach found a rake that would serve as a half-decent weapon, although Phil was undoubtedly armed, reducing the odds considerably. Ted scratched around and found a horse whip that might be useful if he had room to swing it. Warra disappeared, but neither Zach nor Ted had time to worry where he'd gone.

The door rattled open and a blaze of light from a kerosene lamp flooded into the barn. Three figures stood outlined in the doorway. Zach and Ted were momentarily blinded. The constant change of light was playing merry-hell with their night-vision. Zach couldn't make out any guns, but what were the chances of that? But, hang on...

Only three? Where're the other two?

Zach squinted to see beyond the barn door. He wanted to know where all the Harrisons were. He wasn't going to let anyone sneak up and clout him from behind again. The three figures remained still, which puzzled Zach until he heard Warra growl in his best tough-guy voice.

'Okay no one moves,' he growled. 'I'm armed and I've got you covered. One false move and I'll let you have it.'

Oh, very Clint Eastwood, Warra.

'Don't shoot. We're here to help.'

It was Sharon's voice!

Finally Zach's eyes adjusted to the lamp-light and saw Sharon and her twin girls in the barn doorway. They were dressed in jeans, plaid shirts, Akubra hats and they each carried a back-pack. Jet and three other saddled horses stood behind Sharon and the girls. They were ready for travel, Norma even held Ted's bike. It looked as if all their gear was stashed in the saddlebags as well. Sharon was also armed with a .22 rifle.

'What's going on, Sharon?' Ted asked.

'We're getting out,' Sharon whispered, 'I can't take any more of it. I've been thinking about what Bob Brenan said, what with the way Phil treats the girls as well.'

'Good for you,' Zach smiled, 'but we'd better get on with it before they wake up. I dunno whether I'm up for another fight just yet.'

Sharon doused the light and they all mounted up, but Warra remained on foot. He carried a pack too and was armed with only his boomerang. Zach returned his pen-knife. At that moment Sharon gasped as the house door cracked open and a lantern shone onto the verandah. Phil's shadowy form staggered through the door, down the steps into the front yard.

'He's awake!' Ted hissed. 'Let's get out of here.'

Sharon turned with terror in her eyes. There was no going back now. She kicked her horses flank and cantered away with Charlene and Norma close behind.

'You coming?' Zach asked, extending his hand to the Aboriginal boy.

'Reckon I'd better,' Warra replied as Zach hoisted him onto Jet's back behind him.

Zach followed Sharon and the girls along the track towards the highway with Ted pedalling in their wake. They barely heard Phil's screams followed by a shotgun blast as they faded into darkness. The pellets splattered harmlessly somewhere in the bush behind them with Phil's tirade echoing through the night. When they reached the main road Ted opened the gate and secured it after everyone had passed through. They might be running from Phil, but that didn't mean they wanted his stock to escape. Although no one had slept they thought it best to keep going and put as much distance between them and the farm as possible. Adrenaline was pumping and they were all keen to press on anyway. They headed for Emu Creek with just enough moonlight to guide them.

Zach introduced Warra to Sharon, Charlene and Norma.

'Now what gun was that exactly, Warra?' Sharon said with a smile — the first one she could remember for ages.

'I got a boomerang,' Warra said defensively.

'You sounded convincing to me,' Charlene chipped in.

'Don't mess with this bloke's boomerang,' Zach added. 'Take it from someone who knows, it hurts like hell if it hits you. What were you doing sneaking around anyway, Warra?'

'Apari didn't like the look of them boys,' Warra said. 'He reckoned they were shifty and up to no good, so he sent me back to see that you jokers were okay. He likes you, see? He said the mob would hang around for a couple more days. He didn't fancy the way they tried to push us around either. He said if you were in trouble, I should come back to camp for help. If not it might be a good idea to tag along with you or meet up back at Albury later on – whatever I thought was best. I guess you're safe now. Mind if I come along?'

'Be my guest.'

'What about you, Sharon?' Ted asked, pedalling his bike beside her horse.

'I thought about what Bob Brenan said. Phil's beaten me up for the last time and he won't be pawing the girls no more, either. I guess I chose the wrong chap all those years ago.'

'Can't say as I blame you. Phil was always the handsome, blokey one while I was a nerdy wimp.'

'From what I've seen, you don't seem so wimpy now.'

'Do you really think Phil would have killed me -- his own brother?'

'I believe he's capable of it, even the Mark of Cain isn't beyond him now. He's been getting worse for a year now. Headaches and crazy dreams that drive him mad. I tried to get him to see a doctor, but he refused. The grog doesn't help. I think it's finally pushed him over the edge.'

'You did well to get all our stuff together without being caught. That was pretty gutsy.'

She smiled.

'The boys didn't unpack much, so we were able to gather it up easily enough after they went to bed.'

'You know Phil will come after you?'

'I don't think he cares.'

'He don't care about no one 'cept himself,' Norma added.

'Maybe, but he cares about his pride. In his eyes you belong to him and I just don't see him tolerating you girls running off,' Ted, the amateur psychologist, said.

'We're not his property,' Sharon whispered through clenched teeth.

'I bet he doesn't see it that way. He'll come for you, so we'd better be ready.'

'*We*, Ted?'

'Yes *we*, Sharon.'

'As if we don't have enough problems already,' Zach sighed.

He reflected how different Sharon was with Ted than Phil. Her voice had lost its harshness and anger. Charlene and Norma had mellowed to. They chatted to their Uncle Ted with what appeared to be genuine warmth and affection and giggled without inhibitions when he said something witty. They were quite likeable girls when they weren't trying to be slutty.

It was mid-morning when they rode into Emu Creek. Zach saw that Bob Brenan and the citizens had been busy. Firstly, local kids were posted in relays as lookouts. They'd equipped themselves with coloured flags and devised a simple semaphore system. One of the kids, who recognised Zach as a good-guy, explained they only needed a few variations to report approaching strangers. Yellow and green – small friendly group: yellow and red – small enemy group: blue and green – large friendly group, etc. He added Sergeant Bob had limited the combinations to avoid mistakes and rotated the kids every half hour, which was pretty much their attention span.

Bob met them at the top of Main Street. Activity continued all around town. Warra was the first to jump down. Riding bareback was a testicle-challenging experience.

'Got yourself quite a little entourage there,' Bob said as Zach dismounted and shook his hand.

Bob had organised the townspeople to build barricades from crates, sandbags, fence palings and whatever else they could find. Zach was amazed how much barbed wire they'd integrated into the town protection system in such a short time.

'Looks like you're defending the Alamo,' Zach commented.

'It might come to that. We're going to have to live with a fort mentality from now on.'

Karen and Mike strode along the street to meet them.

'Someone's glad to see you, and someone isn't,' Sharon observed, eyeing Zach with amusement.

'Very astute, Sharon, thank you,' he said.

Karen flung her arms around Zach's neck and kissed him unreservedly.

'Welcome back, stranger,' she beamed, 'I thought you were going to Albury.'

'Change of plan,' he said, untangling her arms. Nice as it was to have Karen in his embrace, he and Bob needed to talk. There was also Mike to consider as Zach gave him a questioning look over Karen's shoulder. Mike shrugged.

'I think it's pretty well settled, mate. She's been moping around for the last couple of days,' Mike said, extending his hand in a *can't-say-I'm-pleased-to-see-you-but-the-better-man-won* gesture.

'So, what have you got to tell me,' Bob said. 'Obviously something's up, or you wouldn't be back so soon with half the state. It's nice to see you decided to come into town, Sharon – you too Norma and Charlene. You'll be safer here.'

Sharon nodded and smiled while the girls waved. Their animosity towards the law had also vanished.

Bob shook Ted's hand.

'Not so good in Bright, then?' he surmised.

Ted shook his head.

'Who's the *boomerang kid*?' Bob asked with his usual sensitivity.

Zach once again introduced Warra, suggesting his skill might shortly come in very handy.

'Sorry, Warra, just kidding,' Bob said.

'No sweat, it's not bad. That's what I might call myself anyway.'

Bob nodded. He was neither a racist nor male chauvinist, nor any other '*ist*' for that matter. He took people as he found them, but expected them to be thick-skinned enough to take a bit of friendly ribbing. One thing that angered him beyond all else were touchy individuals who took umbrage at the slightest remark that didn't fit in with their narrow view of the world. Bob knew where to draw the line, so political correctness wasn't on his radar. He despised anyone who relied on PC to get by.

'I reckon there's serious trouble heading this way, Bob,' Zach said, 'and not much time to do anything about it.'

'Okay, let's get you all back to the station. I bet you're starving. The fire's going so I'll put a billy on. Thank heavens for all the bush gear in the camping store.'

'Good idea, Bob. What would we do without tea?' Sharon sighed.

Chapter 10 — Build Up

Bob listened as Zach and Ted told him about the Bright disaster. He was a copper so he took notes of estimated gang numbers, time-lines and other variables that came to mind. When that was finished, he asked Sharon, Charlene and Norma for statements as well. He waited patiently until they too had given their version of events although it consisted mainly of bad-mouthing Phil for being plain mean and the boys for letting him get away with it. Sharon felt her sons weren't lost causes if they could only crawl out from under their father's influence. Charlene and Norma agreed that if they were going to be touched-up, they'd choose by whom as they eyed Zach, Warra and Mike.

Bob knew it was time to up the planning ante and find out exactly what his town was really made of.

Excerpt from Mike Farrow's Personal Journal:

I guess I always knew Zach would return, although I rather hoped he wouldn't. Karen was never really mine after he showed up. Sure we had a great couple of nights. She tried hard, but she didn't fool me. I

don't know whether it was guilt for letting me down or what. If she'd fantasised about some film star, that was one thing, but I know her heart is set on Zach McAlister. It's just a chemistry thing. It boils down to the fact that she LIKES me, but she LOVES him and that makes all the difference. Even if he'd never come back, she'd probably have gone looking for him in the end.

Now I can get my guts in a twist about it or concentrate on trying to survive in this mad-house we call our world.

Bob -- funny I don't think of him as 'Sergeant Brenan' any more, but he's still the boss – has called the whole town together at the RSL hall. He sent Karen and me door-knocking. He wants EVERYONE there. Men, women and kids — everyone — so there is no misunderstanding about what we're facing. Bob has an old Webley revolver and ammo that his grandad brought back from some war or another. I tried a couple of practice shots. I didn't hit much, but scared the crap out of a couple of greenies walking past. In the end we stuck to our police issue weapons and handed the Webley along with its spare ammo over to one of the RSL Vets.
RSL Hall, Emu Creek

Emu Creek had about thirty service veterans who ran the unofficial RSL Hall. Neither the National or State executives thought there were sufficient numbers to form a viable sub-branch, so members of Emu Creek RSL legitimately belonged to either Bright or Omeo. Normally they gathered on Fridays for a few beers and played golf on weekends. It wasn't a formal venue, and they used the pub as often as not. The men and women of Emu Creek RSL had served in Vietnam, Timor, Rwanda, Somalia, Bougainville, Iraq and Afghanistan. None of the WWII or Korean War veterans remained, but at 6pm whenever they got together, the surviving vets recited the ANZAC *Ode of Remembrance* in honour of their departed comrades.

Bob planned to use this core of military expertise to co-ordinate the town's defence.

Karen and Mike rounded everyone up, even several young mothers nursing infants with toddlers in tow. Fitting the entire town population in was a squeeze, but after some shuffling around, they all found space in the end. Bob didn't waste time. He quickly outlined the threat that Zach and Ted anticipated. A buzz of conversation followed. Bob let them go until the initial talk turned to babble then he called the meeting to order.

'Okay,' he yelled, 'settle down. You've got your concerns off your chests. Now we have to decide what to do.'

Like all meetings the outcome boiled down to a simple choice. Stay and protect the town or abandon it and flee. Once that was established Bob needed to keep the agenda tight. In his experience, when people discussed matters, the longer they spoke the more complicated issues became as even more red-herrings were created. Most people said exactly what he expected them to anyway.

One group of greenies who'd moved to the country to get away from mainstream life were all for pacifism and being neighbourly to the bikers. Why not extend the hand of friendship? Why not appeal to their better nature? Bob pointed out that a gang who called itself `Satan's Scrotum` was unlikely to have a better nature.

About half the town were middle-of-the-road and perfectly aware that they weren't warriors. They entertained the idea of taking to the bush until the bikers had passed through. Ted then explained what had occurred in Bright and how there would be nothing left to come back too.

The veterans, including a tough octogenarian who'd fought at the battle of Long Tan, were all for staying and giving the bikers a sound thrashing. Many of the teenagers and younger adults agreed with them.

'I don't think we have a choice,' Bob concluded. 'If we go bush, it'll be every man, woman and child for themselves. Our only chance of surviving this crisis is staying together as a community.'

'Surely, this power-cut can't go on for much longer,' one of the 'rose-coloured' greenies insisted. It appeared being a greenie was okay, so long as you still had all the comforts of home.

'We can't count on that,' Bob retorted. 'There's no doubt that the blackout is connected with the crazy meteor showers and there is no indication that the cosmic activity is lessening. Remember, if the bikers come, they'll be here in the next couple of days.'

'They might pass us by. We're two kilometres off the main road.'

'You want to bet on that?'

The discussion went back and forth without resolving anything, just as Bob knew it would. Finally he felt they'd gone on long enough and were only wasting precious time.

'Right! This doesn't even come down to a vote. I'm staying with my coppers. I can't force anyone to remain. Go if you must, but you'll be on your own. I won't have time or the resources to come and bail you out of trouble. If you stay you'll have to agree to do exactly what I say. This town won't be a democracy. If you think I'm not the best choice to lead you, by all means nominate someone else, but one fundamental rule still stands. Everyone obeys the leader!'

'Surely we can talk to them – make them see reason.'

That bloody greenie pacifist again.

'Go to Bright and you'll see their idea of reason,' Ted said. 'Get real, people. If this town survives the bikers it won't be the last threat by a country mile. Get used to the idea that if you don't defend your territory, sooner or later others will come and take it from you. Check your history – it's the way the world works.'

Good one Ted, that's got them thinking. That was exactly what Zach said.

The veterans voted in a block that they'd fight and the younger people supported them.

'I mightn't have as many years left as most of you,' the old Long Tan hero said, 'but if you run from this, you'll have to keep running and life won't we worth living. So you might as well die trying rather than die without lifting a finger to help yourselves. Look, even if you're not a combatant, you'll be needed in support roles.'

Good on ya! That'll shut the conchies up.

Everyone cheered the old boy. That was the sort of talk they wanted to hear. Even the greenies clapped.

'Right, Emu Creek!' Bob yelled above the uproar. 'It's time for us to stand together!'

Zach might be right about defending the Alamo.

So Emu Creek prepared to fight to the death.

Ovens Highway at the Harrison Property Gate

The bikers had indeed bled Bright dry. The gang numbered nearly a hundred members when they first hit town, but they'd suffered from serious attrition. Nearly a quarter of their people were dead or abandoned. Major Rogers' troops had certainly given the gang a bloody nose. Some had simply fallen by the way-side, too exhausted to continue on foot or bicycle, while others had received fatal wounds in domestic squabbles.

Goliath and Sumo, the *ZZ Top* gang leaders hadn't so much lost control, but rather they'd never been in charge at all. Unlike most outlaw biker gangs that had a strict hierarchy, SS had always bounced from one mob-rule antic to another, mostly involving brawls, alcohol, drugs and skanky chicks. Nothing else interested them much.

So when they grew hungry and found nothing left to scavenge, they took to the road with no survival skills whatsoever. Those who couldn't find bikes were simply left to make their way as best they could. There should have been enough bicycles to go round in a town the size of Bright, but its citizens had taken most of them when they'd fled for their lives. They were not known as early risers, but hunger urged them onto the highway by first light.

What the gang found along the road was close to a scorched-earth landscape. Those property owners who'd remained had mustered their stock into high country far from the highway. Even Phil Harrison had enough sense to take that precaution. He hated the McAlister kid and Ted for running off with his missus and daughters, but he took their warning seriously.

Apari saw the bikers from a hill-top a kilometre off the road. The women and children were well hidden as the gang passed by. With Warra gone, Apari was the only adult male in the group. His wife stood beside him as they watched the rabble below.

'Emu Creek's in for big trouble,' she observed.

'Looks that way to me,' he replied.

'Warra has gone there, then?'

'Yes. He'd be back here if he hadn't.'

'It's just as well Ted and Zach have gone to warn the town.'

Phil Harrison realised he'd need to be pro-active if he hoped to protect his property. Gary and Andy had ridden to the gate and removed the mail box, highway number and any other obvious signs that the path led to a farmhouse. However as there had only been light rainfall in the past fortnight, tyre tracks were still visible and the bikers spotted them. Goliath and Sumo sent a half-dozen strong contingent to investigate. A farmhouse, even if abandoned, was their best chance of finding food.

Phil may have been insane, but he knew how to deal with bikers — shoot first and ask questions later. From the cover of dense bush he levelled his rifle and waited for the gang's recon party to approach. They advanced without caution. The military aside, they were used to getting their own way. Phil aimed with care and patience, placed light pressure on the trigger and squeezed. The slug slammed into the leading biker's chest. He grunted, dropped to the ground and lay still. He'd been killed instantly.

The remaining bikers dithered and scanned about, but saw nothing. Phil dropped another biker and the others dived for cover. Shallow ditches eroded by downpours ran either side of the path, but offered little cover for the beleaguered bikers. Phil shot another gang member's buttocks that were not quite hidden by the trench.

Crows and lorikeets squawked and flapped skywards at the sound of gunfire before silence descended on the bush once more. The only sound was moaning from the wounded biker. The others lay trembling in what they considered might now become their shallow graves. No one dared to lift their head or make a run for it, the sniper was too good a shot for that. Then they heard the clatter of hoof beats and jingling bridles.

Five apocalyptic riders advanced line abreast along the track, the sun at their backs and steam snorting from the horse's nostrils. The bikers raised their heads when they heard the sound and stared transfixed at the silhouetted death approaching. They simply gaped, mesmerised by fear.

'Stay where you are,' Phil growled as he drew alongside the surviving bikers.

His boys surrounded the gang and all pointed rifles or shotguns at the grovelling men.

'Now, we can kill you right here and now,' Phil continued, 'and I don't mind if we do. But, bullets are precious and I don't feel like wasting them on scum like you.'

That was a bit rich coming from Phil, but the bikers didn't know what he was like other than ominously dangerous.

'Whatcha doing on my land anyway?' Phil demanded.

At first the gang members were too petrified to speak.

'Well..?'

'Looking for grub,' one of the bikers finally said.

'You won't find any here, so you'd better bugger off before I change my mind about the bullets. There's a town up the road, go and annoy them and don't even think of telling that lot back at the road about coming up here. Ammo might be precious, but we've got plenty to go around for the lot of youse, and my boys are crack-shots.'

The bikers were only too happy to comply. They took off instantly.

'Oi! You forgot your mate,' Phil called after them, but they kept going.

He turned to the wounded man who was struggling to his feet. Tried to stagger away, but collapsed after a few steps.

'I can't walk,' the biker stammered, turning towards the riders.

'Pity,' Phil said, 'but I can't have you hanging around here.'

Phil levelled his rifle and shot the biker between the eyes. Hearing the shot, the running gang members flinched. One dived to the ground then kept going without looking back. Phil's boys looked on nervously. They'd just seen their father kill three people in cold blood. Bad people maybe, but it unsettled them all the same.

Goliath and Sumo heard the gunfire and stood nervously with the gang at Phil's gate. It wasn't long before the survivors dashed into view and arrived panting at the road. After a heated discussion in which the three scouts insisted they weren't going to take one step back along the track, the gang decided to follow Phil's advice and head for Emu Creek.

Emu Creek, Victorian High Country

Bob Brenan discovered that with expert help, organising his town was falling into shape rather better then he'd expected. He delegated Karen, Mike and Zach as lieutenants and realised that people seemed to work best in small groups — half-a-dozen or so was proving a good number. Ted had taken a contingent away for training in his particular sphere of expertise. Bob's resources also included the RSL members who recalled much of their military training and experience that they were now keen to put to use. One of the vets had been an engineer and was working on a project with a team of townsfolk.

The oldest vet, Stanley Whiting, marched up to Bob, halted military fashion, snapped to attention and saluted.

'Ex-Regimental Sergeant-Major Whiting reporting, sah,' the octogenarian declared.

'Stanley, I know who you are. How many times have we propped up the bar together? Now stop the *sir* crap. What do you want to do?'

'If you don't mind my saying, you are now the officer commanding this post. Whether you like it or not, this *is* a post and you have assumed command. As you said, democracy is over. You are going to have to be harsh, even cruel at times. These people may resent what you'll want them to do, but until this is over they must follow orders — no questions asked and no debate.'

'Yeah, Stan, you're dead right, but I think we can get it done if you still call me Bob.'

'Okay, I was just making a point.'

'Right, chain-of-command is as follows: me, then my two coppers and Zach McAlister. You ex-military blokes are heading up the specialist teams already. That work for you?'

Stan nodded. He was a fit old bloke and wanted to be of use.

'Now what have you got to tell me?' Bob finally asked.

'Back in 'Nam we used to patrol villages all the time trying to ferret out *Charlie*.'

'And ..?'

'I might be an old duffer, but I remember most of it. I've got an idea, but I'll need a team.'

Stanley outlined his plan – the quick version, Bob didn't need minute details.

'How many people do you want?'

'As many as you can spare.'

'Those greenies aren't doing anything useful, will they do?'

'They'll have to, but they won't like what I want them to do.'

'Good, there's nothing I hate more than a bunch of bleeding-heart conchies who want someone else to do their fighting for them. If they give you any grief I'll come and crack a few heads together.'

'I hope there's enough time.'

'Don't we all?'

Stanley was not the only Emu Creek resident with ideas. Warra had taken another group to the Emu Creek tourist shop and then the timber yard where they were planning their strategy. Everyone was kept busy all day, but as Stanley and Bob feared, time was running out fast.

Chapter 11 — Siege at Emu Creek

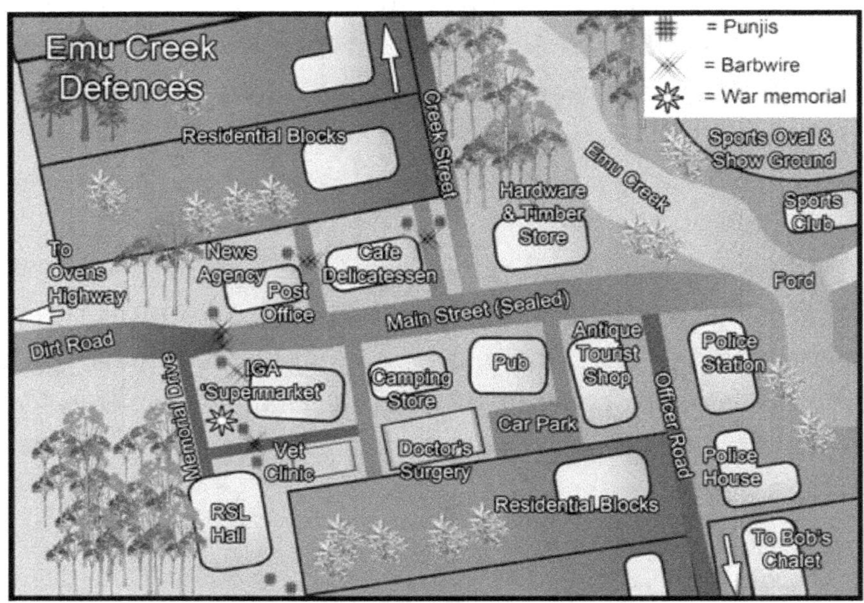

Emu Creek, Victorian High Country

'Remember, they're just bullies,' Bob said to the worried crowd before him. 'They're not superhuman. They're hungry and tired. We can see this through if we stick to our guns and hold together.'

There was no time for fancy speeches. The lookout kids had signalled that SS had reached the highway turn-off and were on the way. Much to their mother's relief, the last of the youngsters were accounted for when they pedalled their bikes at full tilt into town. They slalomed through a narrow path flanked by metre high flag markers.

'They're right behind us, Sergeant Brenan!' one boy yelled as he sped past.

'Well done kids,' Bob called, removing the markers.

Now the children were safely back Ted and a few other townsfolk hauled a tangle of coiled barbwire across Main Street and attached it to star pickets that had been driven into the gravel.

One of the greenies hugged those around her and whispered 'stay safe,' which Bob thought was the damn stupidest thing he'd ever heard. In his opinion there was far too much hugging these days and Emu Creek was going to be a *very unsafe* place *very* shortly. So how anyone was going to *stay safe* was a mystery to him.

Emu Creek had five main weak points where the bikers might breach the town defences. Main Street was the obvious striking point, but barbwire now straggled across the road forming a barricade. There were only narrow access paths at either side close to the newsagency and IGA store, which were the first buildings on the west side of town. Of course the bikers could simply by-pass Main Street and circle around the commercial buildings to attack from the side using several laneways that led into town. One of these had been blocked with barbwire and a few other nasty surprises devised by ex-Sergeant-Major Stan Whiting and the ex-military engineer.

The RSL hall and cenotaph stood isolated and potentially vulnerable at the end of a gravel lane rather grandly called Memorial Drive. Mike commanded the RSL veterans who were posted to defend that area. Karen, Stanley, the engineer and Warra's group were in charge of the laneway defences north of town while it fell to Ted and his people to protect Main Street. Bob took a central position beside the IGA store to coordinate operations. Mounted on Jet, Zach was to act as messenger and support wherever he was needed most.

The greenies were far from happy about their role in the preparations, although they cheered up after being assigned as stretcher-bearers to carry any wounded to Dr Nandamuri's surgery. The town vet, George Grimshaw, was also at hand to assist with medical matters.

'It's the best we can do,' Bob sighed as he eyed the defences.

'Yeah, the only weakness is if they go way north through the residential area, outflank us and have a go from the east,' Zach surmised as he swung into the saddle.

'Atta boy, cheer me up,' Bob mumbled as he turned to the people around him. 'You all know what to do so let's get cracking. Now everyone out of sight — Good luck.'

With a murmur the residents melted away from Main Street, turning Emu Creek into a ghost town.

Great Alpine Road several klicks north of the Emu Creek Road intersection

Phil Harrison rode at the centre of his boys who were spread across the highway. They negotiated the occasional abandoned vehicle, but they were in no hurry. They paced themselves to stay about a kilometre behind the bikers. Phil didn't want the gang to know they were being followed, but intended to stop anyone who might decide to turn back. They did glimpse the stragglers from time to time, but the bikers were concentrating on what was ahead and didn't notice the Harrisons.

However someone knew exactly where the Harrisons were. Apari might have been on foot, but he covered ground fast enough.

He was armed with an axe and machete he'd found in an abandoned barn. No good against guns perhaps, but he didn't intend to be caught in the open.

When the SS gang reached Emu Creek Road they stopped for a moment. Then, with a unified roar they turned off the highway and surged towards town. Although they carried a number of guns, they were short of ammunition and were prepared to rely on the bludgeoning effect of clubs, cricket bats, knives, rifle butts and tree branches. It wasn't long before they approached town where the gravel road changed to bitumen.

The place was deserted.

Main Street, Emu Creek

They reached the barbwire barricade and after looking perplexed for a few seconds, the gang leaders exploded with laughter.

'They think this'll keep us out, do they?' one bearded lout yelled. 'Look it don't even go all the way across the bleedin' road.'

Goliath and Sumo divided the gang into three roughly equal groups, sending one right and the other left.

'Circle round back,' Goliath ordered. 'We'll meet up on the other side of this wire.'

The pack spread out while the centre group started edging around the wire. They were half way through when the ground gave way beneath them. A biker on each side of the road sank into waist-deep pits. They screamed in agony as a dozen stakes, shaved to wicked points pierced their legs and groin. Impaled as they were, they couldn't wrestle free. The agony was excruciating, but doubled when they moved even slightly. They begged for help, but no one could reach them through the tangled barbwire.

'Clear the fence away!' someone yelled.

The bikers clambered to pull the mesh aside. Two more shrieked as they plunged into another punji-pit below the barricade. It didn't take long for the remaining gang to clear the wire, but in their haste they forgot the two men skewered with punji-sticks. Their torsos were shredded as the barbwire ripped over them. They slumped into the pits where other punjis stabbed their bellies. They bled to death in minutes.

Some bikers struggled to rescue their other four comrades, but arterial blood spurted across the road as they were dragged free. The bikers were cautious now. No one wanted to breach the opening until one bold soul wrenched a picket from a nearby fence. He jabbed it at the road as he edged forward, knowing he'd be safe once he reached the bitumen. The others followed using their weapons to test the road ahead.

There were no more unpleasant booby-traps as Stanley's team didn't have time to dig further holes in the road. It was tough going through the blue metal, but the pits had done their work — in this part of town at least. The bikers poured through the breach and were out for blood, but the street was deserted in front of them until Sergeant Bob Brenan stepped from the alley beside the IGA store.

'Stop right where you are!' he bellowed. 'You blokes turn around and bugger off before you regret it. There's nothing for you here.'

He stood alone armed with only his riot-stick, but the bikers pulled up short in pure surprise. They didn't stop for long though.

'You're joking, right?' Sumo said.

'Nope, you heard me.'

'Bugger that. Grab him, boys. Toss the bastard in one of them pits.'

'Ted!'

Ted led his group of young townspeople into Main Street. They raced to the centre and stood in two ranks. Ten people stood shoulder-to-shoulder. They were all armed with sling shots and carried bum-packs full of pebbles, marbles, ball-bearings and fishing sinkers. Once again the bikers halted in sheer surprise.

'Front row, aim!' Ted yelled. 'Fire!'

A salvo of missiles slammed into the bikers who tried to dodge, but there was no respite.

'Front row kneel – reload. Back row, advance -- aim -- fire!'

Another hail of missiles hammered the gang. At such close range every stone hit a target.

'Back row, kneel. Front row, advance – fire ...'

Ted's people rolled on, slamming a continuous stream of painful and potentially deadly missiles into the bikers. They'd trained well, and soon had driven the bikers back past the bitumen. Still there was no let up. The shanghai contingent carried more than fifty missiles each and the punishment went on and on. Then Zach joined the fray, adding his own deadly dimension to the mix.

An arrow pierced Goliath's chest, killing him instantly. A second arrow took out Sumo, while the relentless hail of catapult-fire continued. Several bikers were knocked unconscious by head shots. No amount of ducking and dodging could evade the pellets. The bikers edged away under the continual onslaught. They'd fired a few shots, but with little effect other than causing Ted's people to flinch now and then. He'd drilled them like robots, or lines of 18th century infantry that faced each other and thought about nothing else but loading and firing. Once the Emu Creek defenders reached the gravel road they split into lines and carefully made their way past the punji-pits. They reformed and continued their mechanical, relentless pursuit until they reached Memorial Drive where they were in danger of being outflanked by the second group of bikers.

Around the RSL Hall, Outskirts of Emu Creek

The second team of bikers rushed along Memorial drive. They vented their rage by urinating on the war memorial and smashing the plaques naming Emu Creek's war dead. This was a big mistake because the veterans were waiting for them behind the IGA store and saw the desecration. These men had held a dawn service at the cenotaph every ANZAC day for as long as anyone could remember and they took their war memorial very seriously. Their first impulse was to charge forward and lay into the bikers, but Mike Farrow held them back.

'Hold your position, fellas,' he called. 'You'll get you turn. Steady now. Sling a bit of abuse their way.'

So the vets yelled profanities at the bikers who replied in what turned out to be nothing more than insult-trading, but Mike had his reasons.

Let the bastards get good and mad — and reckless.

It didn't take long. The gang charged in a fury. It was a fearsome sight, but the veterans had faced Viet Cong, Taliban guerrillas, suicide bombers, artillery bombardments and more, so they stood their ground. They also knew that ex-Regimental Sergeant Major Whiting and his team of greenies had been digging around here too. The ground was softer than at the road, so they'd made quick work of the pits. More bikers screamed as they crashed through the camouflage matting and were skewered by lethal punji-sticks. The greenies had dug four holes that all claimed victims.

Fearful of more traps, the bikers hesitated. They were only metres from the vets who knew they were now safe to advance. And advance they did – meting out a terrible vengeance. SS paid dearly for defiling the war memorial. The vets slammed into them wielding axes, cricket bats, machetes and they weren't squeamish about shedding blood. The bikers had never met such ferocious resistance. The clinical and restrained efficiency of Major Rogers' troops was nothing compared with the brutality of the incensed veterans. The bikers turned and bolted before they were decimated, but still left half their force either dying in the punji-holes or beaten senseless. The retreat turned to a rout as the bikers raced down Memorial Drive throwing their weapons aside for better speed. They charged straight towards Ted and his sling-shot squad.

The Northern Edge of Emu Creek Commercial Area

Unaware of the tragedy unfolding for their comrades, the third section of bikers dashed behind the newsagency. Another punji-trap claimed a further victim, but the laneway that led back to Main Street was bitumen sealed so there were no more traps other than a barbwire barricade that three bikers pulled aside with some difficulty while the others continued behind the town café to another lane that ran parallel to Creek Street. This area was too wide to be protected by punji-pits or coiled barbwire so it was a potential weak spot. Bob had counted on it being furthest from the town's main entrance and more likely to be overlooked.

Unfortunately the bikers had spotted the gap. Karen, Warra, Stanley and the engineers would take the brunt of the onslaught.

Once the three bikers had dragged the barricade clear, they decided to take a short-cut beside the newsagency. The lane was narrow and only about twenty metres long. The bikers' bravado was now well and truly squashed and they advanced cautiously. The lane proved empty and they could see Main Street beyond. Suddenly there was a crack from above. The bikers' eyes shot upwards. Two metal bars spanned the alley from the newsagency roof across to the café. A pair of stout nylon ropes were attached to one pole. Forty kilo cement bags were secured to each rope and suspended from the other pole. Each sack was held in place by a cord tied with a slip-knot.

Two youngsters crouched on the roof holding the lines.

'Now!' one of them called and they both released the slip-knots,

The bags swung down and smashed into the bikers, crushing organs and breaking bones. One biker managed to remain standing, but was thumped to the ground as the cement sack cracked into his back on its return pendulum swing. All three bikers lay still. No one had time to check whether they were dead or injured, but they were certainly no longer any threat.

There were still a score or more bikers to deal with as they emerged from behind the café. Karen and Stanley stood side-by-side to meet them. All that stood between them and the gang were two strands of barbwire strung across each end of the alley. These wires were hooked onto metre-high garden stakes close to the cafe and hardware store walls. Karen brandished her riot stick and Stanley was armed with an L1A1, 7.26 SLR he'd souvenired from his days as an army cadet marksman instructor. There was no ammunition for the rifle's magazine, but the bayonet was fixed and he knew how to use it. Once again the bikers dissolved into peals of laughter.

'Is this all yer got — bloody hell, a piddling little fence, an old git and a sheila ...?'

'Never underestimate your enemy,' Stanley muttered with a grin.

Karen and the old man edged backwards as the bikers advanced. Forcing back panic, it took all Karen's resolve not to turn and run. Stanley sensed her fear.

'Steady, lass,' he said keeping his eyes on the bikers. 'Just one step at a time, we want to keep them focused on us.'

The gang was growing impatient. They heard screams and yelling from the edge of town. One of the bikers unhooked the barbwire and let it drop to the road. The gang stepped over the wire and advanced menacingly. They were less than twenty metres away when they charged just as Karen and Stan backed out of the lane into Main Street. Now only one strand of barbwire stood between them and disaster. Just at that moment the bikers heard cries from behind them.

Warra and his people streamed from the rear of the hardware store only metres behind the bikers. Warra screamed a command, no one remembered what he actually said, but a dozen boomerangs sliced into the gang. The boomerangs were hastily made and some were no more than throwing clubs, but they were carved from solid hard wood. Even with limited practice, the townspeople couldn't miss. A second volley followed instantly, then a third. Many bikers went down as they were struck while others threw their arms into the air to try and protect their faces.

In the confusion four men, including the ex-engineer, implemented his plan. They wore protective gloves when they emerged from the front of the café and hardware store. They worked in pairs, grabbing the barbwire strand and pulling it tight about waist-high. They charged along the flanks of the bikers. The barbwire grabbed the gang members who shuffled in confusion as the townspeople flashed past. When they we just beyond the bikers they ducked as Warra and his people picked up the barbwire that lay on the ground behind the gang. They swept past the bikers in the opposite direction, trapping them completely in a mesh of metal thorns. The more the gang tried to escape the worse they became entangled. The barbs cut through their leathers and blood washed across the lane.

Warra's people surrounded the embattled bikers and battered them into submission with axe handles, stakes, stout branches and cricket bats. The bikers thrashed in their torment, but Emu Creek's newly formed militia showed no mercy. Soon there was no more movement from beneath the barbwire. A handful of bikers avoided the net and retreated behind the cafe back to the west end of town. Karen was sickened by the barbarity before her although, acting as a decoy, she had taken little part in the brutality. It was Bairnsdale all over again.

'C'mon, lass,' Stanley nudged her elbow. 'It's not over yet. There's mopping up to do. Remember — don't give the enemy a chance to regroup.'

Enemy, she thought, *OMG, it's come to that. They were just a band of hooligans once and now they're 'the enemy'.*

But that was all the time she had for reflection. Everyone was needed at the Main Street-Memorial Drive intersection. Urgently!

Chapter 12 — Battle Scars

Ted's squad was managing well, they'd expended less than half of their ammunition and driven the bikers back in confusion. Although Goliath and Sumo were only nominal leaders, they had held the band together. Now they were dead, the bikers lost all cohesion. But, just as victory seemed assured, the right flank of the gang barrelled into Ted's group. They weren't really attacking, but fleeing the war-vets and Ted's people just got in their way. Two things happened almost at once. Initially, the bikers started lashing out at anything that stood in their way. They'd abandoned most of their weapons and now only had the use of their fists, teeth and booted feet. Next the fleeing centre section of bikers rallied when the hail of pellets slackened and then stopped altogether.

Ted's people were wrong in assuming SS was beaten because the bikers regained their bravado and charged headlong back into the melee. The catapult platoon was now fighting for its survival and was certainly boxing above its weight. The bikers were bigger and tougher, but Emu Creek citizens had quickly developed a ruthlessness of their own. Sling-shots weren't much use for hand-to-hand fighting, so Ted and his troops resorted to punches and kicks too. Despite their bulk, the bikers were outnumbered, which made the contest practically equal with both sides slowly pounding each other into a stalemate.

The survivors from the left biker group joined the edge of the skirmish just as the crowd from the RSL crashed into the fray. The veterans were right on their heels and piled in with fists and weapons flying. Bob and Karen charged into combat swinging their riot sticks effectively while Stanley pranced around the battle's edge jabbing his bayonet into any part of a biker that came within range.

Zach's bow was now useless. He couldn't see a clear target in the confusion, so he charged Jet into a group of bikers pummelling them apart. Now they were more vulnerable and instantly set on by groups of townspeople. He dismounted and led Jet clear of the conflict, before racing back into the thick of it with a knife and axe-handle ready to do business.

The bikers had cut their teeth (literally) on bar-room brawls and had gained street-smarts in numerous skirmishes, while Emu Creek's residents were new-comers to barbarity and it began to tell. Townspeople were knocked down by the sheer weight of their opponents who knew instinctively to follow up with a savage kick to the kidneys to make sure no one got up again. They could easily out-bludgeon two of Emu Creek's best and it looked like the tide of battle had turned.

Yet one person no one had counted on arrived at that moment. Apari had easily slipped past Phil Harrison and his boys who had stopped at the Highway intersection. He jogged through adjoining paddocks and leapt over a fence onto the gravel road a few hundred metres from town. He'd heard the hullabaloo from a kilometre away and quickened his pace. One glance summed up the situation. He thought he saw Warra somewhere in the mayhem and without a second's hesitation dashed towards town. The bikers had their backs towards him when he reached the fight.

He sank the machete into a biker's shoulder-blade where it lay imbedded as arterial blood sprayed in a crimson mist. The blade was wedged tight, so Apari grabbed his axe with both hands and swung horizontally into another gang-members neck almost decapitating him. He wrenched the axe free and cleaved the skull of one more biker. In seconds the axe had claimed five bikers, but Apari still surged on right to the centre of the fight, carving a path of gore and driving a wedge between the gang.

The bikers staggered in the path of Apari's bloody onslaught allowing the townspeople an instant's respite. They recovered and once again went on the rampage. The gang knew it had been bested. The SS losses were simply too great. Those who could dashed west along the road followed by those who could only stagger. Apari finished off another victim as he lurched past while the townsfolk hounded the remainder, thumping the stragglers into oblivion. Finally Emu Creek's militia were too exhausted to continue and gave up the chase. Barely a dozen bikers escaped and most of them bore serious injuries. With no chance of medical attention their chances weren't good.

The Emu Creek citizens returned to town slapping each other on the back and congratulating themselves. What marvellous chaps they were, even if they hadn't realised just how much it hurt when someone clouted you in the jaw. Their euphoria drained away when they saw the cost. At least half the town suffered wounds from minor cuts and bruises to serious fractures and possible internal injuries. Fortunately there appeared to be no fatalities. The greenies were now put to work helping the worst cases to Dr Nandamuri's surgery. Bob picked his way through the moaning injured and found Zach, Karen and Mike who'd all received minor wounds, but would survive.

'Bloody hell, what a mess,' Mike assayed with both horror and relief. 'We beat 'em though, sarge.'

Bob merely nodded. He'd spotted a body lying at the edge of town. It was Stanley Whiting. He still held his rifle in a vice-like grip and it took all Zach's strength to release the weapon. Karen felt his neck for a pulse, but there was none – he was dead.

'Funny,' Bob observed, 'there's not a mark on him. His old ticker must have packed up. I guess one last fight was too much for the old bloke.'

They called some of Stanley's RSL mates over who'd know how best to lay the old man to rest. Now Bob and his officers had to turn their attention to the biker corpses that littered Emu Creek.

'We're going to have to get 'em underground before they get too ripe,' Bob said. 'Mike, gather as many people together as you can. They'll need spades, shovels and picks. Bury them in a pit in one of the paddocks outside town. As far away as you can manage.'

Mike also commandeered a Clydesdale and dray to haul the bodies out of town. It took several trips which gave enough time to dig a shallow grave. The bodies were dumped unceremoniously into the trench then covered with earth and a top layer of rock to prevent scavengers disturbing the grave. Some of the bikers were still alive although most were critical. Mike wasn't sure what to do about them, but while the dead were being buried, Zach loaded the wounded bikers onto the cart. He led the Clydesdale to the west and didn't return until after sundown. The dray was empty and no one asked him what had become of the bikers.

While Zach was gone, Karen and Bob made their way to Dr Nandamuri's surgery to see if they could help. The vet, George Grimshaw, was an invaluable assistant, but Karen was surprised to find Sharon Harrison and her daughters acting as nurses and doing a sterling job of it. The greenies were making themselves useful too.

'I had to patch up Phil and the boys more times than I can remember,' Sharon told Karen, 'so I've had plenty of practice.'

Dr Nandamuri had set two broken arms and a twisted leg and was busy suturing the worst gashes.

'Makes a change from prescribing anti-biotics and analgesics,' he said grinning. Karen was sure she saw him wink. 'I finally feel like I'm doing something worthwhile.'

'Yeah, pity they had to cop it for you to discover your true calling, doc,' she said.

'Believe me, I am sorry these people are suffering,' he said, 'but that would have happened whether I was here or not. What I meant was I am pleased to be at hand to help. I apologise if I sounded callous.'

'Don't sweat it, doc,' Karen said. 'I shouldn't have snapped at you, it's been a tough day all round.'

'You could do with a bit of attention yourself,' Dr Nandamuri said. 'That's a nasty cut on your forehead.'

'I'll drop by later. It looks like you've got your hands full for a while. Sharon and the girls seem to be managing – I'd just be in the way. I'll see what I can do to help in town.'

'Nice work, girls,' Bob commended.

'Glad to help, Sergeant Brenan,' Norma chirped as Bob raised an eyebrow.

'What happened to dirty, rotten copper?'

'Me and Charlene are sorry we were rude. We saw what you did today and that took guts. Friends?'

'Yeah, friends. Call me Bob and we'll say it's quits,' he smiled and followed Karen out of the surgery.

Excerpt from Karen Davenport's Diary:

OMG. The clean up was horrendous after we beat off that biker gang. Even Bob was shocked by the ferocity of the battle. Mike and Zach worked wonders and did the lion's share of the work. Pulling bodies from Stanley's punji-sticks was the worst job. I feel sorry for those poor people who'd died so horribly. Zach said it was their fault for starting the trouble, but I still pity them dying in such dreadful agony all the same.

Finally Mike told me to find something else to do while he, Zach and the RSL veterans sorted things out. Stanley's secret weapons certainly were as effective as they were gory. Dear old Stanley, he was such a nice man. He always tipped his hat to me when he passed and addressed me as 'Miss Karen'. We'll all miss him at Emu Creek and his mates are planning a special send off for him.

At the moment my hands are shaking so badly I can hardly write. I judged the people at Bairnsdale too rashly. We acted in exactly the same way. I've helped control a few protest marches that got ugly, but they were picnics compared with a pitched battle to the death.

We were lucky this time. Bob said it was because we were ready and had a plan and the bikers assumed we'd be helpless. We'll need to be ready and have a plan all the time from now on. We're going to start properly securing the town perimeter tomorrow.

Dr Nandamuri is awesome .I think everyone will pull through thanks to him and he patched up the wound on my temple. Sharon, Charlene and Norma have been amazing too. They're really nice when you get to know them. They're staying at the pub until they work out where they'll live. One thing is for sure, they're not going back to live with Phil Harrison.

Zach has taken the last bikers away. A few are still alive, but Bob hasn't stopped him. Mike and I saw how ruthless he can be. I don't want to think what he plans for those bikers. But we need someone who can deal with the hard decisions. I don't think I can.

I can't explain why I love him ♡ — I barely know him really. What was it Bob had said? It seems so long ago now.

'Don't dwell, girl, just do it.' — OK I will!

Main Street, Emu Creek, Victorian High Country

Warra and Apari surveyed the devastation while discussing the merits of their traditional weapons. They both agreed that their people needed some serious practice when they returned to Albury. They planned to head home at first light, but right then they were hungry and started a fire beside Emu Creek Ford to cook a possum they'd trapped. They were both well pleased with the way things had turned out, feeling that if violence was going to be a part of their future way of life, they'd better get good at it. Zach joined them when he returned at nightfall.

'I got rid of 'em,' he announced tersely, but neither of the Aboriginal men commented.

Karen and Mike made one last patrol through town. Most townspeople had gone home, although a crowd was celebrating at the pub. Beer supplies were dwindling and it may not have been at an ideal temperature, but after all the excitement and trials of the day, they'd earned it and no one was fussy.

'Our people did well, didn't they?' Mike said as they passed the bar-room that bubbled with exuberance.

'Our people ...?'

'Yes. I know we're new here, but I think we've proved we belong now. There isn't much choice anyway. We have to make Emu Creek self-sufficient or the town will die – literally.'

'You may not have a choice, but ...'

Mike looked at her dully, it was the moment he knew had to come, but he dreaded it all the same.

'So you're not staying?' he asked.

'That's right,' she replied in barely a whisper.

'You're going with *him*?'

'If you mean Zach,' she smiled, 'then yes ... if he'll still take me.'

'I dunno what Bob will say.'

'He won't stop me, he already knows.'

'You haven't said anything to him, have you?'

'No, but I don't have to. You and I both know by now that's he's a lot sharper than a simple country plod ...'

'Like me?'

She smiled and kissed him lightly on the cheek.

'Yes, like you Mike, but I'll never forget my time with a simple country plod. Thank you.'

She left him standing outside the pub and walked towards the campfire by the creek. Mike turned and entered the pub. He needed a drink.

Zach, Warra and Apari sat around the fire drinking tea. They were stewing a possum with native herbs and some potatoes they scrounged. They offered Karen a cup when she sat down beside Zach.

'Staying clear of the celebration then?' Karen observed.

'Yep, we're fine here. Like to stay for supper?' Warra offered. 'There's enough to go round.'

'Thank you, it smells delicious,' she replied.

'Not bothered about possum then?'

'Right now I'd eat grasshoppers.'

'Yeah, they're not bad roasted and we've got damper too,' Apari said.

They sat in silence for a while watching the flames leap about. Occasionally someone prodded the embers sending spark showers into the night air. Karen was wondering how best to bring up the subject of leaving Emu Creek, but Zach pre-empted her.

'Apari and Warra are heading back to their mob tomorrow. I think it's time I did the same. I reckon I've learned all I'm going to. You'll only be able to bring what you can carry on your back.'

'You mean you still want me to go with you?'

Apari and Warra grinned like a couple of kids.

'Of course he does, you duffer,' Warra said. 'Haven't you noticed how he looks at you?'

Zach glared at him.

'It'll be rough going cross-country,' he said.

'I'll keep up.'

'The bike won't be much use,' Zach said. 'We'll take turns on Jet and ride double if we get into strife.'

'We can always rustle another horse somewhere.'

'Yeah or break in a brumby,' he laughed. 'I wonder if Bob will let you keep your police pistol.'

'It was issued to me, not him,' she said defiantly.

'Good, but remember there'll be no room for luxuries.'

'I've got some steamy lingerie ...' she eyed him coquettishly, '... that won't take up much room.'

'Okay, I'll make an exception just this once,' he said with a smile.

Junction of Emu Creek Road and Great Alpine Road

That afternoon the five Harrisons had watched as Zach approached leading the Clydesdale towards the highway intersection. When he saw Phil and the boys Zach halted a hundred metres short of them. He was armed with the police pistol he'd taken from the Mooney brothers and his bow was ready, but he wanted to avoid a further conflict. Frankly, he'd had enough fighting to last a lifetime so he ordered the injured bikers off the dray.

'Now you guys head that way,' Zach said pointing towards the riders. 'Those riders up there might let you pass by or they may shoot you out of hand. I really don't know and I care even less. One thing is for sure, I'll be waiting here and if one of you bastards takes a single step back in this direction, I'll kill you myself.'

Most of the gang could barely stagger let alone walk and some even crawled. It took an interminable amount of time, but finally the bikers reached the highway. Phil Harrison and his sons merely eyed them curiously as they came to the intersection. One biker turned right and Phil shot him at point-blank range. The others took the hint and disappeared southwards.

Zach turned the Clydesdale, climbed onto the dray and rode back to town.

'We gonna follow him, dad?' Gary Harrison asked.

'Not now, son. I'm not really interested in that bastard. Tomorrow will do.'

Chapter 13 — Showdown on Main Street

West Bank of Emu Creek

A mist hovered over Emu Creek edging down Main Street. The night's kaleidoscope of colour faded quickly as sunbeams lanced through the bush heralding another clear day. Apari awoke and declared rain was on the way although how he divined that fact was unclear.

'What, you're a weather chick, now?' Warra challenged.

'I feel it in my bones.'

'Yeah, right. You know it's a waste though, all those satellites floating around up in space and now they're as much use as a fart in a diver's helmet.'

'I miss those weather chicks,' Apari lamented.

Zach awoke, kick-started the fire and brewed some tea. He'd chosen not to accompany Karen back to the police house. Although she insisted she'd been no one's girl until now, he felt he'd white-anted Mike and didn't want to rub his face in it. *'Friends-with-benefits'* was how she'd described the relationship with her colleague. Zach didn't actually want to discuss her previous boyfriends at all – whatever their official status might have been.

'And ours is …?' Zach had insisted.

'… That's quite different,' she replied after some thought. 'You'll soon find out.'

She'd left then and told him she'd be ready at dawn.

True to her word, Karen arrived early, dressed in military combat kit, baseball cap with her hair tied back in a neat ponytail. She wore tough, Doc-Martin boots. Her *weapons-of-choice* were her police-issue pistol, riot stick and mace spray strapped to her belt along with a litre water bottle. Her light back-pack contained only the 'essentials'. She also carried a carton of eggs.

'You look pretty smokin' hot in that kick-arse outfit,' Zach observed cheerfully.

'Into dress-ups, are you?' she replied with a sparkling smile. 'I thought you'd like some breakfast.'

'Ripper,' Warra eyed the eggs keenly. 'Boiled, fried or scrambled — how do you like 'em?'

'I don't mind,' Zach said and, as the others shrugged, Warra placed eight eggs into the billy.

'Boiled it is then. I'll toast the left-over damper as well.'

It turned out that Apari was right as heavy clouds rolled in from the west, bringing a grey drizzle with it. It dampened the town's already low mood as yesterday's fighters nursed their injuries and the impact of the action sank in. They'd regret losing their pretty young police constable too. Karen was a popular officer who worked well with the community. Bob lamented her leaving as much as anyone, but it was not his business to prevent her finding what little happiness she could in the turbulent world that now enveloped them. He admitted there was nothing he could do to stop her anyway.

'Come back anytime if it doesn't work out,' he whispered as she kissed his cheek.

She squeezed his hand and nodded.

'Thanks, sarge. You've taught me more in a few months than all my time at Glen Waverley. You've shown me what it is to be a thoroughly awesome human being and you're an amazing copper.'

Mike shook Zach's hand as they exchanged *I-guess-that's-how-it-goes* looks. He gave Karen a brotherly peck — there was no point in drawing out the heartache. Emu Creek's entire population gathered in Main Street to farewell Karen, so it took some time before she'd embraced everyone and finally headed east with Zach. They rode double across Emu Creek Ford then dismounted and led Jet along the dirt road before disappearing around a bend. Karen turned and waved just once before she was gone. When they were out of sight Zach took her hand.

'You know I'm a pretty happy guy right now,' he said.

Karen just smiled. That was probably about as mushy as he was going to get, but it told her all she needed to know for now.

The crowd slowly dispersed. There was work be done. People required attention and so did the town defences. Food, water, shelter, sanitation and protection were all high on the agenda and it was time to get on with it. Emu Creek routine may not have returned to normal, but it returned.

Mike went back to the police house, but only stayed a moment. Karen had packed up what she couldn't carry and stacked her belongings neatly in a corner of her room. Leaving her stuff there was a painful reminder, but Mike had no idea what to do with it for now.

C'mon, Mickey, buck up. She never led you on. She never promised you anything. Bugger Zach McAlister – trouble is he's a pretty decent bloke.

Then he heard Bob bellowing from the station and he left with relief. Bob found a dozen jobs to keep Mike busy and figured he'd share some creek-chilled beer with him that evening — or something stronger if that's what was needed. Right now Mike was manning the front desk and filtering the delegations that bombarded the station wanting Bob's advice. In the meantime Bob met with several of the townsfolk who seemed to have top priority and together they started developing strategies. Bob was a natural co-ordinator and people automatically deferred to his judgement.

He was just finishing off a plan with George Grimshaw concerning the sustainability of local livestock when Mike knocked on his office door and entered.

'Can I have word, sarge?' Mike asked.

'Sure, we're finished here.'

'Sharon Harrison is at the front desk and in a right old state. Phil's back in town ...'

'Bring her in and let's hear what she's got to say.'

But, when Mike returned to the front desk, Sharon was gone.

'C'mon, Mike, we'd better take a look for ourselves,' Bob said strapping on his utility belt and putting on his hat. Whether he was still officially a copper or not, people respected the uniform — except maybe Phil Harrison. When they reached the Main Street they pulled up short.

'Holy crap,' Bob murmured. 'I don't believe this ...'

Main Street Emu Creek

The crowd was gone when Phil Harrison and his boys rode through the drizzle into Emu Creek. Ted and Sharon were seated at the pub window and saw them arrive. Sharon was taking a break from the surgery and sharing a coffee with Ted. They'd been considering what to do once the dust had settled in Emu Creek. Ted knew what he wanted and had proved he was no longer the wimpy nerd he'd been branded by Phil. But, as with Karen, Mike and Zach — it was complicated.

Sharon was facing the window and Ted saw her freeze with the cup touching her lips as she stared through the glass. Ted spun in his seat and his jaw dropped.

'Oh, great timing, Phil,' he muttered under his breath before turning to Sharon. 'Stay here, I'll sort this out.'

'Be careful,' she whispered, 'they're all be armed.'

'So am I,' Ted said patting the sling-shot sticking from his jeans pocket.

'Don't be silly,' she admonished.

'I won't be, but this is something *I* have to do. It's high time I stood up to Phil instead of letting him run roughshod over me all the time.'

Ted walked onto the pub board walk, but Sharon didn't stay put and followed him outside. The Harrisons had reined to a stop at the start of the bitumen. Phil seemed unsure what to do next. He'd come for Sharon, but had no idea where she was and knew the townspeople wouldn't be disposed to tell him. He was sharp enough to know that getting Sharon and the girls to return to the farm would be messy so he wanted to avoid Bob Brenan and his coppers. But his dilemma was resolved without him even trying.

Less than a hundred metres ahead he saw Ted walk onto the street and there was Sharon right behind him.

'Sharon, I want to talk to you,' Phil bawled.

'Quick, get Bob Brenan and Mike Farrow,' Ted hissed. 'I'll stall Phil.'

Sharon darted along the boardwalk past the antique store and disappeared down Officer Road. She barged into the police station.

'Phil's in town with the boys,' she blurted. 'Me and the girls ain't going back with him. Not now we've made the break. Ted's talking to him on Main Street.'

'Okay, you don't have to do anything you don't want to,' Mike said. 'Stay here and I'll get the sarge. We'll sort out Phil.'

Sharon only waited at the police station door until Mike entered Bob's office then she raced to the pub where a back stairway led to the first storey bedrooms. She clambered up the steps and bolted inside.

Meanwhile Ted edged into the centre of Main Street trying to look as casual as possible although his knees were quaking. He thought it strange that facing the bikers yesterday hadn't frightened him. Maybe things had happened too quickly for him to be scared. Meeting Phil's icy stare was quite different.

'Stay here, boys,' Phil ordered, 'this is between me and your uncle Ted.'

He nudged his horse's flanks and it stepped forward.

'Don't come any closer, Phil,' Ted warned. 'You're not wanted in town. Turn around and go home.'

'What, you're not content humpin' my missus, you're giving me orders now?' Phil stormed.

'No one's *humping* anyone, Phil, but Sharon's not going back with you.'

'Says who?'

'She does.'

At this point Ted didn't want Phil to come any closer. He was armed with a rifle, but who knew whether he was prepared to use it on his own brother? Ted rummaged for one of the lead sinkers in his pocket. He loaded his sling-shot and fired the missile into the horse's withers. It whinnied at the impact, reared and tossed Phil from the saddle. Phil was a good horseman, but he was taken completely by surprise. Normally he'd handle a bucking horse with ease, but with one hand gripping his gun and the other only loosely on the reins, he was thrown to the street. He hit the asphalt with a thump, badly grazing his palms and chin. He'd been angry enough beforehand, but now he was furious.

The horse bolted forward, cantering past Ted until it reached Emu Creek where it stopped for a drink. Its shoulder probably smarted, but otherwise the animal appeared unhurt. Ted vaguely made a mental note to get George Grimshaw to take a look at the poor creature before Phil left town. Because, by God he was going to leave town if Ted had anything to do with it.

Phil staggered to his feet, remembering to pick up his rifle.

'You bastard!' he yelled followed by a string of expletives.

Bob and Mike raced onto Main Street just in time to see the two men facing off in the centre of the road.

'What the hell do they think they're playing at?' Bob said. 'This isn't Tombstone ...'

At that second Phil raised his rifle and fired. A crack rattled through the street and echoes clattered between the town buildings as Ted slumped to the ground.

Mike and Bob dashed forward, but they knew they were too late. Both policemen drew their pistols on the run, cocked their weapons ready to fire. They yelled for Phil to drop his gun, but he ignored them. He was so intent on Ted that they were of no consequence at all. Normally Phil would have done the job with just one bullet, but maybe the shock of being dismounted, the drizzling rain or just plain rage marred his aim. Ted was struggling to his knees. Blood seeped from his shoulder where he'd been hit. Phil levelled the rifle and aimed at Ted's forehead.

'I'm finished with your bullshit ...' Phil hissed as a second gunshot rang across Main Street.

The town fell silent as if frozen in time.

Bob and Mike exchanged glances, but neither of them had fired their weapons. Phil stood exactly as before with his rifle still pointing at Ted who still knelt on the bitumen. Then a red patch spread across Phil's chest and more gushed down the back of his shirt. Phil dropped the rifle and clutched his shirt. More blood oozed through his fingers as he gasped a final curse and collapsed to the ground. Everyone stayed riveted to the spot.

Then all eyes turned to the pub door.

Sharon Harrison stood on the verandah holding the .22 rifle she taken from the farm. The barrel was red hot from the single shot and a wisp of smoke coiled upwards from the breech as she ejected the spent cartridge.

'The only useful thing the dopey bugger ever did was teach me how to shoot straight,' she muttered, dropping the gun.

She raced across the street to Ted who'd been winged, but was still conscious. There was no doubt that Phil was dead, the bullet had passed straight through his heart. Sharon cradled Ted in her arms and burst into tears of relief. Her torment was over at last. Bob and Mike approached from the east while the Harrison boys advanced from the west.

'How is he?' Bob asked.

'We've got to get him to Dr Nandamuri,' Sharon said.

'Yeah, give her a hand, will you, Mike?' Bob replied.

'What about them, sarge?' Mike indicated the approaching riders.

'Leave them to me.'

Bob walked to meet the Harrison boys who sat nervously in their saddles. He waited until they were only a few metres away before raising his arm in true policeman fashion.

'Okay, hold it there, lads,' he said. 'Stow your weapons. There's been enough shooting today.'

'Is Dad hurt bad?' Gary asked in a tone expressing his contempt.

'He's dead, Gary. I'm sorry. Your mum shot him to save your Uncle Ted.'

Bob wondered if Gary might try to shoot him and the thought crossed the boy's mind.

'Stay cool, Gaz,' Andy, the second eldest said. 'Dad was nuts, he was just killin' anyone he wanted. There's nothing we can do about him now.'

'Are Charlene and Norma safe, Sergeant Brenan?' Clarence asked. He was the youngest Harrison boy and closest to his sisters.

'They're fine and doing a good job in the surgery. Now put the guns away and get off those horses. We'll have a cuppa at the station and talk this over.'

'Are we under arrest, then?' Gary challenged.

'No one is under arrest, or likely to be in my opinion,' Bob replied with a sigh.

'What about Mum? She shot our dad.'

'I think that was pretty much self defence, or at least in the defence of someone in danger. Come on you lot, let's get out of this bloody rain.'

The Harrison boys were so numbed by their father's death, they didn't protest and followed Bob to the police station. Meanwhile Dr Nandamuri examined Phil and officially confirmed he was indeed dead.

'I'll sort out the body, sarge,' Mike said.

Emu Creek didn't have a cemetery, so funerals were usually held in Bright or Omeo. Church services were occasionally conducted at the RSL Hall if the faithful could muster a minister who was prepared to come from other parishes. The RSL vets had decided to lay Stanley Whiting to rest in a paddock beside the hall. Mike thought it would be a good idea to use the plot as the future town graveyard as transporting coffins elsewhere was now impossible.

The veterans agreed to make the arrangements for Phil Harrison. They didn't have any time for him, but he was a local citizen, even if not a particularly likeable one. They'd bury Phil at a suitable distance from Stanley who was a man they greatly admired. With yet another task completed Mike returned to the surgery to see how Ted was, but he wasn't there.

Dr Nandamuri reported the bullet had passed cleanly through Ted's shoulder causing only a flesh wound and missing any vital organs. The doctor had disinfected the wound, closed it with a few stitches, bandaged the shoulder and put Ted's arm in a sling. He'd given Ted a course of antibiotics to prevent infection and sent him on his way.

'You know we're going to rapidly run out of medicine,' Dr Nandamuri reflected. 'Once we do, infection will become as big a problem as it was a century ago.'

'Looks like I'll be off on scrounging raids before long, doc,' Mike said. 'I'll check all the pharmacies I come across.'

Mike found Ted in the pub lounge surrounded by Sharon and all her children. They were chattering away excitedly and, if they regretted their father's death, they showed no lingering signs of grief. Even Gary had lost his truculence and was sharing a beer with Ted. He even smiled a greeting when Mike joined them.

'Well, well, what's going on here?' Mike asked.

'Just taking care of our hero here,' Sharon beamed.

'I was lucky,' Ted admitted. 'I thought Phil was a better shot than that, but he was so steamed up that he wasn't thinking or shooting straight.'

'So have you decided what to do next?' Mike asked with genuine concern for the family.

'We're *all* going back to the property,' Gary said cheerfully. It was the only home he'd known and he liked rural life. 'Emu Creek will need surrounding farms to produce enough food to keep going.'

'True enough,' Mike conceded. 'Will you be okay out there?'

'Nowhere is going to be safe from now on,' Sharon said, 'but there are enough of us to deter vagrants. We'll stay alert and we can always scuttle back to town if anything crops up we can't handle.'

'Yeah, Uncle Ted's coming with us,' Charlene said with a knowing look. 'You'll come and visit, won't you, Mike?'

'Every chance I get,' he replied and he meant it.

It's funny how those girls have changed with a decent bath, brushed hair and an attitude adjustment. In a few years ... who knows ..?

Once the decision was made Sharon insisted they leave straight away and get to the farm before dark. Dr Nandamuri fretted about Ted's wound, but judging by the way Sharon and the girls were fussing over him, he'd be fine. Warra and Apari joined the Harrisons and would accompany them as far as their farm before rejoining their own people and returning to Albury.

Mike, Bob and the doctor saw the small contingent off as they rode towards the highway. The rain had finally swept eastwards and the sky cleared. Bob slapped Mike on the back.

'C'mon Mike, it's way past lunchtime and I'm famished. Let's see what we can rustle up.'

'We're going to be busy men from now on, aren't we, sarge?'

'You said it Mike, but we've got a tough little town here so there's every chance we'll pull through ... and call me Bob.'

Part Two — Filling the Void

Chapter 14 — Warlords' Return

Beyond Emu Creek

Emu Creek and Mactown, as the McAlister place became known, were indeed remote enclaves in a barbaric wilderness although they were by no means the only communities to survive the holocaust. It boiled down to a simple formula in the end. Less developed, isolated communities fared far better than those over-crowded centres that were so reliant on technology they were incapable of fending for themselves. Population-stressed metropolises all buckled in quick, smoking succession. Third World cities were the first to descend into anarchy, but western civilization collapsed within days or weeks at best.

So how do you survive when the food supply is dwindling before your eyes and there is no chance of replenishment? You form a gang and the biggest, meanest tough-guy takes control. At first the gangs battled for territorial supremacy, then for food and women.

The First World tumbled back 10,000 years to somewhere in the late Stone Age. Well, probably not that far as people still had the use of metal tools. The skills required to manufacture them were however virtually lost. Those few who still possessed metallurgy arts were either prized members of gangs or poached by others and held as slaves. Some gangs merged to form tribes while others simply shrivelled into oblivion.

It was years before the desolated, deserted cities were safely rid of the diseases that became rife and were spread by scavengers that gorged on rotting corpses. Crows, rats, feral cats and dog packs roamed the vacant concrete canyons of Sydney, Melbourne, the other great capitals of Australia and the World. Initially many humans had resorted to cannibalism to survive. A few managed to, but mostly it was simply a matter of time before all but the most resolute perished.

At first there were guns and ammunition aplenty. Bullets sizzled through cities as battles raged and homemade bombs reduced historic buildings to rubble while dead bodies piled higher. Petrol bombs made a brief appearance, but by the time all the cars had been drained the fuel had degraded and become useless. Those who died in such fire-fights were probably lucky compared with others doomed to slow starvation. Once the status quo was established the survivors protected their turf to the death. Market gardens burgeoned in vacant blocks surrounded by crumbling masonry, shattered glass and twisted metal. Yet victuals were still at subsistence level and tribes guarded their food sources tenaciously. Any one venturing into enemy territory could expect no mercy and received none — there were no exceptions, charity meant death.

Sailors and coastal fishermen were better placed than most. Many yachtsmen sailed to sea with what provisions they could store on board. Many of these mariners resorted to piracy in their own desperation, so any respite was short-lived. They were forced to return once their fresh water ran out. Most had become heartily sick of a fish and seaweed diet anyway. Of course when they returned there was little left, but they bartered their catches with other survivors and formed small communities much like Emu Creek. These centres were no more than villages and only supported minute populations. More than a hundred people in one place was extraordinary.

Indeed the ocean's bounty was seriously challenged for generations. Wallowing super tankers drifted at the current's whim. In most cases they finally grounded somewhere, breaking up and dumping millions a fuel oil into the sea. These ecological disasters manifested themselves as vast, black sludge smeared along thousands of kilometres of coastline. Life in those areas was decimated until the oil formed in amorphous globules. There they lay until some enterprising survivors learnt to use them as heating fuel for which there was a seemingly endless supply.

Age-old skills such as weaving, carpentry and the return of the forge developed quickly enough. There was an unlimited supply of scrap metal to be had and it wasn't too long before blacksmiths emerged to fashion it to some utilitarian purpose. Car bodies were transformed into kitchen utensils, tools and of course weapons.

So people clawed their way to a primitive life reliant on what they could grow or hunt in their local area. Of course there was fierce competition from marauders who had failed to establish a viable patch of their own. Native forests regenerated with remarkable speed. In a few decades bushland had recaptured much of its lost territory. Outlaw bands roamed the forests although the term 'outlaw' was moot as 'law' had ceased to exist long ago. Each settlement developed its own rules and methods of enforcing them. For this they needed ruthless, strong fighters. And of course leaders emerged.

The age of Warlords had returned.

Bob Brenan's Place, Emu Creek

'You know what I still miss?' Old Bob mused, sipping a mug of homemade beer.

He was well into his eighties now and, although he was still fit for his age, he was feeling the effects of arthritis — especially on cold days like this.

He and his good mate Mike Farrow were sitting in front of a roaring fire and had been chewing the fat for most of the evening. Bob's wife was gone now, but his adopted son and daughter only lived a short distance away. They visited daily and often brought him fresh damper and kangaroo stew, which were his particular favourites.

'I dunno,' Mike replied. 'I do know that we've never been able to brew beer as nice a VB. Do you remember VB, Bob?'

'I have trouble remembering what happened last week, but I can almost taste an ice cold Vic. But it's the newspapers I miss.'

'Naw, they were all full of crap anyway,' Mike said dismissively.

'Maybe, but I liked reading the headlines and sport with a cuppa first thing.'

'Yeah, I recall you doing that when we arrived at the station every morning. Remember when Karen and I first moved up here straight out of Glen Waverley Academy?'

'Yep, couple of wet-behind-the-ears young pups if ever I saw them,' Bob chuckled. 'Nice girl, that Karen, I know you were pretty torn up when she ran off with that young fella from Merimbula way. Mactown they call it now, I think.'

'I guess I missed her pretty badly at first — funny how things turn out, though.'

'Yeah, who'd have thought you'd settle down with *both* those Harrison girls, but that went well. Charlene and Norma still get along fine and four of your kids survived. Not bad going these days. And you're a grandad now.'

'I couldn't pick between them. I was going to toss a coin, but *they* came up with a better idea,' Mike smiled. 'You didn't do badly yourself taking on Morrie Sparrow's girlfriend and her two kids.'

'Yeah, Sandra turned out fine considering I shot Morrie, not that he didn't deserve it. It's probably just as well the lights went out. I'd embarrassed the commissioner enough times already and offing Morrie would have been the last straw. In all fairness he'd probably have liked to stick up for me, but he was so far up the politician's and lawyer's aresholes right then. Now there's something I don't miss,' Bob chuckled. 'Getting rid of the pollies and legal-leeches was about the best thing that happened. Mind you, Sandra was a good missus and I don't have any complaints on that score. As you know the kids have coped well too.'

'They were pretty much the first generation to have lived all their lives in the blackout. They were too young to remember what it was like before.'

'It's been hard for them — hard for all of us really. We've been pretty well culled by cold, starvation, disease, bandits and accidents. Who'd have thought we'd have a smallpox epidemic or deaths by lockjaw after a scratch from barbwire?'

'Yeah, but we're a bloody tough bunch now,' Mike grinned.

'Makes you wonder though,' Bob mused.

'Wonder about what in particular?'

'Electricity. I mean, we all reckon the comet or meteorite-shower or whatever it is blazing away in the sky each night stopped electrics, right?'

'Yeah.'

'So why do we keep going? Old Doc Nandamuri was always banging on about human bodies just being a lot of electro-chemical reactions. If we're so full of little electric impulses, I can't understand why we didn't just conk out too.'

'You've got a point, but we did a pretty good job of conking ourselves out. Remember those last big raids ten years back. That was touch-and-go. Just as well we had the palisade reinforced and the Harrison boys came in to help. Now, that was a killing ground if ever I saw one. Those Harrisons certainly earned a place in Emu Creek on that occasion.'

'I'm glad to see it. I don't think it's a good idea for them to become isolated like in Old Phil's day. But, it still doesn't answer my question, why is it only our spark that works?'

'We're organic, I suppose. You know — mortal — perhaps the cosmos simply accepts us.'

'Tolerates us more like.'

Bob reflected on that for a while and drank a little more beer. Then he shrugged. Pondering deep, philosophical issues wasn't something he was prepared to dwell on.

'Talking of Karen,' Bob continued, changing the subject randomly as he tended to lately. 'Now there was a complex girl. She seemed so prissy when I first met her, but she had plenty of grit.'

'She was a little hottie for sure,' Mike added with a slight sigh of regret.

'Have you heard from her lately?'

'Not really, we're all getting a bit long in the tooth for traipsing across country these days. One of Warra's boys passed through here a month back. He was over at Mactown trading, and said they were doing fine.'

'It's a good thing we've got three strong communities situated where they are. Sort of a triangle I guess. It's easier to keep in touch and help out if needed.'

'We weren't so flash in the beginning, especially that first year after Karen left? Thank heaven for spuds and apples, is all I can say. I don't reckon we'd have made it if they didn't grow so well up here.'

'Too right. We just about lived on spuds — gave us enough to go on until we built the perimeter fences and learnt how to grow other stuff. Bloody locust plagues nearly wiped us out a couple of times, but I guess we had plenty of roo meat to rely on.'

'It was rough until we worked how to grow hops and barley,' Mike recalled. 'Geez it was touch-and-go once the pub ran dry.'

'Yeah, but that was a clever idea of yours to go and pinch those vines from Rutherglen. It took a few years of producing vinegar, but I don't mind our reds now.'

'Do you know what Karen said was the hardest thing for her? Well, after her pill supply ran out and she started having babies,' Mike grinned while Bob simply raised his eyebrows. 'She said it broke her heart not to see her mum and dad again, or know what happened to them.'

'It was the same for you, Mike. You had a brother up north as I recall and there was never a chance to get to Shepparton to find your folks. There was no time — we were just too busy surviving. Zach McAlister's parents lived in Sydney. I dunno whether he ever got back up that way again. I was lucky I suppose — not having any family living somewhere else.'

'I guess they either survived or died, just like us ...'

So the two friends reminisced into the night. They talked of how they'd rebuilt Emu Creek from scratch. How they learnt to grow food, keep the herds of cattle sustainable and renew ancient crafts. The greenies Bob so despised had proved their worth in the end. Their home-craft skills had been paramount in the town's survival. The hazardous trips to glean the last supplies in surrounding centres and vital information they'd discovered in books from Bright and Omeo libraries all contributed to their success.

They beat off a stream of invaders, thanks in no small part to timely warnings from the outlying properties. Ted and Sharon Harrison became Emu Creek's chief eyes and ears and its truest ally. In time the Harrison boys all had families of their own. They married town girls, but stayed on the property to maintain a robust satellite community with strong links to Emu Creek.

As the evening drew on Bob nodded off in front of the fire. So Mike pulled a blanket over the old boy's shoulders, put on his roo-skin coat and headed for home next door. The sky was ablaze with another meteor shower as it had been every night for half a century. Charlene and Norma greeted him with a kiss on each cheek as he entered.

'How's the old coot?' Charlene asked with genuine affection as she poured Mike a cuppa for his nightcap. Over the years people had experimented with local herbal mixes and had come up with some tasty alternative brews to the Ceylon teas that were no longer available.

'Same as ever,' Mike replied. 'Bob Brenan's about the only thing that hasn't changed in Emu Creek.'

*

Mike was right about Emu Creek's alterations although the town area hadn't grown or decreased. The residential buildings still stood. Some were reduced to shanty status although others were quite well maintained. It depended on the carpentry skill of the owners with only basic hand tools at their disposal. Many people had died prematurely as medication stocks ran out, but they were replaced by refugees who periodically arrived at Emu Creek.

The newcomers were by no means always welcome. It depended on vacancies. Bob Brenan understood the town resources were finite and he needed to keep a sustainable population. He quickly hardened his attitude and turned away people that he knew he simply couldn't feed.

The greenies bitterly opposed Bob over the matter until he suggested refugees could stay, provided the greenies moved out to make room for them. Survival had come down to a matter of Darwinian nitty-gritty.

The project took several years, but finally a moat surrounded the entire town. Work gangs drove pointed stakes into the trench before diverting water from Emu Creek to cover the tips. Barbwire and pine palisade posts completely encircled the town at last. Armed patrols guarded the perimeter. Emu Creek was by no means unique in its defence. Most communities made similar precautions just to endure. Bob had also developed cavalry units who scouted the surrounding countryside. These patrols generally headed off any danger before it threatened the town.

Another innovation was a water wheel. One of the town's bright-sparks had worked out how to build a mill. At first there was precious little grain to grind, but once farmers realised that wheat was susceptible to disease, they experimented harvesting oats, rye and barley from seeds stored in the pet department of the hardware store. They needed diversity. If one crop failed, the others would get them by. Prior to the mill's construction, pounding grain to flour was a tedious, arduous business. Other developments included a viaduct to convey water from the Ovens River. The Harrisons bred donkeys especially to operate a pump to raise water from the river high enough to allow a gravity flow to town.

Beer and wine production was popular in town and everyone had a favourite brew. In time Bob held an annual contest and was a keen judge to see which vintage was best. As it was a highly subjective topic the result was often contentious.

Wild horses became the preferred mode of transport. They now were so numerous no one bothered to keep domesticated stock that had to be fed. Brumbies crazed on native grassland and bush. Whenever you needed a new mount, you simply rounded one up from a mob. Breaking in feral horses was of course a physical and risky business that not everyone wanted to try, so those prepared to take up the challenge could always earn a decent living.

In time life stabilised. It was still dangerous to roam abroad, but well guarded trading caravans began venturing to other centres. Trade routes were established although they were still plagued by bandits ready to pounce on any unsuspecting or under-defended prey. But as it has proved since the dawn of time, trade makes the world go round and entrepreneurs emerged to fill a commercial void.

Part Three – Brave New World

Chapter 15 — The Word-Keeper

Mactown, Southern New South Wales

It was a clear day in Mactown and most kids wanted to be outside playing marngrook, but the Word-Keeper insisted their lessons came first. He was an old, kindly fellow who had the best interests of his pupils at heart. The Word-Keeper was held in high regard by all of Mactown except the Harrisons who occupied most of the prestigious positions locally these days.

No one quite knew when the transformation had occurred as it was so many generations ago now. They'd come from around Emu Creek in the west and smoothly integrated into the community at first. Somewhere along the line a dominant patriarch emerged and systematically took control. The very easy-going nature and tolerance of Mactown's leaders had been their downfall. At some stage a Harrison alpha-male had declared himself chief and before anyone knew it Mactown had morphed from an elected benevolent oligarchy, to a hereditary dictatorship.

Not that all Harrison chiefs were bad. They came and went in that respect. Right now Zen Harrison was fair enough although his teenage sons were showing signs of the family's dark side. Both lads, Vinnie and Walter, were selfish, greedy bullies. Strangely most Harrison girls were easy to get along with and generally well liked, except Zen's wife.

Having only gained her name by marriage, Alicia wasn't actually a Harrison, but behaved much like her sons. Zen had gained the title of 'chief' because he was a super-tough guy in his heyday who'd defended Mactown effectively again marauders. That was long ago and he'd mellowed with age although he was still man enough to keep his family in check — just.

The Harrisons in general hadn't taken much interest in the lore and history of Mactown. Keeping historical records and educational matters fell to the McAlister descendants after whom the town was named back in antiquity. The Harrisons wanted to change the name after they had tried to redub Emu Creek to Harrison, but it met with such resistance that even they gave up and the sleepy little outback town kept its original title. Mactown was just as resistant to change. The Harrison's might run the place, but the town name remained unaltered.

Zen Harrison tolerated the Word-Keeper because he often came up with clever ideas to solve engineering problems. Raven Mac, who was a particularly gifted calligrapher, was a scion of Zach McAlister and Karen Davenport. She'd learnt to read, write and figure numbers from an early age and was the Word-Keeper's favourite assistant. Raven Mac was a patient and kindly girl who helped the younger children with their scholastic education. As a result he hoped she would succeed him as Word-Keeper.

Raven was approaching her sixteenth birthday. She spent much of her time restoring damaged manuscripts and books or copying text onto vellum sheets. Pencils were in short supply, but feather quills had re-emerged along with ink derived minerals and black wood ash as well as squid and cuttlefish traded from coastal fishermen. Vellum and papermaking were slow and tedious skills passed down by Emu Creek's greenies. Raven not only mentored the younger students, but protected them from the Harrison bullies. She was an active girl, not a total bookworm, who liked nothing better than hunting and fishing with her friends. She came from a family of hunters. Her parents, Jason and Gloria Mac and younger brother, Wombat, were expert archers.

The library that served as a school was a three-bay shed now rusted with age and shored up by endless make-shift renovations. The Word-Keeper had tried to get the building repaired for years, but Zen Harrison had little use for the place. He wasn't prepared to waste resources on something as useless as scraps of paper. Yet the Word-Keeper insisted the books were the community's most important asset.

He knew the lore must be preserved because, without knowing exactly why, one day it would become absolutely vital. Previous Word-Keepers had managed to scrounge plastic sheeting and laid it under the bookcases to prevent moisture creeping through the wooden shelves to the volumes and deterring snails that were everywhere in wet weather. What a wonderful material plastic was. Unlike organic wrapping it was so durable. The trouble was that even it deteriorated with time and nobody knew how to produce or find any more. Especially puzzling were four plastic tablets labelled *kindle.* No one knew their purpose, but they made good drink coasters. The Word-Keeper's mug of herbal tea rested on one right now.

The library stocked a variety of books. Shelves were bolted to one wall of the shed and editions were stacked to the rafters. Many of the works were enigmatic, especially those called 'novels', which described mysterious events that just weren't possible. Objects called planes, submarines, computers, televisions and the internet were so ridiculously bizarre they must be science-fiction. Raven's favourite reading was the *Encyclopaedia Britannica.* She knew the entries were somehow related to the distant past, but it was so confusing. Even the Word-Keeper was perplexed. The information had been passed down through generations and most of the understanding was lost. Fortunately the library contained a copy of *The Macquarie Dictionary* that helped, but was also bewildering because many words seemed to have several meanings and spelling.

There were other books that helped link past and present, although they were by no means always clear either. They were not hard bound like the encyclopaedias, but hand-written journals that were occasionally illegible.

Raven flicked through those books. Word-Keepers over the years had catalogued them, some of which were now known as:

1. *The Word According to Karen*
2. *The Word According to Zach*
3. *The Word According to Daniel*

And most importantly the largest one,

4. *The Word According to Angela*

This last volume was a dozen notebooks bound together in a leather cover. Like the others it was a diary that explained that some catastrophic event had changed the world. Apparently the night sky hadn't always been ablaze with the wonderful lights that amazed everyone. Raven often sat up late with her parents and brother to enjoy the night spectacle. How dull it must have been without the nightly spark-show as it had become known.

There were many intriguingly vague messages in the books, especially the *Word According to Angela.* Raven knew Angela was a wise woman who'd lived long ago and was associated with the Mac clan although not part of the direct bloodline. It was so hard to work out where everyone fitted in although it was clear that Zach and Karen were married and her ancestors.

Many of the entries started with a series of six numbers that the Word-Keeper called dates. He was no longer sure how they worked, but were a system of recording time. It seemed very important to the ancient writers although Raven couldn't really see the point.

Everyone knew there were four season in a year and you could tell what time it was by the weather, sun's position and the moon phases, so why was each individual day so important? Why would you want to write it down? Angela's writing was often hard to understand because she included words that people had either forgotten or simply didn't use anymore. Sometimes the Word-Keeper or the dictionary could enlighten Raven, but more often as not she was still in the dark after her research. It was so frustrating. She wanted to understand everything!

Raven would have liked to emulate Angela's diary, but writing material was scarce and she had little spare time in any event.

Excerpt from 'The Word According to Angela':

It is imperative (I wonder what that word means) *that we do not lose the data needed to rebuild* society. *I am convinced The Spark* (that must be why we call the night sky *The Spark*-show, I guess) *will return although it's unlikely in my lifetime.*

I'm ninety-five years old now. I miss Danny so much. He's been gone six months, but nothing fills the empty space in my heart. Funny, we loved each other when we were young, but we never married. We were so different then, pursuing our separate lives and we grew apart and he found someone else. I don't begrudge that happiness he enjoyed with his wife. I'm just glad we got back together after she died.

Okay, Ange, enough maudlin regrets. Danny was always against dwelling on the past. How right he was.

I digress, but I believe that's an old woman's prerogative. (I must remember to look that word up.) *Now what was I going to write...Oh, yes.*

It's vital we know what to do when The Spark returns. Firstly how will we know? I think it will be like this:

1. *The night sky will clear* (Oh no, I love the light show when it's dark)
2. *Thunderstorms and lightning will return* (That sounds scary)
3. *Magnets and compasses will work again (although who has any now after using GPS for so long. We probably have some of the last hanging outside the shed. That was Danny's idea.)* (What are magnets again? Oh yeah, those three little metal bars dangling on chains from the library eaves. Legend has it that they will all point the same way when *The Spark* returns. I have no idea what GPS means.)
4. *We must watch for these signs in the future and be ready to restore The Spark. Funny how I've got used to the term. We'll need to rebuild generators and batteries.*

Angela had drawn neat diagrams and quoted references, but Raven had no way of knowing how to find the information. She resorted to the dictionary, but the definition of magnet only baffled her more. Raven studied the *Word* volumes whenever she had time, hoping she'd finally discover a clue and be ready when *The Spark* returned.

There was also a large, metal box containing faded images of people long dead. They were often strangely dressed and surrounded by unfamiliar objects although Raven recognised some of them as the rusted wreckage scattered throughout Mactown, much of which now formed part of the defensive wall. The box lid was painted in white lettering. Most of the writing was illegible now, but she could just make out the name *McAlister,* making it a precious artefact. Raven often wondered if the people in the pictures were her ancestors. It seemed possible.

In any event her thoughts were interrupted by her brother. He was known as Wombat although Jason and Gloria had named him William. He was born two years after Raven who thought he looked like a wombat when he was a baby so the name stuck. Wombat wasn't as scholarly as Raven, but could see engineering concepts clearly in his mind. He was a great inventor and had helped with many of Mactown's construction projects since he was very young. Many people though he was eccentric, which was true, but that gave him the insight to come up with useful ideas.

'There's a caravan from Emu Creek,' Wombat announced. 'Mum and Dad want us to help put up our stall. It's time for you to finish up here anyway.'

Wombat dangled a large pocket watch in front of Raven's nose. It was attached to a chrome chain and was his most treasured possession. Unlike Raven, Wombat was obsessed with time and saw it as the orderly answer to most problems. *Time Management* was one of his favourite catch-phrases.

A caravan was a big event as they only turned up a couple of times each year. Normally a town accumulated its special produce and craft until they had sufficient to make the journey worthwhile. Mactown was Emu Creek's favourite trading partner because of their close blood-ties and the route was safe enough when defended by a dozen strong-arm warriors. Over time, some words may have been abandoned, but *warrior* had been resurrected, because that's exactly what the guards were -- the fittest men and women who trained in martial arts, weaponry and battle tactics.

Mactown locals all had stalls and traded whatever they were good at producing. Some families had members who were particularly accomplished in weaving, pottery, basket making and other practical skills. Something that quickly returned to favour after the blackout was jewellery and an unusual breed of people developed to provide it.

They were known as *gatherers* who lived in a solitary and dangerous way. Gold, silver and precious stones had initially fallen the same way as cash. You couldn't eat or drink them, so for a time they were worthless — simply useless, shiny baubles that in no way helped a person survive. But, as communities stabilised, bling became fashionable once more. It was the gatherer's job to locate gems and sell them where they could, and a few always turned up on market day.

The problem for the gatherers was most of the stones and precious metals were found in abandoned cities. They were often stored in secret places and the gatherers had to run the gauntlet of urban gangs, feral dog packs, crumbling buildings to find anything of value. But, the rewards were great. Needless to say gatherers often lived stressful and not particularly long lives.

Unlike Emu Creek, Mactown had not developed from an existing town, but a farm property so it had grown around the main farm building. The old house occupied by Zen Harrison's family, barns and the shed now used as a library, were clustered in the centre of the settlement. Other dwellings encircled those buildings and a palisade surrounded the entire area. Like most communities, Mactown was encircled by a moat. Access to town was via a causeway to the main gate, although there was a small postern that was rarely used and barred most of the time with a drawbridge that was seldom lowered. Markets were held just beyond the moat with stalls either side of the road leading to the main gate. Lack of space within the walls and security were always issues when strangers arrived.

Not that this particular caravan consisted of strangers though. Mactown residents knew many of the visitors from Emu Creek either as friends of relatives, but a handful of wayfarers always joined the traders with an eye on the main chance. They were usually entertainers of some description and generally welcome, although the odd con-merchant or card-sharp occasionally slipped into the mix.

While Raven helped her family set up their stall, she was excited because her father had promised her a special surprise. Well, it wasn't actually a surprise in general terms, only in her choice. She was approaching her sixteenth birthday and was due to be *earmarked*. Most girls looked forward to the annual festival which declared them as women and available to interested young men. The earmarking ceremony was a big social event when girls had their left ear pierced and a jewelled ornament fitted to the lobe. Raven hoped a gatherer might turn up with some especially beautiful gems and that her father had something to trade.

There was considerable status in the earrings and girls hoped their parents could afford a finely decorated piece for them. Often if a suitor was keen enough, he would contribute to the price of the earring. This was not without another cost as the girl would then be obliged to accept his attention, which could even be considered as a betrothal.

Some girls embraced the concept while others like Raven were in no hurry to find a partner. When couples married the bride's right ear was pierced and another earring attached. Some parents were able to provide a matching pair, but that was by no means always the case. Generally grooms donated the second earring. Most brides preferred this as a personal gift from their husband, particularly if it was spectacular.

Couples generally married before they were twenty as babies tended to arrive soon afterwards and, like all other communities, Mactown didn't have the resources for social welfare. There was a zero-tolerance policy towards freeloaders. Extended families certainly looked out for each other, but fathers were expected to provide for their own wives and children. Everyone pulled their weight, even the Harrison bullies, who you had to admit were good at protecting the settlement. There was nothing they liked more than busting a few marauding bandits' heads or driving off a wild dog pack. It was what made the Harrison boys so powerful ... and dangerous.

It was a time when adolescence had long since disappeared and children became adults as soon as they were able to serve in a useful capacity. Many youngsters were skilled jackaroos by the time they reached puberty. There was no room for sentimental compromise, you either grew up quick-and-tough or you didn't grow up at all. About half of those born in Mactown never reached adulthood.

But right now hardship had been put aside and Mactown was abuzz with anticipation as its citizens bustled about preparing their stalls and trade goods. No one was more excited than Raven Mac.

'Honestly, Raven dear, that's no way to talk. I think your upcoming earmarking has quite turned your head.'

'But who is he ..?'

'Oh, he's one of the Farrow boys, but I'm not sure which. There's quite a tribe of them.'

'Can I invite him to supper?'

'It's very forward, but I guess it'll be alright. What if you don't like him?'

'What's not to like?' Raven said and disappeared into the crowd.

Now most teenage girls can be a bit shy and giggly and Raven could girlie it up with the best of them at times, but her window-of-opportunity was limited. She had no time to waste. The best way to meet the new kid in town was to march right up to him and introduce herself. That was precisely what she did.

'Hi, I'm Raven Mac,' she declared as she extended her arm and vigorously shook his hand.

'Hello, I'm Wedge Farrow,' he replied uncertainly, but allowed her to go on pumping his arm. 'Pleased to meet you,' he added uncertainly.

Goodness, I must look a right bumpkin, she thought detaching her hand, but she had his attention at least.

'Would you like me to show you around,' Raven added quickly. 'I mean I know all the stall-holders and the best buys.'

'Can I be sure you're not going to hustle me?' he replied cheerfully.

'Perish the thought.'

'Why not then?' he said. 'Lead on.'

She's a nice cheerful girl, and a little sweetie. Things are looking up.

Raven and Wedge took an instant liking to each other and were totally at ease from the moment they met. Raven took his arm as if it was the most natural thing in the world and they were chatting away like old friends in no time. They browsed around the market without a care in the world until they came to where a gatherer stood. He'd arrived with the Emu Creek caravan, but hadn't bothered to set up shop. All manner of jewellery was simply pinned to his cloak or dangling from his pockets. He leant on a two-metre staff and carried an axe strapped to his belt, which deterred pick-pockets.

'Hello there, pretty girl,' he greeted as Raven passed. She wasn't sure about the gatherer. He looked a bit creepy, but that might have been his ragged clothes and unkempt hair. He was clean enough though, and didn't smell bad like some wayfarers. He also had some wonderful wares on display and dangled them beguilingly in front of Raven's eyes.

'Allow me to introduce myself,' he crooned, 'I am Thornton from distant parts and I have gathered some of the rarest gems to be found. And you, sweet miss, are ripe for your earmarking I believe.'

'That's quite true, Mr Thornton,' Raven said smugly and even bobbed pertly. Earmarking was a proud milestone in an adolescent girl's life.

'Just Thornton,' he corrected and then went on. 'In that case, let me show you my very best merchandise.'

He produced several brilliantly sparkling earrings, each with several coloured stones worked into the design. He purred on about emeralds, pearls, rubies, sapphires and even diamonds, which for some reason were far more precious that the others although Raven preferred coloured gems. So it wasn't surprising when Thornton produced a sample containing four opals. Each stone was roughly the same size with multi-coloured flecks. The gems' background colours varied from almost white, to red, deep blue and finally almost black on the purest one of them all.

Raven gasped as she handled the piece. She had never seen anything so alluringly beautiful.

'What do you want for this one?' she asked.

'That depends on what you have to offer,' Thornton eyed her, shrewdly slipping into negotiation mode. 'This ain't just some small bling I picked up in city wreckage. I travelled all the way to Lightning Ridge. There's only one prospector left who still mines the stones and polishes 'em up like this. They're as rare as rocking-horse poop. Especially this piece made from white, red, boulder *and* black opals.'

Raven knew she was out-gunned in haggling terms, but her father was an expert. Her mother wore two lovely earpieces, one of which Jason had bargained from a gatherer for a brumby he'd recently tamed. Afterwards he'd merely taken the family into the bush, captured and broken in another one. Possibly Thornton would be as obliging, but something about the fellow suggested otherwise.

'I'll get my dad,' she said. 'Don't go away.'

'I'm not going anywhere,' he promised.

She grabbed Wedge's hand and led him away at top speed, chattering with delight at her find. She was sure her father was more than a match for a tatty, itinerant salesman. They'd only gone a few paces when they ran straight into Vinnie Harrison who'd been eyeing them slyly. Walter was hovering by his side. There was something sinister about Zen Harrison's boys. Vinnie was tall and never quite looked you in the eye as if he was always weighing up an angle to spiv you. Walter, on the other hand was just plain thick, but mean, strong and stubborn.

'Look who's got a new, fancy boyfriend,' Vinnie sneered. It was a pretty trite comment, but riled Raven all the same.

'He's not my *boyfriend,* you drongo,' Raven said.

'Oh?' Vinnie replied with a leer.

Wedge seemed mildly amused by the whole confrontation.

'Hiya, Vinnie ... Walter ...' he said, 'you won't remember me, but we met when we were all kids ages ago over at Emu Creek. You don't seem to have changed much, I see.'

'What does that mean?'

'Just what I said. C'mon, Raven, you want to see your dad, remember.'

They disappeared into the crowd. Once they were gone Vinnie and Walter strolled over to Thornton and started speaking earnestly to him. Raven was so excited when she reached her family's stall she was talking continuously.

'Mum, Dad, Wombat, I want you to meet Wedge Farrow,' she blurted. 'He's a warrior with the caravan and has done all sorts of super stuff and ...'

'Hush, Raven,' Jason said, shaking Wedge's hand. 'Nice to meet you son, it seems Raven knows all about you already.'

After the introductions, Raven pleaded with her father to come and see the earring she wanted — *more than anything else in the world!*

Leaving Wombat to mind the store, they hurried back to Thornton. Jason was the family trader, but Gloria wanted to check that the merchandise was indeed as fine as Raven claimed. There was a certain status in the quality of the earring your daughter wore. Unfortunately, in her haste, Raven had made a serious mistake. She should have taken Thornton to her father because he no longer had the earring.

'Young fella came and traded me a good price for it,' the gatherer shrugged.

Raven was devastated. She wanted the opal so badly.

'You knew I wanted it!' she challenged.

'Sorry, miss,' Thornton said. 'First person who antes up the price, get the goods — no refunds, no returns, no exchanges. That's my policy. I learnt that at fairs where folk promise they'll be back, but never show up. It's a tough trade. But, hang on I've got plenty of others ...'

'I don't want others,' she wailed. 'Who did you trade with?'

'Those two young chaps you were talking to a minute ago. Can't say I liked their looks, but they paid my price.'

Thornton didn't divulge what that price was. He liked to keep his dealings secret and his customers guessing.

'Vinnie Harrison! I hate him. Now I'll never be earmarked.'

'Don't fret, darling,' Gloria crooned hugging her daughter. 'We'll find you a piece that is just as nice. We can always approach Zen Harrison and see if he'll make Vinnie sell it.'

'No he won't,' Raven said. 'He knew I wanted it. He overheard me talking to Thornton. I know he did. He bought the earring just out of spite. Why is he always so mean? I hate him!'

There was no consoling Raven and she fled home in tears.

'Sorry about that,' Jason sighed, 'the disappointment has made her irrational.'

'That's okay,' Wedge replied, 'I'm sure she'll get over it in time. I have to get back to Grandad Trilby now. It's been nice meeting you. I hope we'll catch up later.'

He left without even being invited for supper. Raven's day had turned to rubbish.

*

Raven decided to sulk in the library. In time she stopped sobbing, having realised she was over-reacting, but she'd so set her heart on the earring. She found some solace in the old documents, especially the *Word According to Michael*. A wise, erstwhile Word-Keeper had brought the diary to Mactown when it became clear Emu Creek residents weren't particularly interested in preserving the records.

She divined Wedge Farrow could have been related to her if Mike and Karen had married, but Zach McAlister had put paid to that prospect. *Well, that's something,* she thought before realising that her hysterics had probably ruined any chance of becoming friends with hunky Wedge Farrow.

'Revelling in our misery, are we?' a voice said softly behind her.

It was the Word-Keeper who was closing up for the day.

'Oh, I didn't notice you there,' Raven sniffed. 'I'm sorry. I've had a really bad day.'

'You get used to being invisible when you're old,' the Word-Keeper sighed. 'Do you want to tell me your troubles, Raven? Sometimes talking about something helps – then again, sometimes it doesn't.'

'I don't want to talk about it,' she blurted, then proceeded to tell him anyway.

He listened to her without interruption before speaking.

'You know you can look at this in two ways,' he said when she finished. 'One is that your disappointment will wane with time and the earring will become a mere bauble ... or ... you can dwell and let the bitterness grind away until the matter is blown out of all proportion. Which do you want it to be, Raven?'

'You're right ... as always,' she smiled. 'There'll be other earrings. I'll ask Thornton if he'll bring me another one next time.'

'It might be quite a wait. What about your earmarking?'

'It doesn't matter. I think I'll postpone it until next year. There's no rush.'

'You could wear a different one until you find another,' the Word-Keeper suggested. 'There's no rule that says girls can't change their minds. In fact is almost expected of them,' he added with a grin.

'I know, but we feel sentimental about these things. Mum's are nice, but not gaudy like Alicia's and she wouldn't change them for anything.'

'Because your grandparents gave her one and your father gave her the other when he married her. They are very special gifts.'

Raven nodded. She'd stopped sniffing by then.

'Good, you seem to be cheering up already,' the Word-Keeper smiled. 'Just as well because while you've been moping around in here, Zen Harrison and Trilby Farrow decided to have a town barbeque. A gang of people has dug a pit and fired it up. They've slaughtered a couple of steers and broken out kegs of home brew. The meat is turning on the spit right now and should be ready in a few hours. You'd better get off home and help your mum prepare some bread and vegetables to go with the beef.'

Raven brightened up immediately. She loved a party especially if there was dancing and she'd have another chance to meet Wedge Farrow. Mactown had a fine band. Over years they'd acquired a piano accordion, banjo, recorders, ukuleles and their prized guitars that legend claimed went way back to the days when Danny McAlister played them. Wombat was an ace picker with some killer licks.

Several residents had even developed the skills to hand-make new instruments copied from the originals. Many Mactown folk could sing well and never passed up an opportunity to join in. They favoured traditional songs like *Johnny B. Goode, Rock Around the Clock, Old Time Rock 'n' Roll, Great Balls of Fire, Blue Suede Shoes* and *This Old House.* No one remembered where those songs came from, but many people thought they also dated back to Danny McAlister's time. No one cared anyway — they were good fun, easy to play and sing while the entire town loved dancing to them.

'Cool,' Raven said, returning to her usual chirpy self. 'Are you going to be there?'

'Didn't I say they're tapping kegs of home brew,' the Word-Keeper grinned. 'I wouldn't miss it for the world especially if you save one dance for an old codger like me.'

'Wicked, it's a date. I'll see you there.'

She kissed him lightly on the cheek and raced home to help her mother.

'Don't worry,' the Word-Keeper smiled as he collected the books and returned them to their shelves after she'd gone. 'I'll pack up here.'

Chapter 17 — Exile

Everyone pitched in to help and soon the party was a roaring success. The barbeque had been set up in an open space just beyond the market stalls. The beef was soon roasting away with delicious aromas wafting from the pit. Trestle tables were laden with salads, fruit and fresh bread while hot vegetables boiled away in pots placed on the glowing embers. The band kicked off and soon half the town was dancing while others clapped in time to the music and formed a circle around the dancers.

Raven, like all the girls, wore her best dress with flowers decorating her hair and coloured beads around her neck. The dress was white with intricate floral patterns embroidered along the hem and sleeves. With needles, thread and fine linen in short supply, fine clothes were costly and time consuming to make, but every girl and woman in Mactown made it their business to own a pretty gown. Raven had spent many happy hours sewing the dress with her mother and she looked stunning.

True to her promise, Raven danced a couple of lively jigs with the Word-Keeper until he was puffed. She found a chair and brought him a plate piled high with meat, salads and a bread roll. She poured a pitcher of beer and placed it beside his chair before leaving him happily tapping his foot and munching on the huge sandwich he'd made from the food she'd served.

There was no sign of Wedge Farrow so she mingled with friends and strangers for a time and shared a dance or two until she felt hungry enough to tackle the barbeque. She was about to take a plate and help herself when she was once again confronted by Vinnie and Walter Harrison. Vinnie had the earring pinned provocatively to his jacket. She tried to side-step the boys, but Vinnie blocked her way.

'Nice bauble,' he said, pointing to the bling. 'It didn't come cheap either.'

'So what?' Raven snapped. 'You bought the stupid thing, why should I care?'

'Well, we could come to some sort of arrangement, you know,' Vinnie leered and Raven was sure she saw a trickle of drool ooze from the corner of Walter's flabby lips.

'Yeah and what sort of arrangement would that be?' she challenged.

'You're not a bad looking chick when you make the effort,' Vinnie said. 'I bet you'd be a right little raver, especially if the price was right ...'

'Eeeuw, puleease, that's so gross. If you think for one minute I'd let you and your slimy brother touch me, you've got to be dreaming.'

'Maybe I am. You can't imagine what you and I get up to in my dreams ...'

'That's just plain disgusting. Get out of my way, I'm hungry.'

'Not so fast,' Vinnie growled, grabbing her wrist and squeezing it cruelly before she could snatch her arm away.

'Let go!'

She tried to wrench free, but his grip was like a steel trap. The Harrison brothers took sadistic pleasure in her pain until a figure stepped beside Raven and clamped his fist onto Vinnie's wrist.

'Two can play that game,' Wedge Farrow said in an even tone, gouging his fingertips into Vinnie's flesh.

Vinnie yelped and released Raven.

'I think this is my dance,' Wedge said with a smile, guiding Raven away from Vinnie and Walter. 'So you two can push off,' he added over his shoulder.

Wedge and Raven feasted and danced the night away until the band packed up and the barbeque fire had settled to a shimmering glow. Jason and Gloria had already turned in while Wombat and the other band members shared a late-night snack from the barbeque. In the meantime Wedge walked Raven home.

'Thank you for being such a *Sir Galahad* tonight,' she whispered, although he stared at her blankly. 'A knight in shining armour, silly. Haven't you heard about *King Arthur and the Knights of the Round Table?*'

'I don't get to read a lot,' he confessed.

'Well, what do you know?'

'Maybe I know how to kiss a girl ...'

He didn't get a chance to say more. She flung her arms around him and kissed him for all she worth. Yet all too soon it was time to go.

'Would you like to go for a picnic tomorrow?' she asked. 'I'll pack up some cold meat and barbeque left-overs. I can show you around.'

'Yes, that would be nice. I'll meet you here around lunch time if that's okay?'

'Great ...'

He kissed her again then headed back to where Trilby had set up camp. She stood by her front door for a moment, smiling with a contented, warm feeling inside. Suddenly the earring wasn't really very important at all. Once he was out of sight she turned towards the door. She couldn't wait to have a long girlie chat with her mother in the morning.

Mum and Dad met when they were about my age and look how that turned out ...

A rough hand slapped across her mouth as she was grabbed around the waist. The attack was so sudden she froze for a second, stunned and shocked. She tried to scream, but the fingers were clamped so tightly over her lips she only managed a squeak. In a second she recovered from the initial fright and starting kicking until someone grabbed her legs. Her feet were expertly hog-tied and the rope wrenched taut. She was dragged away bucking and struggling, but her attackers were too powerful for her to wriggle free.

They wrestled her to a nearby barn. The door was ajar and they hauled her inside. She was flung face down into a straw pile with the smell of livestock in her nostrils. Her assailant rammed his knee into her back and tied her wrists securely behind her. Hostile hands clawed her and rolled her onto her back. The rope slipped from her ankles only to be looped over her head and around her neck. The noose tightened until she could barely breathe.

The attackers tethered the rope to a roof post and drew it so firmly she felt as if she was being strangled. She was half sitting with her neck held rigidly pinning her to the spot. If she moved she choked as every breath came with a gasp. In the dimness she could barely make out her attackers, but as her pupils adjusted she knew she was in the merciless hands of Vinnie and Walter Harrison.

'Not so high-and-mighty are you now Miss *Raven-too-bloody-good-for-anyone-Mac*. Now you're gonna get what's coming to ya. You'll see what a real bloke's made of. Grab her legs, Walter. I reckon I'll take first crack at this stuck-up bitch.'

Vinnie still had the earring attached to his tunic. He pulled it free and waved it in front of Raven's eyes.

'You wanted it. You can have it, but you're gonna earn it.'

He jabbed the pin through Raven's earlobe. She tried to scream, but the rope choked her cry to a rasping whimper. The initial pain was like a hornet's sting although it lessened to a dull ache as blood dripped from her ear staining the shoulder of her party dress.

'My ... dad'll ... kill ... you,' she hissed, but getting the words out was torture.

'Think I'm scared of a stupid Mac. C'mon Walter, gimme a hand here.'

Walter didn't seem as enthusiastic as Vinnie, but held one of Raven's legs, while Vinnie knelt in front of her and pulled down his pants. Raven tried to kick him with her free foot, but the movement caused the noose to tighten and she gagged. Vinnie was on his knees now and his lust was beyond doubt. He flung her dress above her waist and chuckled with anticipation.

Vinnie's eyes were ablaze with pure hatred and cruelty.

He's barking mad, Raven thought.

Vinnie lowered himself towards Raven and suddenly his eyes glazed and went dull. Raven was sure she'd heard a thud. Vinnie flopped forward and fell limply onto Raven's lap as blood welled from a wound in the back of his scalp. The force nearly throttled Raven and she passed out for an instant. She was vaguely aware of another thump and the pressure on her foot being released.

Fumbling hands finally released the rope from her throat and arms.

'Raven,' she heard a voice as someone gently patted her cheek. 'Wake up, Raven. It's me – Wombat.'

She tried to talk, but only managed to splutter and cough up a lungful of mucus. Wombat helped her up and they staggered over the prone bodies of Vinnie and Walter. A spade lay beside them, which had been Wombat's weapon-of-choice. Raven and Wombat made it to a water tank. He opened the tap and water poured into Raven's cupped hands. She took two long draughts, coughed several times, but soon felt better.

'Come on, Raven,' Wombat urged. 'We've got to wake Mum and Dad.'

They barged inside. The noise of the door crashing open was enough to wake their parents. Raven gasped out the story and Wombat explained how he saw the abduction when he arrived home after the band had finished its midnight snack. At first he was uncertain who was involved. In the dimness he couldn't see that Raven was the victim, but he followed anyway.

Vinnie and Walter had dragged Raven inside the barn by the time he reached the door. Once he recognised the two Harrison boys, Wombat knew they were up to no good, so he scratched around for a weapon. He had no idea what he was going to do. Hopefully he'd just scare them off, but when he saw Raven tied to that post he was so enraged he came in swinging. He took Vinnie out with one blow. Walter was so startled he simply remained stock still with his mouth agape, which gave Wombat time to clout him too.

Gloria removed the earring and dressed Raven's wound. She bathed her daughter's bruised neck and wrists before putting the sobbing girl to bed. She stayed by Raven's bedside all night. Meanwhile Wombat and Jason headed for the barn to see what state the Harrison boys were in. They heard Walter moaning as they entered. He'd managed to sit up and was nursing the side of his head where a lump had erupted and was already turning purple. Vinnie on the other hand still lay face down where he'd dropped. Jason felt Vinnie's neck for a pulse.

'Is he dead?' Wombat whispered in the darkness.

'Who cares?' his father replied.

*

Jason roused Zen Harrison and explained as best he could with justifiable outrage. Alicia Harrison was hysterical and calling for blood to avenge her poor, innocent son. It was hard to guess Zen's reaction. His stony expression was grim, but gave away little else. They brought Vinnie to the main house and laid him on his bed. The boy was breathing weakly, but showed no sign of regaining consciousness.

'I'll kill that little rat and his minx of a sister,' Alicia hissed as she knelt by her son's bed. 'She lured him on and then let that brat attack him.'

'I don't think it was like that,' Jason countered. 'Your boys attacked my daughter. Wombat was defending his sister's honour.'

'Don't tell me what it was or wasn't,' Alicia snarled, 'and I don't need a Mac lecturing *me* about honour. Now get out of my place. Zen will deal with your demon's spawn.'

There was no point in arguing with Alicia, so Jason left to see how his own family was coping. Zen sat moodily in a corner with Walter as if he hadn't yet decided what he intended to do about the whole mess.

Raven had finally drifted off to sleep although Wombat and Gloria were still awake and likely to stay that way all night.

'I'm deep in it, aren't I Dad?' Wombat said.

'From what you said,' Jason replied, 'you were only protecting your sister. There can be no doubt what Vinnie and Walter were up to. Even Zen will have to acknowledge that. Raven is the victim here. Vinnie got what he deserved.'

'The point is Vinnie is a *Harrison*, Dad. We all know they make the rules and they can change them whenever they feel like it.'

'Over my dead body,' Gloria announced. 'Those sneaky bullying louts tried to rape our baby. I won't let them get away with it.'

'If Vinnie doesn't wake up, he won't be getting away with anything. If he doesn't come round he'll die of thirst in a couple of days.'

They debated until dawn, but the situation seemed to only grow more complicated as they talked. Vinnie still had not recovered by morning and Zen finally decided to take matters into his own hands. The Mac family was summoned to the main house and Zen sent a delegation of his tough kinsmen to make sure they obeyed. Raven was still shaken, but said she'd go too. When they arrived Zen was seated in the main room with Alicia and Walter, but to Raven's surprise, Trilby Farrow was also there with Wedge standing by his side.

'Your son is guilty of attacking my boys and possibly murdering one of them,' Zen addressed Jason directly, dispensing with any formalities.

'That's not true,' Jason protested. 'Vinnie and Walter planned to rape Raven.'

'Not according to Walter,' Zen countered. 'He maintains Raven went with the boys willingly. Vinnie offered her an earring she desperately wanted, I believe.'

'That's a lie!' Raven shouted. 'I'm not that sort of girl.'

'According to Walter you are,' Zen said rather too slyly for Raven's liking. 'There are several witnesses, including Thornton the gatherer, who can testify how much you wanted the trinket.'

'I don't believe this,' Raven wailed. 'They tied me up. Can't you see Walter is lying to cover up what he and Vinnie did?'

'I don't see it that way because I understand you still have the earring.'

'I didn't take it! Vinnie stuck it in my ear. Look!' she pointed to the wound on her lobe. The bleeding had stopped, but there was still a livid bruise visible.

'Couldn't wait for the earmarking, could you, whore?' Alicia hissed. 'You're just a cheap slut.'

Then pandemonium erupted. Jason and Gloria yelled for Alicia to take back her insults. A storm of abuse hailed back and forth as everyone yelled at once and it looked like a fight would break out. Raven charged at Walter, wanting to claw out his eyes for the lies he'd told. Wedge grabbed her and managed to hold her before she could inflict any damage. Finally Zen Harrison took control.

'Quiet!' he roared. 'Everyone shut up. I'll flatten the next person who speaks.'

You had to give it to Zen, when he decided to exercise his authority he had a way of making himself heard. Everyone quietened down, but simmering venom still pervaded throughout the room.

'I have decided there is only one issue to resolve. Whatever occurred between Raven and my boys is her word against theirs ...'

'Oh yeah, these rope burns on my neck and wrists got there all by themselves, did they?'

'Silence, girl,' Zen ordered. 'The only case I'm considering is Wombat Mac's attack on my sons. I find him guilty of assault and possible murder ... He is to be exiled!'

Chapter 18 — On the Road to Somewhere

'William McAlister, you are banished from Mactown forthwith,' Zen Harrison announced his official verdict, sounding unnecessarily pompous. No one ever called the Macs *McAlister* anymore. 'You will never return. I declare you an outlaw and if I see you again I will kill you personally.'

'No!' Raven screamed. 'That is so unfair.'

'Fair?' Zen arched his eyebrows. 'It's time you learnt, young woman, that there is no *fairness* in this world. The strong rule and the weak serve or die. Now hold your tongue or I'll cut it out.'

He'd have done it too. No one doubted Zen Harrison's ruthlessness when he was roused to anger. Everyone remembered when he'd led a posse of kinsmen and nabbed a gang of cattle-duffers who'd been raiding Mactown herds. He left the culprits dangling for a week from the nearest blue gum stand. Afterwards he'd had the corpses decapitated and the heads planted on spikes around the area as a grisly deterrent to other would-be cattle thieves.

Jason placed his arm around Raven's shoulder.

'Don't fret love,' he said quietly. 'We'll all go together. We'll stay a family.'

'I heard that,' Alicia snapped. Her eyes narrowed, displaying her natural malice. 'Not so fast Jason Mac, there's the matter of blood debt to be settled.'

A blood debt was a pragmatic way of resolving disputes in Mactown. It wasn't anything new. Vikings had used the system way back in the Dark Ages. Normally if there was a difference between two people or families, they agree to appoint an adjudicator. Having decided, they each put their case and agreed to abide by the judge's decision. Those found at fault were required to compensate the aggrieved with either goods or labour. The system generally worked well, but in this case the judge could hardly be considered impartial.

'What do you mean?' Jason demanded. 'You've already punished Wombat unjustly.'

'I mean,' Alicia hissed acidly, 'that if my darling dies, your pack of filth will be indentured to me indefinitely. You will be slaves for the rest of your lives.'

Jason, Gloria and Raven stood dumbfounded. It wasn't Wombat and her fault Vinnie and Walter were uncouth, lecherous thugs. Vinnie may not even die yet a sentence had already been delivered.

'Don't worry,' Alicia added with relish, 'it probably won't be for too long with the jobs I can think up for you do.'

'I've heard enough of this bickering,' Zen announced. 'You have until noon to get out of town, Wombat. You'd better make the most of it.'

Raven and Gloria sobbed as they made their dismal way home. Wombat would be travelling light, but Gloria started filling his saddle packs with more than they could hold. She fussed and fretted that he'd need this for the cold weather and that for heatwaves and something else for between times. Finally Wombat sat her gently on his bed while he took over the packing, tossing out most of the stuff she'd included. Raven boiled a billy and gave her mother a steaming cup of herbal tea.

'You know,' she said, 'we can all go. We don't have to do what stupid Alicia says. There are plenty of people on our side.'

'Maybe, but I doubt if they'll stand up to the Harrisons when push comes to shove,' Jason reminded her.

'But, how long will Wombat last out there alone.'

'I'm a smart kid,' Wombat beamed.

He looked so cute Raven hugged him, nearly taking his breath away. She loved him so much she didn't think she could bear being parted from him.

'We can all sneak out and meet on the road,' Raven insisted. 'You know a rendezvous.'

'I can't imagine that Zen will tolerate it and I know Alicia won't. All that "darling boy" stuff is pure hogwash in my opinion. It's more of a face-saving thing with her. They'll send their bunch of trackers after us. They'd find us for sure. Remember they're very good at that. Look, things mightn't be as bad as they seem. Get over to Emu Creek, Wombat. You can make yourself useful there and it's not so far away. We'll work things out here and send word when it's safe to return or we'll meet up there.'

'Sorry, that won't work,' a voice said from behind them.

They turned to see Wedge Farrow standing in the doorway.

'I came to see if I could help,' he said. 'That packet of poo they call a kangaroo court back there made me want to chunder.'

'Why can't Wombat go to Emu Creek?' Gloria asked. She'd been clinging to any ray of hope that the disastrous mess would somehow end happily.

'Alicia was like a flea in Grandad Trilby's ear and he's agreed that Wombat is banned from Emu Creek too. He thinks it stinks as much as I do, but he values the alliance with Zen Harrison and is prepared to sacrifice Wombat as collateral damage.'

'So that seems to be that,' Wombat sighed and sat beside his mother. 'Look Mum, I've been out in the bush plenty of times. I can hunt, break brumbies and know all about bush-tucker. I have as good a chance as anyone.'

Gloria sniffed and said nothing.

'Raven, can I have a word?' Wedge said quietly and indicated he wanted to speak in private. They were gone for only a short time and when Raven returned, she seemed a lot happier.

'Come on Wombat,' she said, 'let's make sure you pack sensibly. You may be a bright kid, but you're so impractical sometimes.'

'What are you up to, miss?' Jason asked.

'Nothing, Daddy — honestly.'

'Nothing you're going to tell me more like.'

Much as he liked it, Jason was always suspicious when she called him 'Daddy', but he let it slide. He wanted to make the most of the time remaining with his son.

*

Most of Mactown gathered at the causeway to farewell Wombat. He rode his favourite brumby and led another packhorse, so he was actually able to carry enough to be comfortably stocked up for some time. Zen and Alicia didn't bother to turn up, but remained with Vinnie. They'd have received a cool reception from Mactown's people anyway. Walter stood with a mob of cronies to toss insults and make sure Wombat left town on schedule.

They'd promised him a sound beating if he missed the deadline. Jason and Gloria embraced Wombat for one last time, but Raven couldn't bear to see him leave and had said her goodbyes at home. They left her making a thorough job of crying her eyes out.

Wombat was his usual sanguine self. He kissed his mother, shook his father's hand, mounted the brumby and rode westwards. He waved once then disappeared without looking back. Her loss was finally too great and Gloria broke down in sobs and could not be consoled by Jason or her friends.

In all that commotion no one noticed a lone horseman ride to the back of the Mac place leading three brumbies. No one saw Raven Mac sneak from her home and mount up. She swung two heavily packed panniers over one of the spare mounts. The two riders lead their horses to the postern gate. They dismounted and heaved the locking-bar from the gate before dragging it open. It wasn't a particularly tough job because, although the portal was rarely used, it was well maintained. Zen Harrison saw to that in case he needed to make a quick getaway one day. They lowered the drawbridge using a crank handle beside the postern. The chains were well lubricated with animal grease and ran smoothly with only the occasional clank. The riders remounted and cantered away eastwards. Once out of sight they circled north and galloped full tilt towards the west.

To record that no one noticed the two riders' departure wasn't exactly true. One pair of eyes watched them go with great sadness and a tear in his eye. He would miss Raven desperately, but understood she must follow her own destiny. The Word-Keeper turned back to the library and once again observed the three magnets dangling from the eaves. No one else had detected the fact that the metal strips had been agitated for over a year now. But on that particular day all three lined up in precisely the same direction.

So the prophecy may be fulfilled and The Spark will return, the Word-Keeper mused. He'd no notion what that meant, but sensed the phenomenon was a harbinger of great change.

He entered the library and before long noticed that one of the volumes was missing. *The Word According to Angela* was not in its place on the shelves. He knew exactly where it had gone.

I know you'll treasure it, my dear. I hope it will help you in your quest ... whatever that might be.

*

Wombat was of course distressed at having being kicked out of town, but his situation didn't him fill with dread. He'd spent plenty of time in the bush and knew he could easily hunt food, find water and build a shelter. He figured he'd find a good spot close enough to Mactown to stay in touch, but far enough away to remain undetected. Even if the Harrison louts came looking for him, he knew he could outwit them. They thought they were such smart trackers, but Wombat knew he was better. Stealth and cunning beat brute strength every time.

Wombat could always get word to Raven and his parents. Jackaroo gangs often camped out during roundups. Many of them had no time for the Harrisons and would be happy to relay messages for him. So he ambled along the old track with the sun in his face with no immediate plan in mind other than to stay on the road until dusk then cut across country and camp clear of any travellers.

He was so deep in thought he didn't notice two riders coming towards him until they were only metres way. Admittedly they were silhouetted with the sun at their backs. They were mounted on sturdy brumbies that looked as if they'd been ridden hard. He also made out a pair of pack animals.

'Nice and alert, I'm pleased to see,' Raven said. 'Honestly, Wombat, what if we'd been bandits?'

He was so pleased to see her he forgot she'd gone into 'nag' mode. Wedge Farrow grinned and shook his hand.

'I wasn't hanging around with that bitch Alicia Harrison calling the shots,' Raven declared, 'but Mum and Dad can handle them whatever *she* thinks.'

'So what now?' Wedge asked.

It appeared he had no immediate plans. Wedge was still hopping mad at his grandfather who'd sided with Zen Harrison even though there'd been a gross miscarriage of justice regarding Wombat's expulsion. After a short discussion Raven and Wedge pretty much agreed with Wombat that they'd just hang out far enough from Mactown to avoid trouble, but close enough to see which way the wind blew.

Towards evening they left the track and headed into bushland. Travelling was easy enough through scattered red gums and grassland. They found a spot where scrub acted as a natural windbreak and made camp. A creek ran close by and, after they drank their fill, the brumbies grazed happily on long tether lines for a while. When darkness fell, Wedge brought the horses close to camp in case any wild dog packs passed by. Wombat bagged a small roo while Raven got the fire blazing. They laid their rawhide saddles on the ground and rolled out their bedding. Soon the roo was sizzling away on a spit with tea boiling in the billy.

After supper they chatted for a while.

'We'll have to find more than roo meat to eat,' Raven observed. 'We need fruit and vegetables or we'll develop sore gums and get sick in a week or two.'

'No worries,' Wedge said cheerfully because it meant they now had something positive to do. 'Let's ride over to the Goulburn Valley close to Emu Creek. There are dozens of wild orchards there. People say they were planted generations ago in *The Spark* times. There'll be plenty of fruit ripe for picking at this time of year.'

'Sounds like a plan,' Wombat agreed.

'Sure,' Wedge added, 'and we can always move on over to Albury and visit the Wiradjuri settlement. They've been pretty thick with Emu Creek folk since way back too.'

It seemed like exile wasn't going to be too bad after all. It was just an adventure and a chance to travel where they'd never been before. Wombat checked Raven's ear, which was still swollen and red where Vinnie had driven the pin through her lobe. Wombat took a firebrand and went to the creek where a green mould encrusted some of the plants there. He returned with a pinch of the stuff and rubbed it into Raven's wound. None of them knew why, but the moss had healing properties that prevented infection and blood poisoning. *The Word According to Angela* called the mould *penicillium fungi* and stressed how important it was that people didn't forget about it. Angela even described how to best process the mould, but Wombat didn't have time for that, so he simply plastered it onto Raven's ear lobe. Raven admitted the throbbing had eased and she felt a lot more comfortable.

'What happened to the earring?' Wedge asked. 'It certainly was a fancy piece, but I suppose you never want to see it again.'

'I dunno,' Raven grinned pulling the bauble from her pack. 'I agree it's nice and I'm not giving it back to that pig Vinnie if he ever wakes up. I reckon I've earned it, even if not in the way the Harrison boys thought.'

'You're not planning to wear it for your earmarking, are you?' Wedge asked. 'Surely you'd want something with more sentimental value.'

'Do you have anything in mind?' she eyed him coquettishly.

He just shrugged and looked awkward. Raven's relationship with Wedge was still undetermined and, as they'd only known each other for a couple of days, it could wait. As the night drew on they arranged the guard roster. Wombat consulted his precious time-piece and determined it was nine o'clock, so first watch was until midnight, second to three in the morning and the last duty till six when it was time to get up anyway. They stacked the fire and turned in. It was the watch-keeper's job to make sure the flames stayed high to deter those ubiquitous bush predators -- wild dogs and dingoes. After the day's excitement they were all exhausted and ready for sleep. Unfortunately Wombat, who'd taken the first watch, did just that.

*

They were unlucky as it was probably close to midnight and just about time to change the guard. Also, to be fair, such was the stealth of the attack, no one heard a thing. Wombat jerked awake when he heard a whooshing sound as a heavy vine net landed over his head. Instantly Wedge and Raven were similarly enmeshed. They both awoke with a start and began to struggle free. The brumbies whinnied and stomped their hooves as dark figures rushed past them into the campsite and dived onto the trapped trio.

The attackers were small, but numerous — too many for Raven, Wombat or even Wedge to combat. They were expert too. With at least half-a-dozen scrambling figures swarming over the campers, they were soon tied securely hand and foot. Raven screamed while Wombat and Wedge yelled abuse, but that was all they could do. They were bundled together by their fire and restrained by the gang of sinewy ruffians.

They all ranged in age from barely children to ancients. More tiny tots and a couple of nursing mothers poured from the bush until about twenty-five jittery, gabbling figures surrounded the three captives. Raven quickly assessed the group to be a scrawny, half-starved, motley crew who'd probably have been no threat if it hadn't been for the element of surprise and those wretched nets. They chattered in cut-down English that hardly made sense, especially in the over-all babble.

Suddenly the largest male called for silence. He wasn't particularly imposing with ratty features that reminded Raven of a ferret. Neither did he possess a voice that commanded attention. It was on the squeaky side and complemented his rodent image, but he did appear to be the boss. Soon the only sound was from Wedge who wrestled with the bunch who sat on him. As soon as he shrugged one off another would jump back in his place. Ferret was armed with a club and thumped Wedge on the shoulder to quieten him down. Luckily it was effective and Wedge didn't have to suffer a second blow.

'Yum,' Ferret chirped. 'Big em fire here already — good. Who em we eat first?'

Chapter 19 — Blue Flame

'Eat us!' Wombat cried. 'You've got to be kidding. Look if you're hungry we'll bag a couple of roos no trouble at all. That should do the lot of you.'

But the cannibals didn't seem interested and hovered around their captives deciding who to chew first.

'We'll throw in some trout too,' Wedge offered looking decidedly uncomfortable when a couple of youngsters prodded him to check for tenderness.

A discussion followed, which Wedge and Raven found hard to understand because the tribe used so few English words and had made up many more of their own. However it was all too plain to Wombat and went something like this.

'Look em big beefsteak. This em ... yum.'

'Naw ... tough ... look em gal ...'

'Small em tender em ... like em tops.'

'Want em bit em drum stick ...'

'Em liver em good ... yum.'

'Em gal ... juicy ... em want.'

It seemed that 'em' was a universal pronoun and general purpose word to fill in for almost anything. They appeared incapable of making a decision, but they grew more agitated as they gambolled around the campfire. They snarled, bearing pointed teeth as saliva dribbled down their chins.

Fangs!

'Take em gal,' the leader finally screamed.

'Naw, want em gal ...' one of the youths yelled, but the leader thumped him with his club and that silenced him. He pondered the situation for a moment before deciding the youth had a point. They could always eat her later.

'Take em boy one. Grab em! I bonk em head you chop em!'

Several cannibals grabbed Wombat and hauled him to the fire, but he wasn't going quietly. Others were needed to restrain Raven and Wedge who were frantically struggling against their bonds.

'No, you sick bastards!' Raven screamed. 'Leave my brother alone. I'll kill you.'

Of course, with a feast on their minds, the cannibals paid no attention. They dragged Wombat before the leader who raised his club almost ceremoniously as if he was the only tribe member qualified for the job.

'No ...' Raven pleaded.

As the leader held the club aloft there was a clink sound when a glass bottle landed in front of him and rolled between his spread feet. The bottle contained a clear liquid with a spluttering fuse stuffed into the neck. The next sound was a crack as the bottle shattered and the leader was engulfed in a ball of blue flame. He screamed, dropped the club and raced from the campsite.

Another bottle ...

Another clink ...

Another crack and another whoosh of flame as a second cannibal exploded into a fireball.

An acrid stench spread through the bush. Raven almost vomited as the mixed odour of burning flesh and fresh cow dung assaulted her nostrils.

The cannibals erupted into frenzy. No more fire bombs exploded, but a man fell clutching his chest where a short arrow was embedded. Suddenly another was down with a bolt protruding from his forehead. The tribe wailed as one and streamed in all directions away from the fire. A tall, rangy figure dressed in sheepskins and a wide-brimmed hat strode into camp. He carried a crossbow and led three brumbies that he tethered to a red gum. The weapon was small but lethal at close range. He exuded such an aura of merciless brutality that Raven wondered if they were going to be the next targets. She was wrong.

'Well, well, well,' Thornton said, 'that was bad luck. I mean on your very first night running into a pile of low-life scum.'

Thornton started untangling the nets and untying Raven, Wedge and Wombat.

'Mind you, your luck ain't been anything extra special lately, has it?'

Considering she'd just come short of being fricasseed, Raven though he sounded far too cheerful by half. As soon as he was free, Wedge grabbed his bow and was all for chasing down the cannibals and slaughtering every last one of them.

'Relax, lad,' Thornton said, 'they're scattered all over the place by now. You'll just fall into a rabbit hole and break your leg in the dark.'

'They might come back,' Wombat ventured.

'It's unlikely, they're poorly organised and mostly a sandwich short of a picnic.'

'How come you know about them?' Raven asked. 'Who were they?'

'I've come across a few mobs like that. Normally they hang around the cities where it's easier to trap folk.'

'Eeeeuuww, why eat people ..?' Raven screwed up her nose. 'It's not like there's a shortage of game.'

'They're just not very good hunters, I guess. Mostly they live on snakes and lizards that are easier to catch. But, to tell the truth I reckon they've just developed a taste for human flesh.'

'That's gross, but I'm pleased you turned up. What are you doing here anyway? How did you find us?'

'Found you the same way that lot did — smelt your cooking fire then spotted the flames. I came to warn you.'

'About what?' Wombat asked. 'What else can go wrong for us?'

'Vinnie woke up.'

Raven and Wombat had mixed feelings about that particular piece of news. Wombat was pleased he hadn't actually killed anyone, but when it came to Vinnie ... well ..?

'That's good then,' Wedge said. 'Raven and Wombat can go home.'

'Ahhh, it's not quite as simple as that.'

'Alicia can hardly hold Mum and Dad to the blood debt now,' Raven insisted.

'You could be right although she doesn't see things that way. She's still claiming pain and mental anguish, or whatever.'

'Mum and Dad won't stand for that.'

'Again that could be so and Zen Harrison knows he's on shaky ground. Banishing Wombat wasn't a popular move. Apparently you're a much esteemed young man around town with all your clever ideas.'

Wombat beamed. It was nice to be appreciated.

'So what's the problem?' he asked.

'Vinnie came round only about an hour after you left. You see what I mean about your bad luck? He had a thumping headache, but within minutes was hollering blue murder and vengeance. He and Walter plan to gather their mates and come after you two.'

'Three,' Wedge added.

'Won't matter, I'm sure they'll flatten anyone who stands in their way.'

'Can't Mum and Dad and the others stop them?'

'They were all arguing the toss when I left. It was pretty heated stuff for sure. Zen would be happy to get the boys out of town for a while after the bad feeling they've stirred up. Your folks were giving him a right old tongue-lashing. I thought it best to get out here and warn you in good time.'

'That was very kind of you,' Raven acknowledged.

'Well, I kinda feel responsible. I mean if I'd sold the earring to you not Vinnie, things might have been different.'

'I don't think so,' Raven reassured him, 'Vinnie and Walter would probably have attacked me anyway. They'd just have thought up another excuse.'

Thornton shrugged.

'What were those bombs?' Wombat asked. 'They were awesome. Just like farts.'

'Puleease ... Wombat, you're such a boy,' Raven said.

Thornton reached inside his saddlebag, pulled out a bottle and tossed it to Wombat who caught it nervously.

'Don't worry, it won't go off. Methane mixed with petrol,' Thornton explained. 'You've gotta know where to find both. I carry a dozen bottles with me. Light the fuse, toss the bottle and then bingo ...' He produced a sling shot and lead pellets. '... Smash the bottle and ... Whoosh!'

'Cool,' Wombat said fondling the smooth glass shape. 'How come we don't have these?'

'Petrol's hard to find and it don't always work. There are storage tanks all over the place, but mostly they're full of water and useless. Occasionally I come across a reservoir of good stuff. Methane is a gas you need to get the whole thing going.'

'I guess we know where you get that from,' Wombat chuckled.

'No, I don't have to fart into a bottle. It comes out of the ground in a few places. You've gotta go a long way for it though.'

'How did you find it?'

'Travel broadens the mind,' Thornton grinned. 'Stay in one place and you get used to your limitations. Move around and you have to keep pushing your boundaries -- and learn how to stay alive. Only a bunch of pilgrims would make camp without securing the perimeter.'

He looked at Wedge possibly suggesting he should have known better as a warrior. But to be fair Wedge was relatively new to the game and had only travelled with large groups before. So Thornton spent some time explaining how to prepare booby-traps, trip-wires and alarms. They also discussed what they should do next.

'Look,' Thornton said, 'I reckon the best plan is to stay clear of Mactown for a while whatever Vinnie does. I'm heading up to Canberra Forest, you can tag along if you like — maybe learn something.'

'What if Vinnie chases us?' Raven said.

'He's hardly likely to go that far, is he? And if he does, you'll just have to deal with him and right now, you have to go somewhere.'

'Why not,' Raven brightened, 'I know about Canberra Forest. Angela wrote about it in her chronicle.'

She dug into her saddlebag and retrieved *The Word According to Angela*. Wombat stoked the fire and piled on more wood to give enough light to read by. Raven flipped through the pages. She knew exactly where to find the text as she'd studied the book until she'd just about remembered every word.

'Here it is ...'

Excerpt from 'The Word According to Angela':

The National Library of Australia (NLA) in Canberra may hold the key when (if) the world returns to magnetic equilibrium. We know that electricity (The Spark as I like to call it) relies on magnetic fields. These have been thrown into disarray by the meteor showers. There can be no other plausible explanation. The key to *renewing The Spark will most likely be found in the texts at NLA.*

A copy of every book available in Australia is held there, although what condition they'll be in after time is anyone's guess.

We'll need to rebuild batteries and generators to restore The Spark and that knowledge will be found in engineering and scientific manuals stored in the library.

'How about that?' Thornton pondered. 'Ain't she a wealth of information?'

'Yes, Angela seems to have been very clever,' Raven replied. 'She's always banging on about the future and how things might return to *normal.*'

'When the meteors stop, she says ...' Thornton pondered, stroking his stubbly chin. '... Now that could be sooner than you think.'

'What do you mean?'

'Haven't you noticed?'

'Noticed what?'

'The sky! That's the trouble with you townies, you stop looking. The light show is fading — fizzling out if you like.'

Wombat, Raven and Wedge stared at him.

'It's been happening for months now, but it's been so slow no one has noticed. A mob of Aborigines up north put me onto it. If you can remember back a year or so, you'd be able to see the comparison.'

They all instinctively gazed towards the stars. Lights certainly danced and sparkled above, but now that Thornton had mentioned it, Raven felt sure they didn't hold the same magic she'd felt when she'd first witnessed the spectacle. Could it be that she'd simply grown older and was now used to the night sky? Was Thornton just putting ideas into her head?

And then she knew exactly what to do.

'Okay, Thornton,' she agreed. 'We'll come with you to Canberra Forest and find the National Library.'

Thornton raised his eyebrows.

'Do you know where to look?' he asked.

'Oh yes, Angela drew a map. There's a big lake and the library is close to that. Look.'

She showed him the pencil sketch in Angela's diary.

'Do you think you can find it?'

'Most likely,' Thornton replied. 'I know the lake. Then what?'

'We're going to find all the books on batteries and generators and bring them back to Mactown. We'll be ready when *The Spark* returns.'

'Umm, Raven,' Wombat said, 'don't want to rain on your parade and all that, but will anyone understand the books anyway?'

'You will, my darling brother,' she gave him one of her most ingratiating smiles. 'I have every confidence in you. Look if we bring back the knowledge and you can work out how to apply it, there's no way Zen Harrison can send you away again.'

'Yeah, I suppose I can give it a go.'

'Think of the benefits ...' Raven gushed.

'Think of the power,' Wombat smiled. 'We'll be in control and we can stick it to the Harrisons where it fits best.'

'We'll only use *The Spark* for good,' Raven admonished primly.

'Haven't we all heard *that* before?' Thornton said, 'Of course, that's if we get there alive *and* we can find this NLA of yours *and* we can get past the weirdos who live there.'

'Surely we'll just look around and find a building with a library sign on it.'

'You've gotta understand Canberra is just a great big forest. You can't see anything for the trees. Sure there are dozens of big structures, but they're mostly in ruins now. Mind you the place is a beauty this time of year. The leaves will just be turning to their autumn colours. That's worth a look if nothing else ...'

'What do you mean *weirdoes*?' Wombat interjected.

'Canberra Forest has more than its share that's all.'

'I'm going anyway,' Raven insisted.

'Okay,' Wombat agreed, 'what about you, Wedge?'

'Yeah, I'll stick around. I kinda like hanging out with you guys. It's never boring.'

So Thornton agreed to keep guard for the remaining couple of hours before dawn. When they awoke they discovered he'd made a tasty stew with the remains of last night's supper as well as baking fresh damper in the coals.

'Hearty breakfast to start the day,' he beamed, 'tuck in.'

They polished off the meal in fine style before loading the pack animals and setting off to the north.

'We'll cut through Monaro Pass,' Thornton said. 'The trail will take us directly to Canberra. It can get wretchedly cold at night, so I hope you've got warm kit.'

Raven and Wombat had camped out during winter before and had brought gloves, woollen beanies and sheep skin coats.

Wedge was similarly well prepared. Weather in the South East was changeable at best and it was nothing for the steaming heat of a blistering day to be plunged into the iciness of a sudden, southerly buster. However conditions remained mild. The trail proved passable. There were signs of the early concrete and tar surface and, although it was mostly crumbling rubble, it still marked a way through the bush.

Wildlife abounded. They often chased up massive, raucous flocks of crimson rosellas, rainbow lorikeets, and gold-crested cockatoos. Solitary wallabies grazed in the undergrowth and, as they climbed higher where the bush thinned to open waist-high grassland, mobs of emus and red kangaroos speckled the land as far as the horizon. Small brumby herds mingled peacefully with the other animals. The occasional dingo prowled cautiously on the lookout for a wayward joey while keeping a eye out for irate male roos that could rip its belly to shreds with a single swipe of their mighty hind legs. A brace of wedge-tail eagles soared aloft on the lookout for prey. There was plenty of it around — wombats, rabbits, echidnas and snakes were all on the menu.

'Oh, I just love it out here in the wilderness,' Raven declared, all gushing and one with nature. 'It's so peaceful. Just all these beautiful animals and us — there's not another human to spoil it.'

'I wouldn't bet on that, Raven,' Wedge said and Thornton nodded.

'I spotted them an hour ago,' Wedge added.

'Not bad,' Thornton said, 'I haven't had 'em in my sights much more than that myself.'

'Half a day behind?'

Thornton nodded.

'Six riders?'

Thornton nodded again.

'Harrisons?'

Thornton shrugged.

'I wouldn't be at all surprised,' he added.

Chapter 20 — The Wrath of God

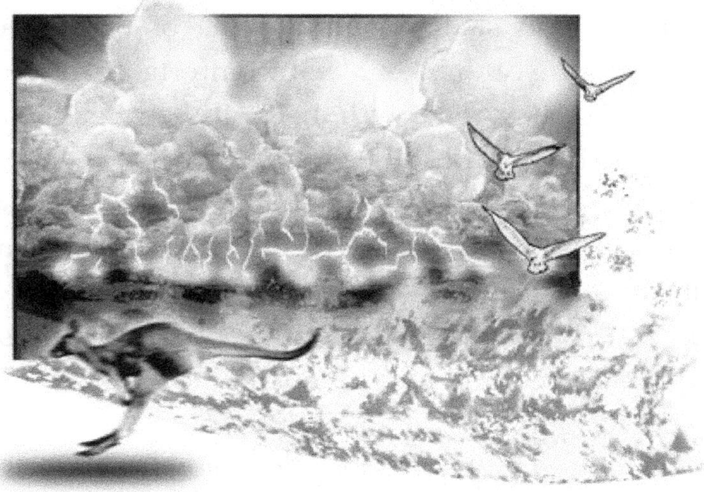

The problem with being tracked in that high country was the lack of any useful cover and there wasn't really any other choice than to follow the trail northwards. Rugged, steep terrain rose a few kilometres left and right of Monaro Pass so there was no chance of dashing to hide on either side. Also Raven and her companions were leading pack animals that slowed them down. The Harrison horses were fit and used to tough terrain.

'Four against six — I've faced worse odds,' Thornton assayed.

'We haven't,' Wombat pointed out glumly, 'and those Harrison boys are pretty good bowmen.'

'Not as good as us,' Raven claimed.

'If it comes to a shootout we could be in deep strife,' Wedge warned. 'The last thing we want is anyone getting hurt out here even if we manage to beat them off.'

'You might as well make your minds up to it right now,' Thornton warned, 'you won't be rid of Vinnie and Walter unless you terminate them once and for all and that means their gang along with them.'

'What if we find shelter behind some of these boulders?' Raven suggested. 'We can make it so uncomfortable for them they might just skulk off back home with their tails between their legs.'

'Even if they do, they'll still be waiting when *you* get back. We either finish them off out here, or they'll forever be a thorn in your side. Are you ready for that sort of commitment? There can be no half-measures.'

Raven and Wombat exchanged uncertain glances while Wedge's expression remained inscrutable.

'What do you suppose we do, Thornton?'

'Right now I haven't got the foggiest notion.'

'I think we should press on and keep as much distance between us as possible,' Wedge suggested. 'Maybe we'll come across somewhere for an ambush or we might lose them altogether.'

'Maybe,' Thornton said, 'unless they've got a black tracker with them, then they'll be hard to shake off.'

'Dunno where they'd find one, the nearest Aboriginal settlement is out Albury way.'

'They're hunters like us, but we might get a chance to cover our trail up ahead,' Raven said.

So they rode on, scattering groups of wildlife in their path. There was no doubt that the pursuing riders had spotted them. There was simply nowhere to hide. As the day wore on a gusty northerly wind picked up and it became oppressively hot on the plains. The humidity was up as well and sweat poured from the riders. They were forced to stop often and water the brumbies whenever they crossed a mountain creek. Dozens of small streams snaked through Monaro Pass. The horses could easily step over them, but the water was fresh and clear.

They often spotted tiger snakes and eastern browns and their greatest fear was that one of the horses would be bitten. Of course the Harrisons faced the same threat and maybe, with a bit of luck, they'd be put out of action, but it didn't appear so. With fitter mounts and no pack-animals to lead, the Harrisons were gaining. Soon they were close enough for the fugitives to see why.

'They'll catch up before nightfall at this rate,' Raven wailed. 'We'll never outrun them.'

'Just keep going, girl,' Thornton said. 'We might be lucky and still be ahead by nightfall. No one will risk riding at night over this country.'

He didn't mention that even if they beat the Harrisons into the night, they wouldn't be able to go any further either, so they'd just be prolonging the inevitable. It looked like it'd come to a shootout after all. By late afternoon they could make out the individual riders with Vinnie and Walter in the van. Four of their most loutish cousins rode closely behind.

They were so intent on keeping an eye on the Harrisons it was some time before anyone became aware of the darkening sky to the west. Huge cumulonimbus clouds billowed skywards above the Snowy Mountains. The last of the late summer fronts was surging across Victoria. A mass of Antarctic air gouged its way under the hot, muggy atmosphere blown down from the tropics. Moisture was dragged upwards and a phenomenon not seen for centuries re-emerged.

The storm clouds turned purple with splashes of green indicating hail and then the riders saw the first lightning bolt followed seconds later by a thunder-clap.

'What the ..?'

More lightning flashed to earth and the hollow rumble of thunder filled the sky.

'Angela's prophecy,' Raven gasped. '*The Spark* is back.'

'Yeah right, it could have chosen a better time,' Wombat yelled.

Any rain was still kilometres away yet lightning bolts preceded the storm. Every single animal on the high plains erupted in panic. None of the creatures had experienced anything like this and bolted in all directions. They had no idea in which direction to turn as lightning flashed from everywhere. The brumbies were just as skittish and it took all the riders' horsemanship to stay in control and not be thrown from their saddles.

'We've gotta get out of here fast,' Thornton yelled. 'If a big red bowls us over without thinking ...'

He heard a sound like a whip-crack and a burning smell wafted through the air accompanied by spasmodic crackling sounds. A shaft of lightning exploded several kilometres behind the riders. It blasted a black hole into the ground and flames fanned out with the wind drawing the fire south. In early autumn the grassland was tinder dry so flames instantly took hold. Kangaroos, horses and emus stampeded ahead of the wall of fire that quickly spread into a front several kilometres wide.

'Stay on the track! The last thing we need is a horse stumbling,' Thornton yelled as he kicked his brumby's flank and galloped northwards. The others needed no encouragement and raced away hot on his heels with a menagerie of wild-eyed creatures bounding beside them. The riders were forced to abandon their spare horses, although they galloped alongside the fleeing group anyway.

Raven and her friends were in luck as the northerly wind still blew, driving the bushfire south right into the path of Vinnie's gang. They were just as startled as anyone. None of the Harrisons had seen a thunderstorm of course, but having read so little, they had no idea of what caused the aerial maelstrom either. What they did see was a mob of frantic roos and emus hurtling towards them ahead of a ten-metre high wall of flame.

'What the ..?' Walter stammered.

'Who freaking-well knows?' Vinnie screamed. 'C'mon, let's move — now!'

The six riders cursed as they tried to turn their horses, colliding with each other as they hauled on the reins. One of the boys was thrown from his mount as it reared and bolted away.

'Wait!' he screamed, but the others were so intent on escape they either failed to hear or simply ignored him. In any event riding double would have slowed a horse to the point where the flames would overtake it.

He turned and stared in horror as a three metre male red boomer smashed into his chest and leapt away leaving the boy sprawled unconscious. Other roos thumped over his body probably finishing him off and sparing him the agony of the advancing inferno. Another rider was pitched from his horse when it stumbled into a wombat hole. The brumby's leg was broken and it was also swamped by the stampede and flames. Its dazed rider suffered the same fate.

As the Harrison horses tired, another one stumbled, throwing its rider. The horse regained its footing and galloped on. The forth horse tripped, breaking its two front legs and now two Harrison boys were on foot as the flames swept relentlessly towards them. Both boys were up and running as the frenetic horde of animals flashed past. They were spared a trampling, but the blaze raced on urged by a twenty-five knot fire-storm wind that engulfed the boys whose screams were lost in the fire's roar.

Only Vinnie and Walter remained, and it looked as if they'd never outrun the fire front. Walter was blubbering and swearing in a right old funk until Vinnie hollered at him to shut up and save his energy, but he still snivelled as he rode just ahead of the firestorm. The emu and kangaroo mobs had either outpaced them or succumbed to the flames.

And then the rain arrived.

It was a downpour like nothing the boys had experienced. They were nearly washed from their brumbies by the sheer force of water. Fortunately they just reached some granite outcrops and gum stands when the hail hit. They would never have spotted shelter if they hadn't been right beside it. The deluge had reduced visibility to only a few metres. Vinnie and Walter dismounted and led their two remaining mounts to the cover of the boulders. Hail stones smacked into the rock, shattering in shards of ice. The noise was deafening. Walter crouched under the rocks and clamped his hands over his ears as he blubbered pathetically.

'What is it? What is it ..?' he mumbled over and over again.

'How the blazes should I know?' Vinnie shouted above the roaring storm. 'Be thankful it's put the freaking fire out. We're safe here, so just shut up. We'll wait it out. It can't last forever.'

So he squatted beside Walter. The trees and boulders appeared to be effective storm protection, but Vinnie ensured he had a tight hold on the reins. The last thing he wanted was the horses bolting if they were struck by a wayward hailstone or spooked by lightning. Walter calmed down when the hail eased to rain and the thunderbolts moved eastwards.

A cool breeze followed the front that chilled them to the bone until it eased, but Vinnie knew they still needed a fire. He scrounged around for dry gum-leaf kindling and branches. Despite the downpour, the leaf mulch under the tree canopy was so dense that he had no trouble digging out dry combustible material. Everyone carried a flint and tinderbox while eucalyptus growth sure burnt well. Soon Vinnie had a healthy fire going. Another good thing about gum tress is the number of dry, fallen branches lying about, which the boys piled onto the flames. Vinnie was truly thankful that the rain halted the blaze before it reached bushland, because there'd have been no stopping the fire then.

'Funny how we were running away from the fire and now we can't make it big enough,' Walter observed through chattering teeth.

Vinnie tethered the horses that had finally calmed down. He took a billy and tea makings form his saddle panniers. There was no shortage of deep puddles to fill the billy, even if the water might have been a bit muddy. Walter cheered up once the flames were roaring away and there was tea brewing.

'Don't worry, Walter,' Vinnie said stoically. 'We'll kip here tonight and head home tomorrow. A night without grub won't do us any harm. I'm too buggered to cook anyway.'

'What about them other boys?' Walter stammered. 'They're dead, ain't they?'

'Most likely. I don't see how it can be otherwise.'

'We left 'em. We just ran away.'

'Listen you big oaf, there was nothing we could do about it. If we'd stopped for a second, we'd be dead too. Even a half-wit like you must be able to see that.'

'We were cowards. I was so scared I nearly crapped myself.'

'Of course you were scared, there was a great, freaking bushfire just about to charcoal us. It doesn't make us cowards.'

Who was he kidding? Hadn't he attacked and tried to rape a girl three or four years younger than him? There's nothing much more cowardly than that, but Vinnie didn't seemed to think so. He was just feeling chuffed that he'd survived the day. He really didn't feel any great loss for his four cousins. Sorrow and pity for others were simply not emotions he possessed. What he did feel was anger -- deep, consuming rage. Raven Mac had escaped and right then he couldn't think of a blind thing he could do about it. He'd have to deal with her later. She'd return to Mactown one day … and he'd be waiting and then revenge would be sweet … and total.

*

On the other side of the flame-front four riders were galloping pell-mell along the Monaro track. They were less threatened as the flames drifted away from them. When he realised the immediate danger had passed, Thornton signalled everyone to slow up in case the horses tripped. The wildlife had scattered, bounding away to anywhere they hoped was far from thunderbolts. Thornton was the first to notice the wall of rain and hail bearing towards them.

'I don't like the look of that,' he muttered while the others eyed him uncertainly.

They galloped on and reached the ruins of Rock Flat just ahead of the hail bombardment. It had been a small community in antiquity, but was now mostly a cluster of rubble. At least the ruins were surrounded by tall white gums that offered some protection.

254

Not much roofing remained, but they found a building large enough to accommodate them all. They took advantage of the slate and terracotta tiles that remained. Remarkably their spare horses had simply followed them. Perhaps they hoped for safety in numbers, but the riders managed to grab the trailing halters and pen all the horses inside the ruins.

There was no time to start a fire before the tempest struck. The noise of hail clattering onto the tiles was unnerving especially when the occasional tile smashed to shrapnel. Lightning intensified and seemed to be crackling everywhere. The wind swirled so violently it uprooted a tree beside the riders' shelter. The trunk slammed against the sandstone structure smashing several blocks, but the wall held. The branches of the remaining foliage added to the riders' protection.

They huddled for what seemed hours while the skittish horses chafed and fought against their reins. The fallen gum had blocked the entrance so there was no fear of them escaping. The main threat was they might become so restless they'd kick someone. Thornton seemed to have a way with animals and managed to soothe them by whispering into their ears while holding the reins firmly and tethered them securely to the branches that now filled their shelter.

As it had done for Vinnie and Walter, the storm moved on leaving a calm void with only a gentle southerly breeze behind it. Like the Harrison boys, Raven and her companions' first thought was to build a fire and dry out. They too boiled a billy as soon as the blaze was roaring away.

It took all four of them to clear the entrance and then lead the brumbies to another ruined building that acted as a stockyard.

There was plenty of grass within the walls, so they left the horses for the night after barricading the entrance.

'I don't think we'll get a repeat of that performance,' Thornton opined as he eyed the calm evening sky.

'Whatever *that* was?' Wedge queried.

'That, my boy,' Thornton replied, 'was the *Wrath of God,* no doubt about it.'

'*God?*' Wombat said. 'Surely no one believes that old legend anymore?'

'Don't bet on it,' Thornton replied. 'Remember I told you Canberra Forest has more than its share of weirdos, and some of them go on something fearful about this god or that. God is alive and well in many quarters.'

'What about you, Thornton?' Raven challenged. 'Do you believe in the legend?'

'I'm not saying I do, but I'm not ruling it out either.'

After supper they sat around the campfire drinking tea and discussing the storm and its meaning until Wombat chanced to look up beyond the flames.

'Blow me down,' he gasped.

The others stared at him blankly as he pointed into the night sky. The darkness was complete apart from a distant shimmering of the Milky Way and tiny points of light from individual stars. A full moon was on the rise, but other than that the sky was completely clear. Raven thought she may have possibly seen one shooting star, but no other heavenly bodies streaked across the indigo night. Raven leapt to her feet and rushed beyond the walls so the campfire didn't mar her vision. She stared in disbelief. Much as she'd loved the nightly light show, she couldn't believe what she now saw in the still silence could be so amazingly and serenely beautiful.

She sensed an overpoweringly spiritual presence ... Could there be any truth to the legend?

*

Vinnie and Walter were so exhausted and cold they simply piled the fire as high as they could before huddling together and drifting into fitful sleep. As they warmed up and the fire dried them they grew more comfortable and fell into a deep slumber. They failed to hear any rustling in the bush around them. They failed to hear any hushed voices. They failed to hear the swish of flying nets until they were entangled and a score of writhing, chattering figures pounced onto them. They were overpowered and trussed up in seconds.

'Yum, em good. Em wanna yum now.'

'No muck em about. Bonk em.'

'Hold em. Not move em.'

Thwack! Thwack!

A club swung twice.

'Yum em got blood on em 'ands. Em yum ...'

Chapter 21 — The Librarian

Nights were cold in the high country, especially when the sky was clear. It was something Raven hadn't expected as she huddled close to the fire. Wedge had gathered a store of dry wood that he heaped onto the flames. Raven snuggled into Wedge when he sat down and he didn't object. She'd just reached an age where her emotions were decidedly confused. Although she hardly knew Wedge there was an instant connection that she hoped would develop beyond a *just-good-friends* or *big-brother* status. Unfortunately — or fortunately — Wombat and Thornton were at hand to keep an eye on her, so she'd have to let her feelings and hormones settle for the time being.

Wombat knew as much about electricity's return as Raven did and spent much of the night explaining the intricacies to Thornton and Wedge. They were both intrigued, but Wombat could see they were baffled by the theory much of the time.

'Yeah, it needs going over a few times to understand how it all works,' he confessed. 'It took me ages to get my head around the whole *invisible electrons* business. I mean even if we find enough manuals to explain how to make a generator or batteries, we may not have the technology to do anything with it anyway.'

'Do you think it's wise to try?' Thornton asked.

'Oh, yeah. It'd be so cool. Why wouldn't we?'

'It seems to me from what you and Raven have said – and from what I already know, we're not all ignorant savages out here in the wilderness, you know – that this *Spark* of yours may have been more trouble than it was worth.'

'What do you mean?'

'From what I can make out, the world used to be an evil, polluted place because people had the means to build factories and machines that pumped poisonous gas into the sky. There were huge piles of waste no one knew how to dispose of so they chucked it into rivers and the sea, which killed off all the marine life. You say that all you need is *The Spark* to return and we'll go back to the past. Maybe it's better to leave things the way they are. At least the air is clean and there are plenty of fish around now.'

'If we don't discover how to use it, someone else will,' Wombat said with a disturbing gleam in his eye.

'We'll be in control, we'll make sure *The Spark* isn't abused,' Raven insisted.

'Is that so ..?' Thornton murmured.

'I wonder what happened to the Harrisons,' Wedge commented, deciding it was a good time to change the subject.

'Scuttled back to Mactown with singed arses, I'd say,' Wombat grinned.

Thornton set up the perimeter warning system nevertheless that included the building where the horses were corralled.

'Surely no one would be prowling around after that storm?' Raven said.

'It might seem isolated and cold up here, but I've learnt to assume someone or something is always prowling around,' he replied.

And he was proved correct. A disturbance occurred during Wombat's watch at dawn when there was just enough light to distinguish features among the shadows. The horses sensed a movement first. Wombat awoke his companions putting his finger to his lips. They grabbed their weapons and crouched beside the doorway. Scuffling sounds came from just outside as two shadows darted past. The dog-like animals sniffed around the horse corral. They paced nervously about the trip ropes, but hadn't set off one of Thornton's warning bells yet.

'Feral dogs?' Wombat hissed. 'Dingoes?'

At that moment the sun's first rays sliced over the horizon and the dogs stood illuminated for just a second. The creatures were indeed the size of large dogs and a similar colour to dingoes. Their jaws were disproportional to their heads and bodies — huge and gaping. Other than that the animals were unremarkable except for rows of dramatic dark stripes around their rumps.

'Where are the rest of them?' Thornton said. 'The pack has to be somewhere close, but I've never seen dogs like that. Not anywhere.'

'That's because they're not dogs,' Raven smiled. 'What you're seeing is a miracle.'

They all stared at her.

'They're thylacines — Tasmanian tigers — they're supposed to have died out centuries ago. People hunted them because they thought they'd kill sheep.'

'In case you haven't noticed, Raven,' Wedge said, 'this ain't Tasmania. I dunno where it is exactly, but I know no one goes there. You've got to cross a lot of dangerous sea I think.'

'Tigers once lived all over Australia,' Raven said. 'Tasmania was just the last place where they were seen.'

'With jaws like that I'd say they're serious carnivores, so we'd better shoo 'em away from the horses,' Thornton said.

'They might bite,' Wombat added uncertainly.

It turned out that thylacines were a nervous breed and vanished as soon as Wedge and Thornton confronted them.

'You're a very knowledgeable girl,' Thornton said. 'I'm impressed.'

'I've read everything in the Mactown library,' she replied smugly. 'I'm probably the only person except the Word-Keeper who's done that. That's why it's so important to keep the books. If they get damp at all they just crumble to flakes in no time. I try to make new copies to replace damaged texts, but it's such a slow process.'

'What condition do you think the books will be in if we find this NLA in Canberra Forest, then?'

'I can only hope for the best,' she replied. 'Maybe they have a Word-Keeper who's trying to preserve them. I'm not going to let pessimism discourage me especially after seeing something as marvellous as we did this morning. Thank you for waking us, Wombat. Now I think it's time for breakfast.'

*

They followed the Monaro trail for three days passing through a large rubble pile that had once been Cooma. From there the open plain became more wooded and soon they were trekking into dense forest. The trees were unlike the eucalypts around Mactown, but Wedge said there were many similar types close to Emu Creek.

'They look pretty special in autumn,' he said. 'It's a little early yet, but you can see some of the leaf tips are starting to turn red and yellow. Wait another month and this will be a real spectacle. The ground is smothered with golden foliage. It's a bit depressing in winter when the trees are bare though. It makes me really look forward to them budding and sprouting again in spring.'

'You're really quite poetic when you put your mind to it, aren't you?' Raven said.

'Dunno about that, but I do like the autumn colours, maybe we'll still be here to see the leaves fall.'

'Yeah, but it'll be getting pretty cold in a month's time,' Thornton said without relish.

'I hope we've found what we're looking for by then,' Wombat added.

The forest appeared devoid of human denizens which was fine by Raven. Maybe they'd all taken off to avoid the cold weather. She wasn't happy about the *weirdos* Thornton claimed lived there. That aside the rest seemed simple -- find the lake and Thornton would lead them to the library with the help of Angela's sketch-map. It shouldn't be too hard to get in even if the place was locked. What she hadn't expected was the sheer vastness of the forest. It stretched for a hundred kilometres.

They'd penetrated the wilderness for two days before the ruins appeared. Hundreds, maybe thousands of debris-piles appeared in regular patterns that were more-or-less evenly spaced.

Sometimes they were in straight lines and sometimes they were curved or even in circular patterns. Thornton explained that each ruin had once housed a family.

Raven found the number of them staggering. Even more startling were the crumbling monoliths they encountered every few kilometres. Thornton thought the huge masses of concrete, steel and shattered glass were markets and gathering places, but he didn't really know for sure. The structures were pocked with massive caverns filled with rusted metal hulks that had once been a common form of transport. Once again Raven wondered how there was room for them all on the tracks, although Angela's diary indicated the roads were wider then.

'The lake is not far,' Thornton finally announced.

Navigation wasn't so difficult. Thornton explained they'd simply follow a north running river until they came to a lake.

'That lake's called Burley Griffin after the man who designed the town,' Raven announced. 'Even though Walter Burley Griffin got all the credit, his wife Marion had just as much to with the town's concept.'

'Well, aren't you the *Miss-Know-It-All*? But what town would that be? There's nothing but rubble left now. There is only one place left standing as far as I know and that's a huge domed building on the north shore. Apparently the lake used to be much wider and deeper, but it's silted up a fair bit over the years.'

As they picked their way along the lakeshore they saw the building across the water. It could be clearly seen at the end of a kilometre long straight break in the forest. A causeway made from wooden planks stretched across crumbled pylons and miscellaneous wreckage. The structure looked in poor repair and crossing could be hazardous. They saw no one, but now Raven sensed that life was all around them. The question was whether it was human or dangerous.

'We're not alone, are we?' she whispered to Thornton.

'More of your thylacines perhaps?' he grinned.

'Aren't you concerned about weirdos?'

'We're being watched no doubt, so keep your eyes peeled. According to your map, we're nearly there anyway.'

Finding the library was ludicrously easy in the end. They simply followed the lake shore until they stumbled into the ruin. By comparison with the rest of the forest debris the building wasn't in bad shape. It was certainly a huge structure perched on a high concrete slab. Steps led to an entrance that was surrounded by pillars. Much of the ceiling and walls had fallen into disrepair, but enough evidence remained to suggest it had been a magnificent edifice in its time.

The usual hills of masonry and shattered glass lay haphazardly around the building. Raven was amazed at the size of where the glass panels had been. Glass was difficult to produce from sea-sand and no one bothered with it much. The amount of glass that must have been produced was astounding.

They dismounted and tethered their horses to some of the bushes that surrounded the library. Wedge volunteered to guard the mounts and equipment.

'Whistle if you need help,' he said cheerfully. The idea of going into a ruin didn't seem to appeal to him.

'You do the same,' Raven replied. She couldn't wait to see what was inside.

They had to scramble over debris and past more ruined car shells that were no more than hollow, rusty frames although formed in neat lines. They climbed the steps leading to the main portal, and to their surprise the main doors were open. Apparently they were far too large and heavy to close and led to a hallway the size of an auditorium. Tables, bookcases and statue plinths were scattered about in no particular order. They appeared to have no current purpose as they were all empty.

'You're not allowed in here,' a shrill voice cried.

They turned and saw a middle-aged woman seated at a large desk. An open tome lay on the desk and a wooden beaker containing pencils stood beside it, which was remarkable as pencils were a rarity.

'What is the meaning of this?' the woman demanded.

'Meaning of what?' Raven said.

There was something about the woman that immediately made Raven's heckles rise.

'Why, this intrusion of course. You are trespassing. No one is allowed in here.'

'Why ever not?'

'It's a rule.'

'Whose rule?'

The woman seemed a little uncertain for a moment before replying.

'Umm ... the library's of course ... and I'm the librarian so I uphold the rules. I'm also a public servant so you have to do what I say.'

'If you're a public *servant* don't you have to do what *the public* say?'

'Good gracious no that would never do. Public servants make the rules and give orders. *I* certainly don't *serve*. That would be totally inappropriate and quite unacceptable.'

'Look, all we want to do is look at some books,' Wombat interjected.

'Well, that is out of the question, young man. This is the Australian National Library and no one is allowed to look at the books except during conducted tours on Thursdays and Saturdays and then they certainly can't *touch* them.'

'Doesn't that defeat the purpose of a library?' Raven suggested.

'What has purpose got to do with it, miss? We public servants have no time to bother ourselves with *purposes*. We're far too busy making rules. Today is Tuesday anyway and there hasn't been anyone available for guided tours since I've been here.'

'Just tell us, why can't we read the books?'

'Because, as I said — *it's the rule*. Goodness me, you are a foolish girl.'

'It doesn't make sense,' Raven was about to explode. *And I bet she doesn't even know whether it's Tuesday or not — she just said that to sound smart. It's a pity Wombat's fancy watch only tells the time and not the day. Then we'd sort this crazy woman out.*

'It does to me,' the woman gave her a laboured smile.

'Listen,' Thornton said as he pulled his knife from his belt, 'what's to stop us just going in ... you?'

'Oh, don't be silly. How could I possibly do that?'

'In that case, we'll just be about our business and see what's inside.'

'Oh, I wouldn't advise that. Oh no, that would be most unwise.'

Just then they heard Wedge whistle.

'I think you should go and see what that's all about,' the woman said calmly.

Thornton glared at her and Raven was sure he was about to slit her throat, but Wedge whistled again.

'You need to see this,' he called.

They raced outside, sliding to a stop at the top of the steps. Wedge was standing at the base, bow drawn with an arrow nocked. A group of a dozen robed figures stood before him in a half-circle. Their hoods were drawn up revealing only occasional flashes from the reflection of their eyes.

They weren't armed. But they didn't have to be. Each figure held a snarling dog on a short leash. The dogs were fierce mongrel crossbreeds that exuded menace and were more than ready for a fight. They tugged at their rope leashes to the point where they almost gagged on their leather collars.

The centre figure handed his leash to the man next to him who now held two dogs with difficulty. He pulled his hood back revealing a bearded young man with shoulder length hair.

'Why have you come?' he asked simply.

'Blimey, we only came to read a few freaking books,' Wombat said. 'What's the big deal?'

'It's forbidden,' the man said.

'So the witch-woman in there said,' Raven said.

'Show some respect, she's a public servant.'

'She said that too.'

'Look, what harm can it do? *What's* the big deal and *what* gives you the right to say who reads what?'

'We are the *Guardians of the Words*,' the bearded man declared. 'It is our hallowed duty to protect the knowledge and prevent anyone purloining the words.'

'You can't steal words, they've already been written.'

'Nevertheless the words must remain secret. *You* are Harbingers of Chaos. Look at the sky if you need proof. The night lights have gone and you appear straight away. That can only spell evil. We cannot go back to the dark days of technology and mass destruction. It has been our sacred trust to guard the works through countless generations. The words represent evil and cannot be revealed.'

'He's got a point,' Thornton reminded Raven of his earlier misgivings.

'Oh great,' Raven threw up her arms in exasperation. 'You might just as well burn the whole lot down then. Why not do that and save yourselves all this trouble?'

'What do you take us for — Nazis?'

'Nazis?' Thornton looked at Raven.

'Bad guys, really bad guys from way back,' she replied.

'That won't be necessary,' the bearded man said. 'Normally our public servant is enough to deter meddlers.'

'I can understand that, she has a way about her,' Wombat muttered.

'But I don't think so in this case,' the leader said taking the leash back from the man beside him and reaching to unleash the slavering dog.

Chapter 22 — Colonel Charlie's Campaign

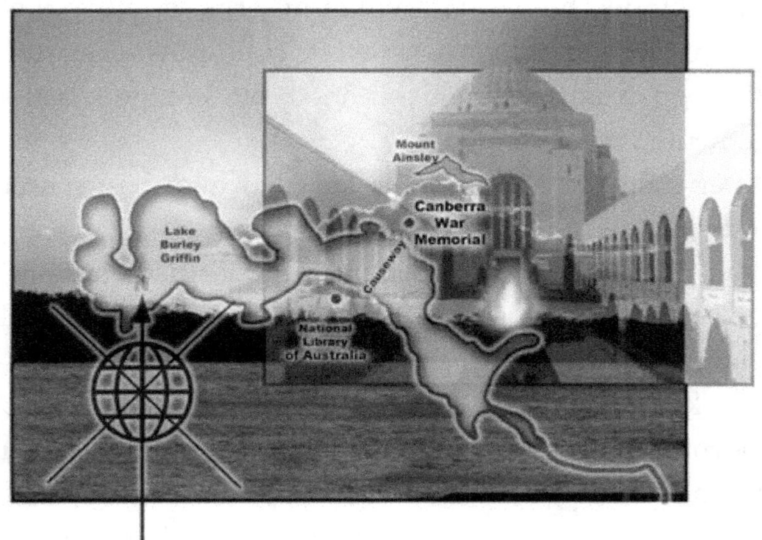

The guardians' lack of coordination gave Wedge and the others a fighting chance. The leader released his dog, but the others appeared unsure whether they should do the same. They dithered as if they were waiting for direct orders.

'Time to get out of here!' Wedge yelled as Raven, Wombat and Thornton raced for their horses.

Meanwhile Wedge launched into the warrior's role he'd been trained for. He drew his knife as the pit-bull leapt. The animal only had one tactic -- go for the throat. Wedge swung the blade and sliced a chunk of the animal's head clean off. It howled yet came on in blind, primitive rage. It tried to latch onto Wedge's arm, but its jaws were too badly damaged by the knife-wound. Wedge struck the dog again and this time it fell silent.

The guardian leader screamed in distress, but it was his own fault for setting the dog loose. Wedge felt no pity for him or the mortally wounded hound. He swung into the saddle and galloped after his three companions who were riding away at full speed. The other guardians seemed stunned by Wedge's actions and stood cemented to the spot.

'After them, you idiots!' the bearded guardian roared. 'Free your dogs.'

Now they had definite orders the guardians sprang to life. They unleashed the dog collars and a dozen hysterical hounds chased after the riders with only one thing on their minds — hunt down and kill the prey.

Thornton knew that the dogs would eventually outrun them. The brumbies may have had a chance without riders, but loaded down there was no hope. He led them to the shattered causeway across the lake knowing full well that the horses would be unable to cross the crumbling structure.

'Get the horses into the water!' he yelled. 'They can swim across. We'll go on foot.'

The horses needed no encouragement as the baying dogs were almost upon them. They splashed into the lake which wasn't particularly deep at first, so they waded out some distance before being forced to swim for it. Squawking, honking flocks of egrets, ducks and black swans flapped skywards in their path. Raven, Wedge, Wombat and Thornton only managed to cover a few metres before the pack arrived and scrambled onto the causeway. Several animals even hurtled into the water and swam alongside the causeway until they were abeam the fugitives.

Wombat took a dog out with his bow while Wedge dealt with another in similar fashion to his first victim. Thornton managed to clout a beast senseless with his staff while Raven hit another in its shoulder with an arrow, putting it out of action. The remaining dogs may have been in battle frenzy, but they backed off when they saw a third of their number dead or wounded in seconds. They were trained to kill. They knew nothing else and, although they now advanced cautiously, retreat was not an option. They snapped at their quarries' feet as they edged along the causeway.

'I never thought I'd say this,' Raven gasped, 'but I wish Vinnie and Walter were here right now.'

'Yeah, they sure could deal with feral dog packs,' Wombat agreed.

Wombat led the way while Raven and Thornton protected the flanks and Wedge held the toughest position as rearguard. It was hard enough scrambling over the rough surface, but he had to walk backwards and often stumbled. Once he went down and a dog pounced, latching onto his arm. Thornton swung his staff with little effect even though he struck the animal several times. Raven pulled the knife from her belt and rammed the blade up to the hilt into the dog's eye. The knife pierced the animal's brain killing it instantly, but its jaws had latched onto Wedge's arm like a vice.

It took all Wombat's strength to part the dog's blood-soaked teeth while Thornton and Raven held the others off. Wombat helped Wedge to his feet and they staggered on, leaving Raven and Thornton to deal with the remaining dogs. Raven skewered another hound with an arrow into its slathering chops and Thornton hammered out more murderous blows that silenced two more dogs. Wedge recovered enough to return to the fight with his knife flaying. The razor edge cut up the remaining animals so badly that they were unable to continue the chase.

'That'll teach the buggers,' he muttered, nursing his injured arm.

'Come on. No time for victory speeches,' Thornton admonished. 'Let's get across this wretched bridge.'

The brumbies were making good progress while their riders had been engaged with the dog pack. They certainly didn't wait around and were about a quarter of the way across. Despite Wedge's injuries the riders were feeling pretty good about having sorted out the dogs even though they hadn't managed to get inside the library.

They were about half way across when they heard the baying of more hounds – many more. The wild moans came from the forest just beyond the tree line along the southern shore. The howls came faintly at first, but quickly rose to a crescendo of hideous canine wailing. Then the pack burst from the forest onto the causeway.

'There are hundreds of them!' Raven screamed. 'We'll never outrun them and we can't fight them all off.'

The guardians certainly had no shortage of dogs to call on. The beasts surged onto the causeway or ran straight into the lake and swam alongside the ramp until they found a foothold to scramble onto dry land. The eerie howling echoed across the lake, closing with alarming speed. Even if Raven and her companions reached the causeway end they were still in open country and it was a long sprint to the nearest trees. The horses may have swum across the lake, but they'd all scattered so far away that there was no hope of capturing and remounting in time.

They were less than a hundred metres from shore when the first dogs started yapping at their heels. The pack had taken up so much of their attention that they scarcely noticed anything else. In fact they had hindered their retreat by continually looking back and checking the pursuit. It was only when they heard a voice hailing from the north bank that they became aware of several figures standing on the shoreline.

'I say,' a man called, 'it'd probably be a smashing idea if you blighters jumped for it.'

'What?' Thornton yelled.

'Stand aside.'

'There's only water ...'

'Then jump in if you know what's good for you.'

Wedge and Raven had no idea what the fellow was blithering on about, but Wombat and Thornton looked ahead and saw the reason for his warning. Thornton grabbed Wedge and Wombat heaved Raven from her feet and the four of them splashed into Lake Burley Griffin's icy waters just as they heard a call from the bank.

'Fire!'

They felt the blast as a shower of shrapnel blasted along the causeway smashing into the pack. Bricks, rocks, metal shards and other debris sliced into dog flesh. There were shrieks and howls from the beasts when another salvo cut through it. The pack was reduced to a bloody pulp. Over half the animals had either been killed or sustained serious wounds. These dogs apparently didn't have the suicidal fanaticism of the first dozen and the survivors turned and ran or limped back along the causeway to the curses and threats of the guardians waiting on the southern shore.

'I think it's safe to come out now before you catch your deaths,' the voice called cheerfully.

Raven and the others were close enough to wade ashore. They clambered up the bank and trudged, dripping wet, towards the group of figures standing beside their war machine. It was a ballista and resembled a massive cross-bow, but fired a missile-filled pouch rather than bolts. Winding mechanisms had been attached to either side of the catapult and it took a team on each to ensure enough tension for the firing cord to be effective.

'Isn't she a beauty,' the spokesman gushed with pride. He was about forty with close cropped hair and sported a dapper moustache.

'Saved our bacon right enough,' Thornton conceded uncertainly. 'There must have been hundreds of those wretched dogs.'

'I think no more than a couple of dozen is more like it,' the fellow said, 'but we shooed 'em all back where they came from. Those rascals haven't tried that bally trick in yonks. You must have upset 'em pretty badly.'

'I think we insulted one of their sacred institutions.'

'Yep, they can be a touchy lot. Allow me to introduce myself, I'm Colonel Charlie and my four lieutenants here are Percy, Caroline, Denis and Joyce.'

'Colonel Charlie ..?' Raven said, suggesting something more formal.

'Well, it's actually Colonel Charles Rogers, but that all gets a bit confusing. You see the militia was formed way back by three Australian Army officers, Major Rogers, and Lieutenants Goddard and Kildare. Somehow they felt the need to move up here and defend this shrine. We're their descendants so we only have three surnames between us. We use our first names to stop getting muddled up.'

'I see ... so there are others?' Raven said, noticing that Colonel Charlie and his lieutenants were all dressed alike. They wore roughly woven khaki shirts and pants, brown untanned leather boots and broad-brimmed hats. They were also armed with uniform knives and clubs.

'Affirmative, most of our frontline joint-strike force is up at the Memorial on guard duty, you see. So stand to and identify yourselves.'

Thornton introduced them all and Colonel Charlie greeted them cordially even kissing the back of Raven's hand.

'I'm so pleased you turned up,' Raven said. 'We were dead meat back there.'

'Oh, we didn't turn up. We're here all the time. We saw the whole little episode unfold, so we got ready. You were just too busy to spot us.'

'Only five of you?'

'That's all we needed,' Colonel Charlie smiled smugly. 'You don't over-commit your manpower. Bad tactics and all that, what? You're lucky the causeway is here. Wasn't always, but silt and rubbish have built up from way back and it's a way across. Bit of an inconvenience really because we have to keep it guarded.'

'Guarded from what? Why are you here?'

'We're barracked at the War Memorial. We're charged with maintaining the monument and keeping the Eternal Flame alight. So it's, you know — *eternal*.'

Oh no, not another load of nutter sentries, Raven thought. *And only three surnames can't be good.*

'People around here seem to think there's lots of stuff to guard around the lake,' she observed.

Colonel Charlie explained that his predecessors had guarded the War Memorial for as long as anyone could remember or record.

They believed that it was vitally important to preserve the monument, but had to admit the reason was now lost in history.

'Then why do you do it?' the ever pragmatic Wombat asked.

'Duty, dear boy,' Colonel Charlie replied, 'we can't let tradition lapse and what else can we do if not our duty? You have to have purpose. There'd be no point in anything if a chap didn't have a purpose in life. Come on I'll take you up to HQ.'

Not like the librarian then. She certainly didn't need a purpose. Still they're all stark, raving bonkers, the whole lot of 'em, Raven thought, but at least these guys aren't hostile -- towards us anyway.

They walked up the slope to the Memorial, or rather Raven and her companions walked while Colonel Charlie and his lieutenants marched. Sheep and cattle grazed in the long paddock. They'd been startled by the baying dogs and had scattered towards an enclosure at the meadow's top end, but quickly returned after the pack was driven off. The gene-pool wasn't quite as limited as Colonel Charlie might have suggested. Some outsiders with a similar military disposition had joined the militia ranks.

'Aren't you worried about the dogs coming back, Colonel?' Raven asked being careful to use his service title because she thought she'd read somewhere that military-types could be touchy about that sort of thing.

'Not at all, my dear girl,' Colonel Charlie replied with confidence. 'A pasting like that should last for ages. I don't think they're really interested in us right now anyway. They were always causing mischief years ago -- trying to pinch our manuals and historical records for their library. They're fanatics you see, but they haven't bothered us for a while, so I deduce it's *you* they've got a grudge against right now.'

'We'll round up your mounts, ma'am,' Lieutenant Joyce said and left with her three fellow-subalterns to gather the brumbies and lead them to the enclosure. Later Raven was pleased to learn Angela's diary remained undamaged and still securely packed in its leather pouch.

As they approached the War Memorial they saw a dozen tents standing in two precise rows in front of the main structure. Further to each side were other, large marquees where children played. They'd been too far away to take any notice in the dog-pack decimation, but didn't appear particularly interested anyway. Action must have been an everyday event for them, or they were simply calm and disciplined. Laundry hung on lines that were placed with equal precision to the tents. An Australian flag flapped languidly from a tall white post. Colonel Charlie also pointed out the mess tent, kitchens, arsenal, storehouses and latrines. He was obviously proud of his orderly base.

'Single officers' billet here,' Colonel Charlie announced pointing to the smaller tents, 'and married quarters over there.' He indicated the marquees. 'We even have a forge and a couple of capable blacksmiths.'

'How many people do you have?' Thornton asked.

They discovered the good colonel certainly didn't command a regiment, or indeed a battalion, but a cut-to-the-bones half-company at best. The force strength was about fifty people who all held the rank of lieutenant. There were no privates, NCO's, captains or majors in Colonel Charlie's unit. It didn't really matter because Raven was the only person who'd read anything about military rank structure and she hadn't understood it anyway.

'Come along, I'll take you to HQ and we can discuss strategy,' Colonel Charlie said.

They entered the War Memorial via a long courtyard flanked by arched walkways with a pool in its centre. The eternal flame flickered in a shallow chalice that stood just above the water surface. Buckets of what appeared to be gelatinous goop were placed, like everything else, in exact rows.

'We send patrols to the coast to collect the oil balls,' Charlie explained. 'There are deposits all along the shoreline. We merge the mineral with organic material so it burns for ages.'

'Impressive, but what's the importance of the flame?' Wombat asked.

'I'll show you, young man,' Charlie replied.

For the next couple of hours Colonel Charlie conducted Raven and her companions through the galleries and chambers that made up the building. The gamut of memorabilia, artwork, photographs, dioramas, uniforms and military hardware was simply staggering. The now-defunct war machines were simply unbelievably awesome.

Despite the images of cheerful Anzacs, GIs and Tommies, Raven was struck by an overwhelming sadness at the misery and suffering they must have endured. She only vaguely knew who the Japanese were and had no idea why they'd waged war so ruthlessly. And yet they were only one of the country's enemies. Turks, Boers, Germans, Italians, Koreans, Malays, Vietnamese, Afghans, several Arabian and African nations had all been at war with the Diggers at some stage. She wondered what Australia had done to inflame so much hatred. The point was moot of course because all those nations had long since ceased to exist. Warfare was now waged on a far more personal level.

'How did they justify the fighting?' she asked Colonel Charlie.

'It was simply what people did all the time,' he declared.

'What just fought wars?' Raven said in disbelief.

'Goodness me, yes. There was a time when millions upon millions of people were killed in two world wars in just over thirty years and many wars lasted much longer than that. There were so many people then, I suppose they must have been terribly overcrowded and had to kill each other off just to make space. No one really knows except that wars were fought on a massive scale. There certainly aren't enough people around these days for that sort of thing.'

'It still doesn't explain why you guard this place,' Wedge said.

'Lest we forget,' Colonel Charlie replied solemnly. 'All those people made the ultimate sacrifice and we will remember them. *That* is our purpose. All kinds of vandals, marauders and bandits, including that mangy lot across the lake, have tried to loot the Memorial and generations of our soldiers have driven them off.'

'How have these displays remained in such good condition when everything else has crumbled?' Wombat asked.

'TLC, old chap,' Colonel Charlie replied. 'We have always maintained the exhibits. When we see anything deteriorating, we repair it immediately if we can. We pay attention to detail while keeping an eye on the big picture. That's the key to our success.'

'Do you think the guardians will have preserved the library with such care and dedication?' Raven wondered.

'They're disorganised sometimes, but it's possible. They see it as *their* duty even if they don't want to share it with anyone.'

Colonel Charlie's unit had tried to duplicate many of the weapons displayed at the memorial, but were hampered by technological limitations. They knew how to produce gunpowder, but raw materials were scarce and their supply of pyrotechnics was only used when absolutely necessary. Training was their strong point. Their discipline and skill-at-arms was their best weapon against attack. The same organisation also allowed the community to effectively husband the area around them. Colonel Charlie said they rarely went hungry and their victual-stores were much envied by the guardians on the south side of the lake. He had no intention of sharing any surplus with the guardians, or even trading with them.

Although they'd shown little interest in the War Memorial recently, they were still a strong force close by and he had to keep a constant eye on them in case skirmishes flared once more. Fundamentally he hoped conditions would eventually get so tough for the guardians that they'd simply 'bugger off' somewhere else.

At suppertime everyone gathered in the mess tent where the single lieutenants ate at three long trestle-tables laid out in an 'E' shape with the centre stroke missing. All Colonel Charlie's personnel followed a duty roster assigning cooking, cleaning and standing guard in rotation. The food was simple, but well prepared and there was ample for everyone. Raven and her friends sat at places of honour on the top table with Colonel Charlie.

The mess supplied a tolerable wine and, after a toast to 'sovereign & country' — although whoever and whatever that might be remained unclear -- they all tucked in. The married lieutenants and their children normally ate meals privately, but they all came to the mess-tent to meet the strangers. They were friendly, courteous and impeccably behaved, but genuinely curious about where their visitors had come from. More to the point, they were curious to know where their guests intended to go next and what they proposed to do there.

'We came in search of knowledge,' Raven explained solemnly, which she had to admit sounded a bit ethereal, 'and, I for one don't intend to go home without it.'

'You have a battle plan ..?' the colonel quizzed.

'Well ... not as such ... not just yet ...'

'You need a plan, you know. First principle of war — selection and maintenance of the aim, and all that.'

'That's easy. We've got to get back inside the library and see what's in there.'

'You won't be able to do that with those bally dog-lovers hanging around.'

'It seems not.'

'You'll need someone to see 'em off.'

Raven noticed the colonel was looking particularly sly at this stage.

'Do you have anyone in mind, Colonel?'

'Possibly. It's been a while since we've been on serious manoeuvres.'

He stood and addressed his subordinates.

'Ladies and gentlemen, we have been called upon to assist these young people, and I believe it behoves us all to do our duty. I plan to conduct a raid to this end. Be upstanding. I give you a toast.'

They all stood and raised their cups.

'A raid!' Colonel Charlie declared.

'A raid!' the company chorused in response as they pounded the table-top with their fists.

'A raid it is then,' the colonel iterated with a smile.

Raven smiled in return. Even if there was a grudging truce at present, it was obvious the guardians and Colonel Charlie's militia harboured a festering feud. She was pretty certain the colonel was itching for a fight and she'd arrived at just the right time to give him an excuse to start one. It seemed negotiation wasn't an option and the troops were every bit as feisty as their gung-ho commander.

Chapter 23 — War Footing

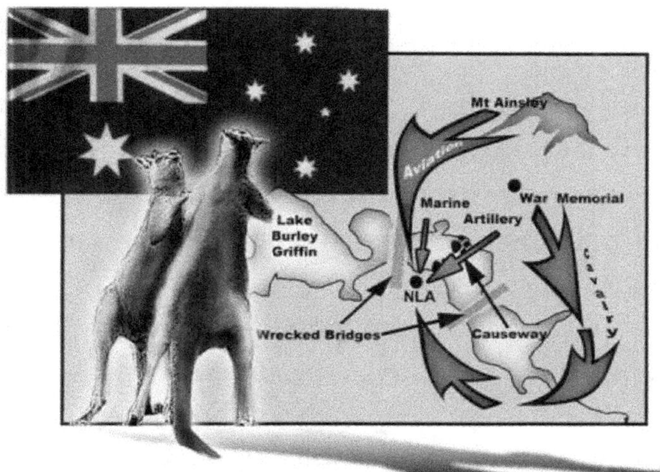

aven and Wombat were assigned to a tent while Thornton and Wedge shared another. At sundown the lieutenants formed three ranks in front of the flagstaff before a bugler played *Last Post* as the standard was lowered. The militia snapped to attention and saluted the descending flag. It was a haunting and moving ceremony and there was no doubt that the militia set great store by it.

Raven said goodnight to her brother who was soon snoring soundly, but she lay awake for a time thinking of the day's adventure that had bordered on surreal. She liked Colonel Charlie even if she thought he was crazy, or perhaps mildly eccentric was a kinder way of looking at it. She'd asked Lieutenant Percy why the colonel spoke so peculiarly. Percy explained the CO liked to read from a cache of ancient magazines that had been preserved in the War Memorial archives. They featured characters like Colonel Blimp, Captain James Bigglesworth and Pilot Officer Prune. Charlie had picked up their mannerisms. Percy assured her that the rest of the militia were quite normal, although she was far from convinced. From a purely literary standpoint, she did admire the fact that they'd preserved the publications for so long. She knew how hard that was.

Raven understood the militia company acted as they did because it was what they'd been taught by preceding generations, even if the precise reasons why had been lost. However bizarre, the guardians' and militia's positions were exactly the same -- except for the savage dogs of course.

With so many muddled thoughts racing through her mind, she finally fell asleep. For the first time since leaving Mactown she felt totally secure and slept deeply throughout the night. *Reveille* sounded at daybreak and Raven quickly revised her opinion of bugle calls. She didn't often feel like sleeping in, but that morning was an exception only to be ruined by a wretched trumpet.

Raven was delighted to discover that hot water was available. The militia had salvaged several copper cauldrons from the old Duntroon training academy nearby. One boiler stood beside the mess tent filled with simmering water heated over a slow fire. Wombat was intrigued by the clever device they'd utilised to hand pump water via a pipe. A wooden shower head with holes drilled through it was attached to the pipe and stood about head-high. The water cooled sufficiently en route to provide a wonderful, refreshingly warm shower that lasted as long as you were prepared to crank the pump handle.

Raven did justice to a steak-and-egg breakfast washed down with strong tea. It seemed every community had worked out how to substitute teas with some herbal brew or another – they varied and the militia's recipe was particularly tasty and refreshing. Now

Raven felt she was ready to take on any number of dog-supported guardians.

Once the mess tables were clear, Colonel Charlie held a council-of-war aimed at inflicting as much mischief among the guardians as possible. He had some surprises in store for Raven and her companions as well.

'First off — the aim,' he declared, slapping his swagger stick against the table top.

Raven stared at him blankly.

'What do you hope to achieve?' Colonel Charlie said after a meaningful pause.

'We want to get as many books about electricity out of the library as we can,' Wombat came to her rescue.

'Have you any idea how many are there?' the colonel asked.

'No.'

"Do you know how or where they are stored?'

'No.'

'Do you know how big they are?'

'No.'

'... or how much they weigh?'

'No.'

'Do they contain appropriate and useful data?'

'Don't know.'

'Is the effort-reward ratio viable?'

'I beg your pardon?'

'Is it worth the *risk*?'

'We hope so,' Raven said.

'You can see they've really thought this through,' Thornton grinned.

It does sound a bit lame when you put it like that, Raven thought, *and I reckoned Colonel Charlie was bonkers.*

'You're not part of this enterprise, I take it?' the colonel eyed Thornton.

'Just their guide to Canberra Forest, that's all,' the gatherer replied definitely.

Colonel Charlie considered the situation for a moment while Raven fretted that he'd dismiss the whole notion out of hand. She had to face the fact that they didn't have much of an idea at all. To her surprise he asked Lieutenant Joyce to lay out a map on the trestle. It showed the lake and both shorelines as well as the surrounding terrain.

'The guardians — or at least their dogs — took a beating yesterday, so they'll be licking their wounds. This will be a good opportunity to kick 'em while they're down,' Colonel Charlie said with relish.

'Won't that have made them wary?' Wedge ventured.

'Then we'd better take 'em by surprise. Here's the plan and afterwards we'll take a quick tour and I'll show you some of the hardware we'll need to carry it out. Joyce, my dear girl, you'll lead the cavalry. We'll need all mounts prepped and ready by 0-six hundred tomorrow. Percy, you'll command the artillery batteries as usual. Caroline, you're OIC amphibious ops and Denis will handle aviation of course.'

Cavalry? Raven thought.

Artillery? Wedge wondered.

Amphibious Ops? Thornton pondered.

Aviation? Wombat marvelled.

Meanwhile Colonel Charlie outlined his battle plan. Timing was crucial. Each team leader was issued with a Seiko, clockwork analogue watch, which they synchronised to make sure there were no mistakes. Charlie explained the watches were treasured artefacts and only used on vital missions. Raven was comforted to know that he considered their operation to be so important. With an air of self-importance, Wombat synchronised his pocket watch with the others and was pleased to note it had kept exceptionally accurate time over the years.

*

The conference lasted over two hours in the end as they huddled around the chart and ironed out details. Colonel Charlie dumped a box full of coloured blocks onto the map and started moving them around. Raven saw they represented his force. Different colours indicated the different roles everyone was to play.

'The main elements are surprise, diversion, decoy and ruse,' he explained.

'I know what you mean,' Wedge agreed. 'When I was a kid a travelling troupe came to town. While we were watching their magic show some of the buggers slipped around behind us and nicked anything that wasn't tied down.'

'Same principle exactly, dear boy,' the colonel beamed.

'I suppose we *are* planning to nick their books,' Wombat conceded.

'The books aren't theirs,' Raven insisted. 'The library should be for everyone's use.'

'*Should*, the most over-used and useless word in our language,' Thornton muttered. 'There is only "what *is*" and "what isn't". *Should* is just a pipe dream.'

Raven stood admonished, glaring at him.

Once they'd settled on a plan, Colonel Charlie dismissed his lieutenants. Percy immediately assembled his gun crews and they busied themselves around the catapults. Joyce gathered her team, which included Wedge, and headed for the stock pens. Caroline disappeared into the woodland beside the shore. Thornton and a group of four enthusiastic assistants accompanied her. The colonel, Denis, Raven and Wombat packed water canteens and lunch before hiking up a trail to Mt Ainslie's peak. Mt Ainslie lay north of the War Memorial via a track that ran for about three kilometres to the summit. Although steep at times, it was an easy enough trek for fit people.

When they reached the top the view was spectacular and they clearly saw the NLA peeking out among the treetops.

'There is our target,' Colonel Charlie observed confidently.

'It's a long way off,' Wombat observed. 'Haven't we come in the wrong direction?'

The colonel smiled and led the way to a shelter camouflaged with felled trees and scrub. Together they pulled away the undergrowth and revealed two glistening metal frames. They were an impressive size, spanning close to ten metres. Another sleek, impossibly light frame was bolted beneath each wing section. Once clear of the shelter, Denis retrieved two packs containing large sheets of fabric that neither Wombat nor Raven could identify. He also opened some cases containing coiled cables, metal fasteners, washers, clamps and hand tools.

'These little babies will get us across in no time and no one will be expecting us.'

'How ..?' Raven was starting to feel decidedly uncomfortable.

'Why fly, my dear. These are hang-gliders,' the colonel declared. 'We'll soar with eagles!'

'Sick,' Wombat purred as the colour drained from Raven's face.

They spent the rest of the day preparing the hang-gliders. Even though Colonel Charlie and Lieutenant Denis were experts, assembling the gliders was tricky. Each piece of the frame had to be carefully secured and the cables correctly attached. The sheeting wasn't a single piece of material, but dozens of small pieces neatly stitched into a gigantic triangular aerofoil.

'Wear and tear, I'm afraid,' Colonel Charlie said with regret, 'so we have to repair the wings when they're damaged.'

Damaged? Raven looked aghast.

'Not to worry, old girl,' Colonel Charlie said, 'our sail-makers have done a sterling job.'

'I noticed Wedge and Thornton managed to get themselves assigned to ground duties,' Raven observed suspiciously.

'It's a matter of weight,' Denis said. 'You two are the lightest and the ones who want to get into the library and hopefully know what you're looking for. Don't worry their job will be diversion and recovery. They'll be in the thick of it and we can't manage without them.'

'How did you make these machines?' Wombat asked.

'We didn't,' Denis replied. 'My great-grandad found them stashed in a cave at some cliffs on the coast when we were harvesting oil-balls. It took a while to figure out how it all worked, but they were flying by the time I was old enough to take an interest.'

'Denis has been our airborne specialist ever since,' Colonel Charlie beamed. 'Great instructor and even taught me how to fly as well.'

*

While Raven and Wombat explored the wonders of aviation, Wedge spent most of the day with Lieutenant Joyce arming and provisioning her cavalry contingent. The troop consisted of twenty riders who prepared for a night away from base. Each trooper was armed with a lance and three-quarter-metre-long cudgel supplemented by optional knives and axes.

'We should be able to bust a few heads with this lot,' Wedge observed.

Lieutenant Joyce frowned.

'I don't think you've quite grasped the concept, sweetie. Our job isn't to actually kill anyone,' she explained. 'Sorry to disappoint you, but our task is to create mayhem and contain the dogs.'

'Stop the guardians releasing them ..?' Wedge ventured.

'Precisely.'

'How many guardians are there?'

'I haven't got the foggiest notion,' she replied cheerfully.

Well, so much for reconnaissance.

From what Wedge gathered the entire militia strength was no more than fifty combatants. Nearly half were cavalry which didn't leave many left over, although they all bristled with weapons and seemed well trained. The guardians on the other hand had so far proved to be poor warriors who relied on their dogs. But even the finest soldiers could be overwhelmed by sheer numbers. Colonel Charlie had hinted that times were tough on the south bank, so

292

how many guardians could there be? Just keep the dogs in their pens and the whole operation would be a pushover.

Wedge rode beside Lieutenant Joyce with the troopers filing behind in two ranks. She led the column east behind the War Memorial, ensuring they remained invisible from prying eyes south of Lake Burley Griffin. Once clear of the lake they travelled some kilometres before finding a suitable site to ford the Molonglo River. They needed to bivouac close enough to be effective the following day, but with enough distance to remain undetected.

'No fire, I'm afraid,' Joyce said. 'Just dried beef jerky, damper and fruit for rations.'

'I've had worse,' Wedge said.

Gender equality was encouraged in the militia and the other lieutenants deferred to Joyce without hesitation. Colonel Charlie had a knack of selecting those most able to lead, but as all his troops were lieutenants, Wedge wasn't sure how that worked. Maybe the ranks were just honorary.

Joyce was in her early twenties, yet she led the cavalry with confidence and efficiency from what Wedge saw. She selected a campsite where the troopers busied themselves unsaddling the horses and seeing to their comfort before settling down themselves. Wedge found a spot under a large oak and arranged his kit into a comfortable bed. He'd kept his bow and hunting knife, but commandeered one of the cavalry clubs. He decided against a lance as he had no idea how to use it and would more than likely wind up stabbing himself in the foot with it.

Once her people were settled, Joyce brought Wedge a steaming cuppa.

'Mind if I join you?' she asked.

'You're the boss,' he said, which he realised sounded terse and ungracious. 'Sorry. Please sit down. Thanks for the tea.'

She didn't seem particularly offended and smiled as she handed him the cup. She asked him about Emu Creek and Mactown while he wanted to know all about the militia's history. After dark Lieutenant Joyce left to organise the guard roster, but to Wedge's surprise she returned once she'd made the arrangements. At night with no firelight, privacy was assured and Joyce left Wedge in no doubt about her intentions.

'You're a good looking boy, you know,' she purred in his ear as she stroked his thigh.

'Um ... shouldn't we be getting some sleep,' Wedge stammered inadequately. 'Big day tomorrow.'

'Nonsense, it may be dark, but it's still early. There'll be plenty of time for sleep later, especially if you're in a relaxed frame of mind — and I know what *relaxes* me ...'

'But ... I'm ... sort of ...' *think quick Wedge*, '... engaged ...'

'What? You're far too young for that sort of nonsense. It's that little scrubber, Raven, isn't it?

'Well ...'

'She's just a girl. What you need is a *woman!*'

'But a promise is a promise,' Wedge lied, '...and she's not a scrubber ...'

'Whatever.'

The situation could have gone badly in any number of directions around then. Lieutenant Joyce apparently took her passion as seriously as leading the cavalry. There was no doubt she was a beautiful woman with a striking figure and Wedge would have certainly been punching above his weight had the situation gone further. Fortunately one of Joyce's subordinates came to the rescue.

In her ardour, Joyce had raised her voice louder than she'd wanted and it travelled through the trees into the night. The militia all knew Joyce was a woman of amorous zeal when she was in the mood and it was no secret she'd set her sights on the handsome young stranger. But he was just so young and the timing was doubtlessly bad. Subsequently they delegated one of their female members to defuse the situation.

'Lieutenant Joyce,' she called from a discreet distance. 'We need to go over a few details for tomorrow, if you don't mind.'

It all sounded pretty lame, but Wedge was off the hook and Joyce had saved face, so no harm had been done. When Joyce had gone the young woman who'd saved the day remained and Wedge was concerned she might take the leader's place, but that wasn't the case.

'I'm sorry, I didn't mean to offend her,' Wedge said, realising how confusing women were. He really needed to pay more attention to females, especially when they were in a frisky frame of mind.

'Don't worry,' the trooper assured him, 'she'll have forgotten all about it in the morning and it'll be business as usual.'

'*Hell hath no fury like a woman scorned,*' he quoted from somewhere.

'Just as well no one believes in hell anymore then,' the young woman smiled and disappeared into the night, leaving Wedge to sleep as best he could.

*

Thornton and Lieutenant Caroline spent the afternoon preparing the waterborne element of the operation. The militia had several watercraft hidden in the forest, but handy to shore. They ranged from crude rafts to dugout canoes and small sailing boats. Caroline fretted over what equipment would serve best. Thornton was of little help there as his sailing experience was limited. Their four assistants offered advice until they settled on two sail boats and rafts secured by towlines.

'We need a test run,' Thornton ventured.

'The guardians will spot us from the south shore,' Caroline warned.

'Yeah, but they won't have any idea what we're up to — if anything at all.'

It was just as well Caroline took Thornton's advice because the rafts proved difficult to tow as their bows tended to cut under the water surface and bring the towing yachts to a halt. They were stumped for a while. They needed storage room for their mission, but the single hull boats were simply too small.

'What about strapping two boats together,' someone suggested, but that was impractical as they didn't have the materials to construct a catamaran from two hulls. Their rope wasn't strong enough and the hulls kept pulling apart. Eventually Thornton came up with a compromise using two of the sailboats with a canoe attached to each by poles. The canoes acted as outriggers while the poles provided just the cargo space they needed.

The work wasn't finished until after dark. While the other lieutenants returned to the mess tent Caroline and Thornton conducted one last inspection by torch-light.

'That outrigger design was a clever idea of yours considering you're a land lubber,' Caroline commented.

'Yep, that's me,' Thornton grinned, 'a right clever fellow.'

'You might even say a right smart arse,' she replied.

Like Lieutenant Joyce, Caroline had taken a fancy to the new-guy-in-town. Thornton was a man who exploited his luck where he found it and harboured none of Wedge's misgivings, but then he'd had a lot more experience.

*

So the land, sea and air elements of the operation were in place. Sentries were posted and the militia hunkered down for the night. Raven and Wombat sat up late admiring the view from Mt Ainslie under a full moon.

'The moon is really beautiful, isn't it?' Raven sighed.

'Yeah I guess so,' Wombat replied, 'but I kinda miss *The Spark*-show.'

'Oh, I don't know,' she replied. 'It all seems so much calmer now.'

They chatted on for a while until the dropping temperature drove them into their bedrolls.

Chapter 24 — Strike Force Go

At daybreak Lieutenant Percy led his team to the shoreline. The previous evening they had positioned their two large catapults as close to the water as possible. The ballista was ineffective at long range, so Percy needed to bring up his big guns. These were counterweight trebuchets that had been constructed from diagrams and blueprints found in the War Memorial archives. Although they were much smaller than the medieval originals that weighed tonnes, they still stood three metres tall and could hurl a ten kilogram missile across the lake. A cart loaded with oil-balls stood beside each catapult while a pile of rocks, metal, shattered masonry, and other suitable material was stacked between them. Two more heaps of what appeared to be hessian sacks had been placed beside each catapult and a pile of spare sacks lay on the grass nearby.

Percy checked his watch for the umpteenth time as the sun cracked past the eastern Gourock Ranges. He knew Lieutenant Joyce's cavalry would arrive soon. He hoped the watch would be superfluous and he'd actually be able to spot the mounted unit, but a dawn mist drifted over the lake and that could hang around half the morning if the weather conditions were right.

*

Joyce mustered her cavalry in the pre-dawn gloom. She woke Wedge by unceremoniously kicking his foot accompanied by a glare that suggested *your-loss-mate* and pretty much ignored him after that. Not that Wedge needed instructions. He was an expert horseman and could wield a club with the best of them. After consulting her watch, Joyce ordered the troop to mount. They rode from the camp in silence. Wedge decided to join the rear guard and keep out of her way.

They followed the shoreline at a walk until they reached abeam the War Memorial. No orders were necessary, the cavalry simply followed Lieutenant Joyce's lead. They hugged the bank clear of the tree line because they needed to be visible from the northern shore. A bugler rode beside Joyce ready to blow the command on her orders. The other contingents would act when they saw the riders or heard the bugle call. The shallow mist still hung a metre above the lake. Only the clatter of hoof-beats and jingling harnesses disturbed the morning calm.

*

Lieutenant Caroline was looking particularly flushed and pleased with herself when she led Thornton and her crews to the lake shore. Using log rollers, they pushed converted outriggers to the water's edge. The vessels were lightweight and manoeuvring them into the lake was easy enough. Although a single person could handle the craft if required, each boat carried a crew of three, in case replacements were needed. Also a little extra combat strength might come in handy if they ran into trouble.

The mist was an advantage for the mariners as they'd stay temporarily hidden from the southern shore. Unfortunately the wind was calm and they'd have to resort to paddle-power.

'We go as soon as the fun starts,' she explained, rather unnecessarily in Thornton's opinion because they'd been over the plan dozens of times.

*

Colonel Charlie and Lieutenant Denis made last minute pre-flight checks to their aircraft and, after some wire-pulling and shaking the frames, they finally seemed satisfied. A zephyr blew in from the southeast that pleased both aviators. Initially Denis had been concerned about the mist that would make landing hazardous, but from his vantage point, he saw the wind would soon clear the fog away. There was another equally important element to the morning breeze.

'Just the job,' Denis beamed. 'Enough headwind to gets us airborne without any turbulence. Super!'

There were a few different harnesses available to attach to the frame. Denis chose a twin bench alternative rather like a swing seat.

'Bit more drag,' he opined, 'but a lot easier to manage.'

Colonel Charlie nodded sagely, but Raven got the impression he'd go along with whatever his trusty lieutenant said. Charlie knew how to delegate and then leave his subordinates to it. It was a lesson many commanders hadn't learnt to their regret. From her reading, a fellow called George Custer sprang to Raven's mind.

Charlie and Denis helped Raven and Wombat onto the seats and secured them by a single lap strap. The breeze caused the wing fabric to flutter, which was alarming at first until Denis explained it was quite normal. Wombat pointed out that nothing about aviation was normal in his view. Denis strapped himself next to Wombat and Charlie took charge of Raven's hang-glider. Perching half crouched with their feet planted on the ground was uncomfortable and a little nerve-racking as the aircraft bucked in the rising wind. Once again Denis assured them everything was fine.

Colonel Charlie peered through a set of small binoculars before nodding with satisfaction. They shuffled to the edge of a cleared area that ran gently downhill for about ten metres before dropping away sharply. Other than a few tracks and that one cleared area, the rest of Mount Ainslie was covered with thick bush, so there was only a single takeoff runway available.

'Percy's on the move and I can see stirring on the south bank. Any minute now, chaps. Stand by.'

*

Percy's trebuchets now stood loaded and cranked for firing. The artillerymen had spent the previous afternoon preparing their ammunition. The hessian sacks were half-filled with a mixture of rubble and oil balls. Percy had stuffed oil-soaked, gunpowder-infused ropes into the sacks with half a metre protruding before tying each bag tightly with twine. The fuse timing was not an exact science and Percy hoped he'd estimated correctly. He held a flaming torch while his gun-commanders stood beside their weapons awaiting his command.

At last he spotted a glint of metal through his binoculars. The riders emerged from a shallow mist and moved cautiously westwards.

'Prepare to fire,' Percy ordered.

The trebuchets were named *Bluey* and *Curly* after two WWII cartoon characters featured in Colonel Charlie's collection of service magazines. Right now the operation relied on Percy's judgement.

He lit the first fuse and the rope spluttered into life.

'Fire *Bluey*!' he yelled.

The gunners released the mechanism and the trebuchet's arm rattled into life and swung deceptively languidly through its arc driven by a whirring counterweight. As the arm reached the end of its travel the bomb was flung skywards into a steep trajectory. No sooner had the ammunition been discharged when the gun crews began cranking the arm back to the loading position. Percy wasted no time and immediately ignited the second fuse.

'Fire *Curly*!'

Another bomb hurtled into the air.

*

A faint clatter floated across the lake as the catapults swung into action. Joyce pointed to the sky where two specks tumbled towards the shore. The balls grew in size as they approached at an apparently slow rate. But it was only an illusion.

Seconds before impact their true speed was evident. Then they smashed into the forest surrounding the library. Percy's fuses were perfectly timed and burnt inside the sacks at the instant the oil balls smashed to earth. The sacks burst open exploding their lethal missiles just as the oil spewed into a thin mist and erupted into flames.

The result was a bombload of vicious fireballs that leapt through the foliage smashing anything in their path, leaving a trail of blazing hotspots. The first bombs had barely dissipated when *Bluey* and *Curly* slammed a second salvo across the lake. The effect was immediate. Guardians spewed from their posts in and around the library. Most were still muggy with sleep and befuddled by the chaos swirling around them.

'Party time,' Lieutenant Joyce said. 'Sound the charge.'

'Forward!' she screamed as the bugle blared in her ears and the cavalry lurched into attack.

As the library came into view the troop broke into a full gallop. As they thundered towards the ruined building guardians erupted all around them. Many of them had dived for cover behind trees but re-emerged with the intent of neutralising any intruders. Joyce led the riders up the library steps. Hooves clattered against decaying, crumbling concrete. The cavalry drove the guardians from the steps into the forest, which wasn't ideal terrain for galloping horses.

Only a few dogs accompanied their handlers and they quickly fell to the lances. Many guardians wisely scattered into the woods, but a couple of courageous fellows tried to fight back only to be silenced by flaying clubs. Those who ran weren't actually cowardly, but seeking a tactical advantage that they found among the trees. A dozen guardians leapt into the lower branches of a massive oak, scrambled into its foliage and lay hidden. As the militia rode past they dropped from the branches and unhorsed a pair of riders. They tumbled to the ground, but quickly jumped to their feet brandishing their weapons. The downed horsemen then had to rely on clubs, axes and knives to fend off the enemy on foot.

As yet there was no sign of any more dogs, but Wedge spotted the bearded guardian chief as he bolted from the library. Wedge was convinced he'd head to wherever the hounds were kennelled and release them, causing mayhem. The cavalry troop had broken into squads of two or three riders that were now more vulnerable to canine attack. Trusting his hunch, Wedge followed the guardian leader. His prime task was to stop him taking control. The guardians were much easier to deal with leaderless.

Around him, Wedge heard the hostile uproar of the conflict. Screams filled the forest as foes met in combat. It was impossible to see anyone or anything in the chaos among the trees. Joyce rode up with her bugler beside her. She'd appeared from nowhere and glared at him. Wedge noticed she'd abandoned her lance and carried a club tipped red with blood.

So much for, 'our job isn't to actually kill anyone', eh Joycey girl.

'That bloke,' Wedge yelled, pointing after the bearded guardian. 'He's their boss. I reckon he's going for the dogs. I've got to stop him.'

'I'll come with you, you might need help.'

They plunged through the forest after their prey.

*

'Time to hit the surf,' Lieutenant Caroline said as she observed the first bomb flying across the lake.

305

The crews clambered aboard, hoisting the sails to take advantage of the freshening wind. They paddled to augment their progress as the outriggers glided across the surface into the swirling mist.

*

'Now it's our turn,' Colonel Charlie announced with relish. 'Tallyho!'

Tallyho?

Raven had no time to reflect further. She squealed as Charlie pushed forward and she was forced to race along with him. Her legs scurried frantically as they were carried forward by the glider's momentum. Denis and Wombat followed in close formation.

'Sick!' she heard Wombat call with glee.

They raced pell-mell across the cleared area. The drop loomed up with alarming speed and just as Raven was sure they'd plunge into the cliff to be impaled on the trees below, the hang-gliders' wings filled, sweeping them skywards. Raven's stomach was still back somewhere on the hilltop.

Her sensational cocktail was a blend of exhilaration, awe, pure joy and abject fear as the hang-glider soared across the lake. The speed at which they were plucked upwards was staggering. She glanced across to Charlie who beamed with joy. He controlled the plane with an aluminium bar that moved forward, back and from side to side. Raven saw that the colonel only needed to move the bar slightly to change the glider's course.

'Super, don't you think?' he cried, but Raven was too breathless to respond although Wombat produced a few whoops from behind her.

'The boats are away,' Charlie reported, although Raven didn't spot them, 'and good old Percy's banging away with his artillery. Let's hope the cavalry can clear a path for us. Don't want to run into any unpleasant surprises, do we?'

The gliders swept across the lake, quickly overtaking the outriggers. Raven cast her eyes down to her feet dangling above two hundred metres of emptiness. Although unnerving at first, she felt better when she simply stared ahead. The view was magnificent and more like looking from a hill top, which gave her some comfort. Indeed she was just beginning to enjoy the ride when Colonel Charlie dipped the glider's nose forward and banked gently to line up on a clear area between the NLA and the lake shore.

'When we land, just keep pace with the glider,' Charlie instructed. 'Don't try to slow down or you'll fall on your face. The glider will pull up at its own pace.'

The ground rushed towards them. Raven gasped and was sure they'd crash, but at the last moment Charlie pushed the control bar forward. The glider reared, slowing almost to a hover and arresting the descent rate so their feet gently touched the ground at a fast walking pace. As he'd predicted the drag on the sail brought the craft to a gentle stop leaving Raven with a feeling of deep regret that the flight was all over.

Denis and Wombat arrived seconds later in another copybook landing. They quickly released the seatbelts. Due to weight restrictions, they only carried a knife each for protection and felt extremely vulnerable in enemy territory. Fortunately there was no sign of the guardians.

'Looks like Joyce's crew drove 'em off,' Charlie assayed with satisfaction. 'You start dismantling the rigs, Denis. We'll see what's in this bally old library.'

'Reinforcements aren't far off,' Denis reported pointing to the outriggers that had cleared the mist about half way across the lake.

'Okay, but let's get going before we lose the element of surprise.'

The concept of not using the gliders at all had been raised at the planning stage. The boats were not far behind, but Charlie thought even a few minutes might be the difference between success and failure. So he opted for an airborne assault, with the outriggers as backup and transport to recover the gliders and carry any library booty back to the north shoreline. The boat crews were kept small to allow for extra passengers on the return voyage. Raven was sure Colonel Charlie just wanted to go flying anyway.

Although they were only lightly armed, Charlie, Raven and Wombat wasted no time dashing up the library steps, disappearing inside in seconds. Denis started to dismantle the gliders into components small enough to carry on the outriggers. The sails were the hardest to deal with because they billowed in the breeze and he had no one to hold them down while he attempted to roll them up. He also had to keep a sharp lookout for any prowling guardians.

While help was on the way, it seemed to take ages. Finally the outriggers nudged the bank and Thornton leapt ashore. He was armed to the teeth with a bow, arrow, club and his staff. He dashed past Denis, leaving Caroline and her crew to help the pilot pack his gliders into manageable sections and load them aboard the escape craft.

Meanwhile Raven, Wombat and Colonel Charlie had charged up the steps, around the outer wall and towards the main entrance. No one challenged them and, although they heard the yells and clatter of battle nearby, they saw nothing of the action. One unconscious guardian was the only evidence of conflict, so the trio stalked through the portico into the atrium.

'What's the meaning of this?' the librarian challenged.

She was seated at her foyer desk with the ledger open on the desk before her, seemingly oblivious of the bedlam unfolding on her doorstep.

'This is highly inappropriate and quite unacceptable!'

Chapter 25 — Out on Loan

'Oh yeah, and what are you going to do about it?' Raven demanded. 'Your bully-boys are all preoccupied in case you haven't noticed.'

'I am office staff,' the librarian replied primly. 'I do not concern myself with the goings-on of outdoor personnel.'

'Fine by me,' Raven said. 'Now you can start by doing your job and serve the public ...'

'... That is quite out of the question. We've been over that before.'

'Just show us where the freaking books on electrics are,' Wombat said, 'before Raven here does something you'll regret.'

But the librarian was adamant. She remained firmly in her seat with her arms crossed and didn't seem inclined to budge for anyone.

'We don't have time for this,' Raven hissed, 'we'll look for ourselves. We're good readers, you know.'

'I don't doubt it,' the librarian said smugly, but offered no more information.

They hurried past her through an open door way and stopped dead in their tracks. The sight was staggering. Canyons of book shelves spread out before them. Each shelf held hundreds of books and each stack held maybe a dozen shelves. There was room for a thousand Mactown book-repositories in the library's maw.

'Oh, and that's just one room of many,' the librarian called over her shoulder.

'This is hopeless,' Raven cried, 'we'll never find anything in this lot.'

'And you don't have a lot of time,' Colonel Charlie reminded her just as Thornton dashed through the entrance hall.

'How's it going?' he asked.

'Nowhere,' Raven replied. 'Miss Brick-Wall here refuses to show us where the books are.'

'Ms ...' the librarian clarified.

Thornton looked around and pulled a large book from the nearest shelf. He then grabbed one of the burning torches that illuminated the chambers.

'Listen lady,' he growled holding the volume just above the flames. 'Show 'em what they want to see or I'll toast your precious tome.'

'You wouldn't dare!'

'Wouldn't I though?'

Thornton torched the book.

The librarian screamed and flung herself at him in a fury. She was surprisingly strong for a small woman, but she was in a vicious mood. Thornton fended her off then grabbed her, managing to control her in a bear hug. Her arms were restricted, but her legs flayed about and connected with Thornton's shin. He yelped and dropped her, but held onto one of her wrists. He slapped her once and then all resistance ceased. He hadn't hit the librarian hard, but she was so startled she was unable to function.

'That ... that ... was ... *inappropriate* ...' she stammered.

'Now listen,' Thornton warned, 'I'm not much in favour of hitting females, but woman, you're trying my patience. Tell us what we want to know or I'll burn down the whole, dammed place.'

'Then you won't find what you want?' the librarian said, regaining some of her stubbornness.'

'I reckon it won't bother me as much as you.'

'Please,' Raven said. 'I promise we'll return the books when we've finished.'

'I suppose I have no choice at the hands of you hooligans,' the librarian sulked, but showed them to a wall panel where several sheets of paper were placed. They were entitled *Library of Congress Classification System*. It was an alphabetical code and under *TK* they found *Electrical Engineering* and *Electronics*. After a little more duress from Thornton the librarian led them to the shelves that contained over a thousand books and journals on the subject.

'Where do we start?' Wombat asked.

'Why not: *Electronics — Circuits & Systems*, by Owen Bishop,' Thornton said, pulling a volume from the shelf.

'As good a place as any,' Wombat agreed.

'We don't have time to browse. Let's get 'em loaded,' Colonel Charlie said. 'Speed is of the essence, you know.'

As no one else had any idea which titles were best either, they simply grabbed the closest. They carried the books, pamphlets and journals in roughly half-dozen lots. By the time they reached the boats Denis had loaded the hang-gliders onto the out-riggers and was busily securing them with rope. Raven dumped her collection of books into the hull of the closest boat and dashed for another load.

They finished their second trip and returned for a third with Denis and Caroline's lieutenants who'd secured the hang-gliders. Raven deposited her load and led the way back. Wombat and the colonel followed so they now formed a trail moving back and forth, rather than a single unit. Raven met Thornton as she entered atrium. He still had the librarian firmly in hand, although she seemed subdued and resigned to her library's violation. Thornton had frog-marched her back to her desk and ordered her to stay put or he'd throttle her. Although visibly seething with rage, she obeyed him.

'What do you want to do with her?' Thornton asked with a little too much relish in Raven's opinion.

'Just leave her and lend a hand. I reckon she's quiet enough now.'

'You stay there, lady,' he said between clenched teeth, 'or I'll really do something *inappropriate!* Understand?'

She nodded and slumped into her chair.

As Colonel Charlie and Wombat raced up the library steps they heard the bugler's call from the woods.

'That's recall,' Colonel Charlie said, 'the cavalry is on the way back.'

'Is that good?' Wombat asked.

'Either they've secured the area, or they've run into trouble.'

As he spoke Wedge came thundering through the woods while other riders galloped from the trees, reforming in front of the library. Lieutenant Joyce shared Wedge's horse, riding behind him with her arms wrapped tightly around his waist.

'Time to withdraw, I believe, Colonel,' Joyce panted. 'We might have bitten off more than we can chew.'

*

While Raven and Wombat flew in and were occupied at the library, Wedge, Lieutenant Joyce and her bugler had dismounted and led their brumbies through the trees. Joyce ordered the bugler to sound recall. Answering the summons, riders appeared in seconds and fell in behind their leader who still followed the chief guardian. They saw other shadows darting past tree trunks -- more guardians no doubt. The cloaked figures had recovered from the first onslaught and made an orderly retreat, rallying towards their principal. The forest became so dense that the only access was by a track that barely allowed two horsemen to ride abreast. Branches hung low and soon all the cavalry were forced to dismount and lead their animals. They saw the trailing guardians scamper ahead, but the horses prevented Joyce's troop from keeping pace.

After maybe half-a-kilometre the forest opened into a clearing where a ruined building stood squarely in its centre. The building was surrounded by a wooden palisade of sharpened poles, but the entry gate was wide open. Cottages, sheds and barns bordered the stockade. There were signs of cooking fires and laundry flapped on clotheslines, but the villagers had all taken refuge behind the walls. The militia had found the guardians' lair where their families lived -- where they were most vulnerable. To date Colonel Charlie had never investigated the site as he simply had no interest in it, providing the guardians kept to themselves. The same could be said for the *protectors-of-the-word* until Raven and Wombat arrived. That should have led to a *live-and-let-live* ethical dilemma if anyone had taken the trouble to think about it. Wedge remembered Colonel Charlie describing the stand–off as a *cold-war*, whatever that might be.

Dogs bayed ominously from behind the fence so the cavalry mounted and formed a single line across the clearing. They drew their clubs once more, anticipating a stiff fight.

'What do you reckon?' Wedge asked. He rode beside Joyce now as last night's differences seemed forgotten.

'I don't like it,' she replied. 'We don't know how many ruddy dogs they've got and they'll play merry-hell if they get among the horses.'

'Percy's artillery must have thinned them out yesterday, but discretion might be the better part of valour,' Wedge suggested. 'Raven should have had enough time to get all the books she wants by now.'

'Maybe, but I'd love to know what's inside that fort.'

It was as if the guardians had read Joyce's mind. The riders could just make out frenetic movements through the gateway. Then a dozen guardians marched through the portal and formed a group to one side in front of the palisade. Each guardian held a snarling dog on a tight leash. The animals were straining so hard the handlers needed all their strength to restrain them.

'Okay,' Joyce surmised, 'that's not so bad. We can handle a few dogs.'

But as she spoke more guardians streamed from the gate. They kept coming until almost a hundred stood before the gates. They were lined in four straight ranks. Their drill was every bit as polished as Colonel's Charlie's soldiers. To make matters worse the guardians each carried a three metre bamboo pole sloped over their shoulders. The spear-tips were sharpened to a lethal point. The guardian leader stepped in front of his men and moved forward. No orders were given and the guardians simply fell in behind him with well-rehearsed precision. They morphed into a column of three abreast which was exactly the width needed to traverse the forest pathway. The leading rank of guardians lowered their bamboo pikes horizontally, forming a deadly barrier Joyce's cavalry couldn't break through.

'Now that's a different matter,' Joyce said, turning to her column of riders now strung out along the path. 'Fall back,' she cried. 'Reform at the library. Quick as you can.'

That wasn't as easy as it sounded as the trailing riders had to turn their mounts in the most confined space of the track. Initially they manoeuvred in an orderly fashion, but confusion erupted as the middle section of the column jostled for space. And all the time the sound of tramping feet grew louder as the guardians marched on. The dog handlers thankfully brought up the rear. Joyce simply stood her ground facing the oncoming armadillo-like juggernaut.

'Come on!' Wedge roared. 'They're almost on us.'

'We'll never get out of here in time,' Joyce gasped. 'The horses are all bunched up.'

She leapt astride her brumby, thumped her heels into its flanks as it bounded forward straight at the advancing column. The leading guardian was undismayed by Joyce and simply raised his hand. The column halted and immediately fanned into three ranks right across the forest clearing. Then in another expertly practised movement they lowered their pikes so they stuck out two metres ahead of the leading rank. The second and third ranks also presented their pikes, adding an impenetrable barrier to the bristling defence. Joyce's charge may have been futile, but it halted the guardian column sufficiently for her own troops to make an orderly withdrawal.

She figured she'd done enough and wrenched at her brumby's reins, dragging the animal's head around and urging it back to the forest. She'd have been successful, but the horse stumbled as it tried to stay balanced after spinning on its shadow. Its leg snapped and the brumby crashed to the ground with a hideous cry. Joyce was flung from the saddle and tumbled a few metres before coming to a halt. She tried to stand, but she'd twisted her ankle and collapsed after a single step.

She was now totally vulnerable as the guardians resumed their march.

Oh boy, this woman'll be the death of me, Wedge thought as he leapt into the saddle, urging his horse on. The spear-points were only metres from Wedge when he reached Joyce.

'Grab my arm!' he screamed as he leant forward in the saddle. She reacted in a second, staggering to her feet just as Wedge reached her. With vice-like strength borne of desperation she gripped his wrist and forearm with both hands. Although limping badly, she toughed it out and launched herself across the horse's back, landing behind Wedge. She flung her arms around his waist and clung on so hard he could hardly breathe.

Wedge turned the horse, batting away the first bamboo pike with his club. A second point grazed the brumby's flank, but the animal was already speeding away from danger and escaped with little more than a scratch.

'Duck or lose your head!' Wedge yelled as they approached the forest where low branches embraced the pathway. There was no time to dismount and Joyce was useless on foot in any event. Foliage swept over them as they hugged the brumby's back. Often they'd suffer a cruel swipe from a whip-like branch, but they hardly noticed. After one slap in the face too many and, as soon as Wedge thought he was far enough ahead, he reined his horse to a stop. He dismounted and led the horse at a walk so Joyce had time to brush any overhanging branches away. They'd caught up with the rest of the troop anyway, most of whom were still dismounted.

'Those buggers have been studying their military history too,' Joyce panted as they hustled along the track.

'What ..?' Wedge had no idea what she was talking about.

'Old fashion square formation,' Joyce said with a hint of admiration. 'Infantry used it for thousands of years. It's rare that cavalry can bust a square and that lot know it.'

I suppose they have plenty of books to study up on, Wedge thought, looking back to see the guardians enter the forest path with their sinister spear-points gliding inexorably towards him. Fortunately the path widened and the congestion melted as all the riders took to the saddle and galloped away.

'How's your foot?' Wedged asked.

'I won't win a race anytime soon, but I'll be okay on horseback. Thanks for what you did back there, *Sir Galahad*. That took guts.'

'I really must read more,' Wedge said realising Joyce was the second girl who'd called him *Sir Galahad.*

'What?'

'Nothing, it doesn't matter. Let's keep going. The guardians are right on our heels.'

He remounted and noted Joyce didn't waste the opportunity to wrap her arms around him once more. She nestled her cheek into his back.

Women!

When they reached the library the cavalry unit had reformed as the stragglers rejoined them within minutes. They'd suffered cuts and bruises, but the entire troop was accounted for although it appeared they'd inflicted no lethal damage on the enemy either. The guardians had made a speedy withdrawal into the trees and even their sole casualty on the library steps was beginning to stir, moaning as he nursed his throbbing head. Still it'd be some time before he'd be ready to rejoin the fight, so everyone ignored him.

Colonel Charlie, Denis, Wombat and two other lieutenants stood on the steps, but Thornton and Raven were still inside.

'We've got to get out of here,' Joyce reiterated. 'The guardians are close and they're mad as hell.'

'Okay, get all your people back along the bank and cross where you can,' the colonel ordered.

'I'll go in the boats,' Wedge said. 'You'll make better time riding single.'

He dismounted much to Joyce's chagrin, allowing her to take the saddle. *See you later,* she mouthed and blew him a kiss before leading her patrol away.

'Denis, it's back to the boats for us too,' the colonel advised.

'I'll get Raven,' Wombat said disappearing through the portal.

Colonel Charlie and his lieutenants quickly made their way to the boats, but Wedge hesitated.

'I'll wait for the others,' he said. 'Hold a boat for us.'

'As long as I can,' Colonel Charlie warned and he was gone.

What the blazes is keeping them? Wedge wondered in despair just as Thornton and Wombat returned with their arms full of books.

'Where's Raven?' Wedge asked.

'Right here ...' Wombat turned, but Raven wasn't right behind them as he'd thought. 'She was ... Oh, shit ...'

As he spoke the guardians stomped through the trees and once more formed into three bristling ranks at the library steps.

Chapter 26 — Lakeside

Raven scrambled for the last books on the *electronics* shelves. In her haste she dropped several volumes that clattered on the floor. The books' condition after so many years was fragile at best. Pages broke away and some of the binding simply shattered to paper shards or dissolved to dust. Raven knew that handling old books needed special care, yet there was no time for that now. Having spent years tending Mactown's meagre library with such diligence, she felt like a vandal.

And she wasn't the only one ...

The destruction of her precious publications was too much for the librarian to bear. Despite Thornton's dire warning, she'd left her desk when she heard the commotion Raven had caused. She stormed into the chamber and stared in horror as her worst nightmare was realised.

'How could you ..?' she wailed. 'How could you be so wanton? These items are precious ... irreplaceable ... now you see why we must guard them.'

'You said you didn't want the knowledge getting out,' Raven challenged.

'The guardians said that, not me ... I'm a librarian ... it's my duty to protect these works with my life if necessary ...'

That's a switch from the meek-an-mild public servant, Raven thought, but it was all she had time for. The librarian charged with a venomous tirade of curses Raven would have thought impossible coming from such a prissy tongue.

The librarian slammed into Raven, fists flaying with surprising power. The books flew from Raven's arms and she found herself fighting for dear life trading punch-for-punch and kick-for-kick with the literary harpy. The woman screamed hysterically as tears streamed from her eyes.

'This is my life's work ... you've ruined everything ... you common slut ...'

Save your breath in a fight, dearie ... and don't call me a slut!

Punch ... slap ... scratch ... kick ... pinch ... bite ...

Fanatical as she may have been, ultimately the librarian was no match for Raven who had youth, strength, match-practice and street cunning on her side. Finally a hefty thump to the librarian's midriff followed by a slap across her cheek and two nasty boots into her shins sent the woman to her knees. One more blow finished the librarian. She lay sobbing on the library floor.

'I'm sorry,' Raven said panting for breath. 'I'm truly sorry I hurt you, but you started it ...'

'No ... No, I didn't. You did when you barged in here.'

'Fair comment, I guess ... sorry again,' Raven conceded dragging the librarian by her collar and hauling her to her feet. She drew her knife and held it to the woman's throat.

'One wrong move and it's all over,' Raven hissed.

Now, whether she'd actually have carried out that threat was problematic (in fact there was no way she'd have knifed the old girl), but she sounded convincing enough for the librarian to believe her. As they stumbled past the hall desk, for reasons known only to her, the librarian snatched her ledger from the desk and clasped it her chest. Raven shrugged and marched outside where Wombat, Thornton and Wedge faced off the guardian cohort.

'Ah, that's not good ...' Raven muttered.

The guardian ranks were composed of men and women, old and young, including many who were barely in their teens. But so were Wombat and Raven. A murmur rattled through the guardian force as Raven and her hostage appeared. The leader looked genuinely shocked as he saw a rivulet of blood seep from the librarian's neck where Raven had her knife point firmly pressed.

'How dare you ..?' he stammered.

Raven sensed that the fanatical intensity of the guardians was shaken now their librarian was at risk. So she was of importance to them.

'Release her at once,' the leader demanded resuming his loud and pompous tone. 'She must not be harmed.'

'Nor will she providing you get out of our way,' Raven replied.

The guardian leader hesitated as Colonel Charlie and Denis raced back to the steps. That showed commendable courage given that they could have escaped in the boats. Indeed they'd despatched one vessel with Caroline at the helm and all the books on board. She'd taken half her lieutenants with her while the others manned the second boat standing by the shoreline ready to launch instantly. Charlie had instructed Caroline to have Lieutenant Percy lob some more fire-bombs into the guardians and hopefully scatter them, but it looked as if she'd never get there in time. Percy probably didn't have a good enough view to act on his own initiative. The last thing he wanted was the whole operation scuppered by the CO falling victim to friendly fire.

'C'mon, drop that lot and let's get out of her,' the colonel whispered. 'We can outrun this lot to the boat, even if they let the dogs loose.

That might have been a bit optimistic. It was well over two hundred metres to the shore. The dogs were fast and there were also plenty of young fit guardians armed with very long spears. As they hadn't moved since they spotted their librarian, it looked very much like a stalemate to Raven.

At that moment another murmur ran through the guardians. Their ranks parted as a young woman came forward and climbed the steps. Glided might have been a better description. She was about Raven's age, dressed in a simple, flowing white shift. Her waist-long golden hair was adorned with a wreath made of autumn rose blooms. She stepped serenely past Wombat, Thornton and Wedge, acknowledging them with a smile and a slight tilt of her head.

But it was Raven she wished to speak to.

'You can let my mother go now,' the girl said. 'The guardians and I have no wish to harm you. The damage has already been done, and bloodshed will serve no useful purpose. It rarely does.'

Raven simply gaped at the girl.

'Your mother?'

Raven found it hard to believe the librarian could ever have possessed enough passion to become a mother, but who knew what hot blood flowed under that cold exterior. She'd certainly fought like the devil to defend her books.

'Yes,' the girl confirmed. 'Now, if you'd be so kind.'

'Watch it,' Wombat hissed, but Raven released the librarian who sobbed as her daughter placed her arm around her mother's shoulder. The girl inspected the librarian's bruises and eyed Raven suspiciously, but made no comment.

'The ledger is still intact,' the librarian whispered. 'I fought to protect it, but *she* was too strong.'

'You did well, mother,' the girl said softly and beckoned the guardian leader who approached and led the librarian away with some comforting words.

'I wasn't going to pinch that book, honest,' Raven declared.

'I'm so pleased to hear that. Did you have to knock my mother around?'

'I'm sorry and I told her so, but she attacked me first.'

'She defended the ledger.'

'What's so special about it?'

'Why, it's a record of our life here. It is our community diary that records salient events. Births, marriages, deaths, anything newsworthy.'

'Raid from across the lake should get a mention.'

'Quite so.'

'Are you in charge?' Raven asked.

'Only that I'm the librarian-apparent and I think my mother will need a rest after today. So I'll take over sooner than expected.

My name is Destiny and I must ask you to leave those volumes and depart or I will order the guardians to take them from you.'

'I'm Raven. This is my brother Wombat and my friends Wedge and Thornton. You probably know Colonel Charlie and his lieutenants ...'

'I know *of* them,' Destiny replied coolly.

'Well I don't think you can beat them if it comes to a fight. They out-tech and out-tactic your people. Anyway, we only wanted to borrow some books now *The Spark* has returned.'

'*The Spark* ..? Oh, yes I see. What a clever term. We've had some spectacular electrical storms now the heavens are clear, haven't we?'

'You know about electricity then?'

'I read much, as it appears you do. I know humanity depended on the electrical phenomena for every single aspect of their lives. It allowed them untold freedom, but also led to overpopulation, greed, war and abject misery at times and ultimate downfall, had things continued the way they were. The guardians were formed generations ago to prevent that knowledge ever being available again. Do you want the world to return to that chaos?'

'As opposed to *this* chaos?' Raven challenged. 'Don't you want life to be easier?'

'The price is too high to pay.'

'What if we promise not to abuse the power?'

'You can promise what you like, but others won't be so accommodating.'

'Someone, somewhere else will already be working on restoring *The Spark* even if it takes years or maybe centuries.'

'I'm sure that's so, but we don't want any part of it. Now leave those publications and go back across the lake. We don't want further bloodshed, but we cannot permit you to take them.'

It was then that Raven realised Destiny didn't know they'd already purloined a boatload of books. She thought this was all they had and her mother was so upset, she'd not yet mentioned the fact.

'Okay, you win. Put those books down guys, we're out of here.'

What they had was better than nothing and would have to do.

'But ...?' Wombat protested.

'Just do what you're told for once, Wombat,' Raven hissed.

There was something in her tone that made him place the books gently on the steps. The others did the same and followed Raven towards the waiting boat. They'd only covered a few metres towards the shore when they heard uproar from the guardians.

'I guess the old witch just spilt the beans,' Raven surmised, 'come on, *Miss Goody-Two-Shoes* Destiny isn't going to hold them back now.'

They bolted for the boat with the entire guardian company surging after them. Their disciplined formation was lost as they abandoned their unwieldy pikes and raced to obliterate the book thieves. In their rage and indignation the youngest and fittest guardians ran like steroid-pumped athletes. Being robbed was bad enough, but being duped was unforgivable.

The leading guardians were about to overwhelm the fugitives at the shore where they faltered in trying to get on board the escape boat. Hands reached out to grab Raven and Wombat as they clambered onto the vessel's transom. Wedge and Thornton beat off as many as they could, but the sheer numbers were unstoppable. Several younger men dragged Wombat from the boat and then yanked Raven by the arm and she fell into the lake. She staggered to her feet panting for air as more hands grabbed her. Thornton and Wedge were set on by more guardians. Colonel Charlie and Denis used their clubs to fend off another contingent of attackers, but it looked as if they would soon be smothered by the throng. The lieutenants on board tried to launch the boat but more guardians grabbed the hull and held it to the shore.

The lakeside dissolved into a melee of screaming, scratching, kicking, punching humanity all trying to tear each other apart in the most inhuman way possible.

And then the crowd parted.

Lieutenant Joyce and her cavalry ploughed into the fray. The guardians were taken by total surprise, falling to club blows and buffeting brumbies. The charge effectively rolled up the guardians' flank and scattered their main force. Colonel Charlie and the others dealt with the remaining enemy with some well aimed blows.

'Get going, colonel,' Joyce yelled. 'We'll keep 'em busy until you're clear.'

They didn't need to be told twice. Wedge, Raven Thornton and Wombat scrambled aboard while the colonel and Denis shoved off. Caroline's people hoisted the sail and the boat cruised out of harm's way. They stared back to where the cavalry fought desperately to extricate themselves from the surrounding guardians who were recovering their senses. Some were even racing back to the library to rearm with their deadly spears. At that moment the dog handlers released their animals into the mix. They yelped and howled as they snapped at the horses' hooves.

'Get out of there, Joyce,' the colonel shouted, but it was unlikely he'd been heard over the clamour of battle.

As it appeared the horsemen were in grave danger of being dragged from their saddles, Joyce ordered the bugler to sound retreat. The shrill notes blasted across the lake as all the horsemen bolted past the remaining guardians and clattered along the shoreline back to their river-crossing. The hounds bounded after them, snapping at the hooves until a couple of dogs were kicked in the face. The pack was discouraged and soon the riders outpaced it. The handlers were last seen chasing their dogs and trying to recall them. Meanwhile the rest of the guardians were left to help their comrades out of the lake, nurse their bruised bodies and wonder how to get their own back. They hurled abuse and a few missiles after the boat, which was now far enough away for neither to be effective.

Colonel Charlie was overjoyed and positively bubbling with bonhomie.

'Damn good show everyone,' he gushed. 'Damn fine. Citations and gongs all round I reckon.'

He seemed to have forgotten that the battalion didn't actually have any medals to issue, but no one was going to rain on the colonel's parade by mentioning the fact right then. As they sailed back across the lake they saw two more fireballs soar upwards and smash into the southern shore. It seemed that Caroline had passed on the message and Percy couldn't help himself even though the colonel's people were all safely away. Those angry guardians who remained on the shoreline ducked in time as the missiles hurtled overhead and disappeared harmlessly into the forest.

'Hold your fire,' Colonel Charlie yelled before Percy could reload. 'Mission accomplished – successfully'

*

The rest of the day was spent taking stock and tending wounds. Most were superficial although there were a few nasty cuts and bruises here and there. The cavalry, who'd sustained the wost injuries, rode back to barracks by mid afternoon. Colonel Charlie and the lieutenants met them with mugs of hot herbal tea laced with moonshine grog.

'Lieutenant Joyce, I take it you know the definition of an order?' the colonel demanded solemnly as she rode up.

She merely nodded.

'And you deliberately disobeyed mine. If I recall, I told you to retreat.'

She nodded again. Her ankle was hurting like blazes and all she wanted was to have a hot shower and put her foot up. The colonel stood in silence, while the troopers waited for a reprimand. There was an awkward pause until Colonel Charlie threw back his head and roared with laughter.

'Thank goodness you chose to ignore it,' he bellowed. 'Good show all round. That's what we need -- initiative -- Ho! Ho! But you should have seen your faces just then. I had you going for a moment. Very droll! Capital fun! Come on let's get those mugs refilled and fix up your injuries.'

Oh, he thought that was a great joke. The colonel's sense of humour tended towards slapstick.

Wedge and Raven greeted Lieutenant Joyce. Wedge helped her from the saddle and they exchanged meaningful glances as she clung to him. Raven simply raised her eyebrows as Joyce placed her arm around Wedge's shoulder and limped with his aid to her quarters.

'Looks like we're square in the *Sir Galahad* department,' Wedge said.

'Who's counting?' Joyce replied. 'But, I can still show my appreciation.'

'You've got a sore ankle.'

'So, I'd better not stand on it then.'

Raven looked on anxiously, but he was gone for only a short while. When he returned she eyed him suspiciously.

'What ..?' he said.

'Oh, nothing,' she replied. 'I think she likes you and she *is* pretty.'

'Not as pretty as you,' he said. 'Come on, we haven't even unloaded those wretched books yet. It won't do to leave 'em out in the weather.'

She followed him with a contented smile.

Epilogue – The Book Club

Although the battalion celebrated that evening, Colonel Charlie posted extra sentries along the shoreline in case the guardians mounted a reprisal raid. Wedge took pains to avoid Lieutenant Joyce whose testosterone and oestrogen levels were off the scale after the day's action. Fortunately for him she was confined to quarters until her ankle healed. Even so Raven stuck close to him to make sure there was no back-sliding anywhere.

Colonel Charlie ensured no one drank too much homebrew and ordered them all to bed early. Most of the battalion were exhausted and didn't complain. The colonel was especially concerned that the guardians might counter-attack at dawn so the bugler sounded reveille an hour early to make sure they weren't taken by surprise.

Raven awoke cursing the bugle. It annoyed her more than squawking crows in the morning. When reveille ceased she rolled over and went back to sleep, but it only seemed like seconds before Wombat nudged her awake again.

'What, can't I get a minute's peace?' she grumbled.

'You'd better come and see this,' he said.

Raven must have been asleep longer than she thought. The sun now clipped the horizon so she was able to see clearly to the causeway where the battalion was lined in battle formation. She and Wombat raced to the shore to find Wedge and Thornton had already joined Colonel Charlie's troops. The guardians were lined up along the southern bank armed with their spears and they all carried square shields as well.

'Pikes and shields in a square will be a hard nut to crack,' the colonel observed.

'They've got to get across the lake first,' Lieutenant Denis replied.

'True, maybe they're just showing us what they're capable of.'

At that moment Destiny stepped onto the causeway followed by the guardian leader who'd tied a white strip of cloth to his spear shaft. She advanced purposely to the causeway centre and stopped. The guardian rammed the spear between some crumbling rocks and they waited. Colonel Charlie and Denis went to meet them, exchanged a few words and immediately returned.

'She wants to talk to you,' the colonel said to Raven.

'Yes, and I think I know what it's about. Do you mind if I borrow a horse.'

'Be my guest.'

One of Joyce's cavalry lieutenants offered Raven a mount and she galloped back to the battalion tents before returning with her backpack. She dismounted and handed the reins to the horse's owner before stepping onto the causeway. Wedge and Wombat followed, but the others remained on the bank.

Destiny stood serenely. She wore a fur robe over her shift as the morning breeze tugged gently at her hair. The guardian leader stood woodenly by her side.

'Good morning, Raven,' she greeted.

'Good morning, Destiny. I hope you're all okay after yesterday.'

'There were no major injuries, so we're recovering well, thank you — physically at least.'

'It was a bit of a blow to the guardians' pride I guess.'

'I think it goes deeper than that. They hold their duty sacred just as the colonel and his battalion do.'

'I'm surprised you two haven't come to blows before.'

'We have — in the past, but lately it hasn't been necessary,' Destiny sighed. 'Our spheres of interest do not coincide.'

'Yeah, I'm sorry. That was my fault, but it's a long story and some of it was out of my control.'

'There's talk among the guardians about regaining the volumes,' the guardian leader said.

'I thought there might be,' Raven replied, 'so I'm here to make a deal.'

'What can you possibly offer to put things right?' Destiny asked.

'I will give you my most precious possession to hold until I return your books.'

She reached for her pack and withdrew Angela's diary. She held the book for a moment, almost caressing the cover before handing it to Destiny.

'This is the work of a very special woman who lived at the time of *The Spark*. It's full of wonderful insights and tips about how people should live. I have tried to be guided by her words. I think you'll enjoy reading her work. I treasure this more than anything else I own.'

She failed to mention she didn't actually own *The Word According to Angela,* but it was a moot point. She'd certainly been primarily responsible for its care since she was a little girl. She was using the book for the greater good and Destiny was moved by her obvious sincerity. The librarian's daughter considered the proposal for several minutes while the guardian leader eyed her doubtfully.

Destiny was then faced with a thorny and complex dilemma. Above all, she wished to avoid conflict with the battalion if possible. As Raven had said, it was unlikely the guardians could best the colonel's troops in a pitched battle. The square formation was an efficient weapon to scare raiders away, but it was unwieldy and ineffective anywhere but on open ground. A raid on the War Memorial would be hazardous and bitterly opposed.

The guardians could ward off a cavalry charge, but were helpless against Percy's catapults. Face would be been saved by the exchange and Destiny hoped Raven would have neither the understanding nor resources to apply the books' knowledge. Unlike the guardians, librarians were more interested in keeping the library intact rather than hiding its secrets.

Destiny had preached the guardians' party line when she'd first met Raven, but was not so sure now. The risk of present-day bloodshed seemed much greater than some perceived threat far in the future. She quickly scanned a few pages of Angela's diary and was intrigued by what it contained. Maybe there was indeed useful knowledge to be gained there. She was a pragmatic girl who now took a huge gamble. Then Wombat produced his prized watch and handed it to Destiny.

'And this is *my* most precious procession – except my sister. You can borrow it until we come back.'

Destiny smiled and took the time-piece. It was the deal-clincher.

'Very well,' she replied.

'Thank you,' Raven said, stepping towards Destiny and hugging her.

It was such a spontaneous gesture that Destiny's usual coolness melted and she returned the embrace. Suddenly a cheer erupted from the battalion and, to everyone's surprise, the guardians joined in. Obviously they'd all done enough fighting for now. Only the guardian leader still maintained a hostile, stony glare. Whether he approved of the deal or not made no difference now.

'I have other journals,' Raven said. 'When I return, I'll bring them for you to read.'

'I'd like that,' Destiny replied softly.

'I hope we shall be friends.'

'I'd like that too.'

The librarian's life was lonely and Destiny realised she'd never had close friends among the guardians' children while she was training and studying with her mother.

Wombat rolled his eyes as it was all getting too girlie for him, but he had to admit Raven had played a master stroke and they were off the hook. Destiny and Raven exchanged looks for a moment more before returning to their separate sides of the lake.

'You didn't have to do that,' Raven whispered to Wombat as they walked away.

'Just got caught up in the moment,' he replied.

'So that's that?' Wedge said as they picked their way along the causeway rubble.

'Yes, and I'm getting us out of here before Lieutenant Joyce gets any more fancy ideas,' Raven warned.

'Jealous, are we ..?'

'It's for your own good.'

'That's what girls always say when they want to spoil your fun.'

*

It was time to go. They'd got what they'd come for, or most of it anyway and Raven wanted to be clear of the high country before the snow season. They packed up and were mounted by dawn the following day. Colonel Charlie saw them off with Denis, Caroline and even Joyce who limped on crutches from her tent. She flung herself at Wedge and kissed him passionately until he was able to untangle her arms and extricate himself. Raven thought he took his own sweet time about it, but eyed them with mild amusement. They'd be gone soon and she'd have Wedge to herself then. The other goodbyes were warm if less demonstrative.

Thornton didn't go with them. He planned to travel north for the winter and Lieutenant Caroline had applied for leave to accompany him. He'd told her about crocodiles, turtles, dugongs and colourful reefs ablaze with millions of glorious fish and she wanted to be a part of that. Her skill with sailing craft would come in handy. He'd promised nothing and she'd asked for nothing, but maybe she'd be a part of his life too. Thornton and Caroline were packed and ready at the same time as Raven, Wedge and Wombat.

'Thank you for all your help,' Raven said to Thornton. 'We'd be dead if it wasn't for you.'

'My pleasure. It's been a good time. You'll be fine if you remember to take the precautions I've taught you.'

So one party left for the north and the other turned east along the lakeside to the Molonglo River ford. The way back was easier for them as they recognised most of the landmarks and camped at most of the same sites they used on their previous journey.

They stopped for a night in the ruins where they'd spotted the thylacines, but the animals didn't return. While Wedge took his turn on piquet patrol Wombat pulled a small paperback book from his jacket and read avidly by the campfire light.

'What's that you've got there?' Raven asked.

'These are wicked,' Wombat replied, handing her a Manga graphic novel.

'Where did you get it?' she demanded.

'The library of course. I found a bunch of them by pure accident and nicked some. No one's going to miss them for ages and I did trade my watch for 'em. Destiny and her mum will be concentrating on the electronics books.'

'Isn't that what *you're* supposed to be studying?'

'Plenty of time for that later. It's a matter of priorities,'

'Oh well, I suppose we can return them when we give the others back,' Raven sighed.

She had to admit the artwork was amazing although the violence was not to her taste, but Wombat found them wonderful.

When they reached the blackened, scarred land left by the bushfire they doubled their vigilance. They weren't going to be taken by surprise in cannibal country again. Wombat was especially alert. The campsite where they'd been ambushed was deserted but there were signs that someone had been there since they'd left.

What they found shocked them to the core. Human bones had been cast around the blackened fireplace and a single skull lay beside a tree. The cannibals had found at least one other victim. There was no trace of clothing so obviously they'd taken that. While Wedge scouted the area confirming no one was lurking close by, Raven and Wombat picked around for clues.

Wombat thought he heard something, but it was probably just his nerves playing tricks.

'Listen,' he whispered, 'do you hear that?'

Raven concentrated and indeed heard a low, barely audible moan. They crept to the foot of a large red gum where the sound came from beneath a pile of leaves and bark. They brushed the debris aside and there lay Walter Harrison. He was naked, filthy and barely alive. His left leg was severed at the knee and had been tied off with a strip of rag. Ants and grubs crawled all over him taking a great interest in his bloody stump.

'What ..?' Raven gasped.

'Please ... please ... don't leave me ...' Walter begged in a whisper that was barely audible.

'You'd deserve it if we did,' Wombat replied.

Raven and Wombat dragged Walter to the fire and wrapped him in blankets. They bathed his leg and applied penicillium fungi to the wound. Walter was dehydrated and suffering from hypothermia, but he was tough fellow. The fact that he'd survived at all made Wombat and Raven think of him in different light with grudging respect. It was unlikely either of them would have survived for days in the cold wilderness suffering from shock and blood-loss. Walter was by no means out of danger, but he did recover consciousness. After several cups of steaming herbal tea he became remarkably lucid.

'What happened?' Raven asked. 'Where're Vinnie and the others?'

'Bush fire got most of 'em. That's Vinnie ... or what's left of him,' Walter rasped indicating the skull.

'You ran into that gang of loony people-eaters ..?' Wombat said in awe.

Walter nodded.

'More like they ran into us,' he said.

'How come they didn't eat you?'

'You're not going to believe this.'

'Try us.'

'Well I like turnips, see. Most people don't.'

Wombat and Raven screwed up their faces. They belonged to the 'don't' faction.

'It saved my life though. They didn't like the way I tasted. They knocked me out and when I came round they'd hacked off my leg for a taste test. I managed to strap it up before they pinched the rest of my clobber and finished off Vinnie.'

Raven and Wombat made Walter as comfortable as possible. They tried to rid the horrific images from their minds although Walter was taking his experience stoically and soon he fell asleep. His tenacity and will to survive were remarkable. Wombat built a travois, hitched it to one of the brumbies and they hauled Walter back to Mactown to a mixed reception.

Gloria and Jason were of course overjoyed to see their children back safe and sound. Alicia, on the other hand was furious.

'You've killed my baby,' she wailed, glaring at Raven. 'This is all your fault'

She launched herself at Raven, but Gloria had heard enough and flattened Alicia with a sharp right hook to the jaw followed by a left jab into her nose. Alicia collapsed to the ground as blood seeped from her nostrils. Previously Gloria would have been in deep trouble, but the situation had changed dramatically. While Zen was totally stunned by the news of Vinnie's death and Walter's maiming, the Harrison ranks were seriously depleted. So Alicia's opinion didn't carry much weight any more. Zen realised how the wind blew now his power-base was decimated. He welcomed Raven and Wombat back, if a little diffidently, especially in light of the promised new technology they'd brought with them.

For all her wailing, Alicia was useless when it came to nursing, so Gloria took charge of Walter's care. She was the best herbalist, physician and nurse in Mactown anyway. He responded well especially when Wombat promised to engineer a prosthetic leg that he claimed would work better than a real one.

Zen Harrison never really recovered from the loss of his son and kinsmen. He handed the reins of chief to Jason who got along with most people and proved pretty good at the job. Alicia spat venom for several weeks, but shut up after she realised no one was particularly interested. There was nothing lonelier than complaining into empty space so she and Zen moved to Emu Creek and never returned to Mactown.

Wedge decided he should return home too and let his family know he was safe. Raven felt her heart sink at the news. She'd decided it was time for a serious boyfriend and Wedge Farrow suited her fine, but now he was leaving.

'I'll be back,' he assured her, 'and I've got something I'd like you to have.'

He took a small leather pouch from his pocket and handed it to her. Raven open the flap and a sparkling earring dropped into her palm. It was the most beautiful thing she'd seen, far prettier than the one Vinnie had tried to tempt her with. The stones were all blue, ranging from pale azure, cobalt to deep indigo.

She simply stared wide-eyed at the gems.

'I got it from Thornton before he left. I don't think he wanted to part with it, but I coaxed it out of him. Do you like it ..?' he hesitated.

'Like it? I love it. Oh, thank you ... thank you.'

She flung her arms around him and kissed him.

'I know you want to put off your earmarking for this year, but I thought next year maybe you'd wear it for me.'

Of course she would.

So they said farewell and she watched him until he rode out of sight. There was an ache in her heart, but how much better it would feel when he returned. Emu Creek wasn't so far away. She could always visit him anytime. And that anytime would be soon.

So she returned to the library where Wombat was still engrossed in his graphic novels. Electricity might have to wait, although Wombat being what he was, it wouldn't be long before he started tinkering again. She greeted the Word-Keeper with warm embrace.

'I'm sorry,' she said, 'I sort of lent Angela's diary to a friend.'

'A friend, eh?' he smiled. 'There's nothing wrong with friends lending things to each other. It sounds to me like you've started a book club.'

The End

About the author

Richard Marman was born in Swindon, UK. His father was a RAF pilot who had served with distinction during WWII. The family moved from base to base after the war, including four years in Germany. They immigrated to Fremantle in 1962. Richard attended six primary and three secondary schools, so he is familiar with the 'new kid on the block' status.

After school, Richard joined the Royal Australian Air Force and trained as a pilot. He served for nine years, including a tour in Vietnam and a significant time flying in New Guinea. In 1975 Richard left the RAAF to fly with Ansett Airlines until the company closed in 2001 at which time he was a Boeing 767 captain. Afterwards he trained Singapore Airlines pilots on Lear Jets until 2006.

Leaving aviation behind, Richard completed a Diploma of Visual Arts at Tewantin TAFE and a Bachelor of Arts at the University of the Sunshine Coast, majoring in creative writing and design. Most of Richard's books have stemmed from University projects.

The McAlister Line

The McAlister Line reviews:

'McAlister's Way is a fast paced page-turning read, the kind of read where you lose track of time. Absolutely enveloping! Highly recommended!'

'...Masterfully handled and quite eloquent — Wonderful.'

'With pirates and secrets set amongst the northern tropics, you're in for a delightful read. It has a really good sense of place and from the voice to the detail, it's a fast moving action story that will leave you wanting more'

'McAlister's Spark is a fast-paced, action-riddled amazing read you will struggle to put down.'

'McAlister and the Great War is a very good and well researched read. I enjoyed it very much.'

Illustrated Books for All Ages

Other Adventure Titles

Approaching his sixteenth birthday, Henry is thrust into a perilous quest when his village chief's wife is abducted. Joined by three companions and his pet wolf, he vows to track down the mysterious kidnappers.

With no magic or special skills, they can only rely on their courage, determination, wits and friendship to survive in a cruel realm which makes no concessions for youth or innocence.

Danger mounts with each challenge until ultimately they face a seemingly unconquerable foe at the gates of a hostile, alien city.

Illustrated Books for All Ages

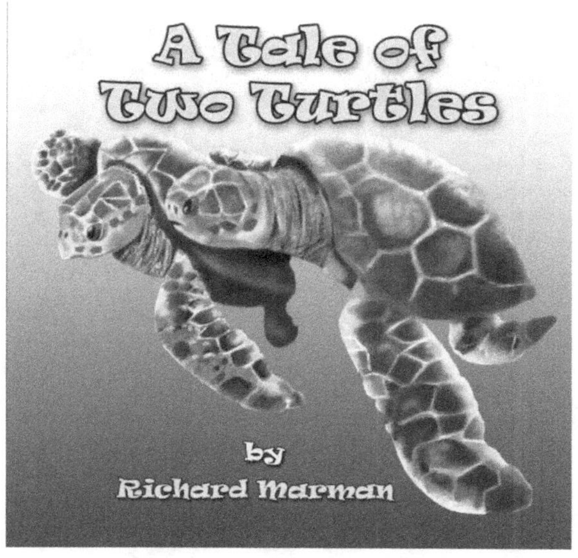

Other Adventure Titles

Approaching his sixteenth birthday, Henry is thrust into a perilous quest when his village chief's wife is abducted. Joined by three companions and his pet wolf, he vows to track down the mysterious kidnappers.

With no magic or special skills, they can only rely on their courage, determination, wits and friendship to survive in a cruel realm which makes no concessions for youth or innocence.

Danger mounts with each challenge until ultimately they face a seemingly unconquerable foe at the gates of a hostile, alien city.

A mighty dragon called Brimstone is terrorising the quiet village of Oak Tree. Prince Roger and his sister Princess Crystal set out to hunt the fiery beast.

They are ably assisted or hindered — as the case may be — by an evil knight, a mysterious good-guy, the local sheriff, loyal men-at-arms, forest brigands, ogres, trolls and Oak Tree's villagers with a bunch of attitude.

There are thrills, spills, romance and heaps of rollicking fun to be had by all.

Illustrations for other Authors